Sleepin' Wit' the Virus

a sequel to *Anonymous*

Karla Denise Baker

First Edition

The characters and events in this book are fictitious. Any similarity to real persons, living or dead, is coincidental and not intended by the author.

ISBN-13: 978-0-9815668-2-5
Library of Congress Control Number: 2008927384

Printed in the United States of America
10 9 8 7 6 5 4 3 2 1

Editor: Chael Needle

Other books by Karla Denise Baker :

Anonymous

To order copies contact: (Enclose *Certified, *Cashier's Check, or Money order for $14.95 + $4.95 for shipping and handling. If two copies are more add an additional 2.00 for shipping/handling. *Bulk orders available at special rates*. Make *check or money order payable to: Karla D. Baker).

Mail to:
The Write Message
P.O. Box 3071
Paterson, New Jersey 07509

E-mail: karlabkr@yahoo.com

Formatting: Karla D. Baker

Hello Everyone,

I just want to express my appreciation to the many of you who have purchased my first book, *Anonymous*. It really means a lot to me. It wasn't easy admitting what happened to me. But the horrific experiences changed me for the better. Yes, I was surprised too. I've gotten a lot of feedback about my life story. Many of you said it sounds like a soap opera. Others said it could be a movie. Sometimes I feel like it is, but when I look in the mirror I am reminded that it is real.

I was quite delighted to see *men* engrossed in my story. That was awesome! Some men said they were hooked. One even stated he stopped watching sports because he was fascinated in knowing about my life. I said, "Ooh!" I wasn't expecting that.

As you already know, I've been through a lot, but I am trying to be optimistic, even in times of doubt. I am surely trying to be a better person. I just want to thank you all for your support.

—Avery

I was lost, then I was found, but now I am uncertain.
—*Anonymous*

Catchin' Hell

"Hello."

"Ah, what's up, Avery?"

"Nothing. Just relaxing till our date this evening."

"Oh, yeah, um, about that…."

"Is there something wrong…?"

"Ah, well, ah, something came up so I have to cancel."

"Oh. No, problem. I guess we can plan this for another evening."

"Well, actually. I prefer not."

Click.

Dang. It never ceases to amaze me how quickly things change from, "Excuse me, Ms. May I have your number?" to "I gotta go check the meter." It is always another lame excuse as to why *time* doesn't seem to be available with a tall, dark, and handsome man. Everything is cool up until I say those magic words, "I am HIV-positive." And zoom, their 10½, 11, 12, 13½ feet rush for the exit. I swear there must be a remix of those same exact words 'cause I'm catchin' hell with these men. Why do you keep putting yourself through this girl, I ask myself time and time again? And I come up with the same response, I dunno.

I will tell you this…Stephanie Mills sang it the best with her song, "Feel the Fire." Chile I am not only catchin' hell with these men I am catchin' hell with this sweltering heat in between my legs. Woo! It is blazing.

I feel like I have weeds growing all around the blackberry bush. Yes, it has been a long time since the weeds have been tugged from the bush. Well, at least a few months. It seems more like eternity to me. I know the blackberry bush needs watering. Now the question is whom I can get to hose it down. I massage my chin. Hmm.

I Jus' Gotta

Moisture is slowly drooling down into the lining of my black boy shorts. I can hear it swishing against my skin with each step I take. Ooh, the sound is turning me on. Impulsively, I want to go into the fitting room and pleasure myself, but I may get carried away like the *"yes, yes, yesssssssss, girl"* and make an embarrassing scene out here in the mall. Dang, it's hot. Ooh, ahhhhh, I can't take it.

I stroll in and around Nordstrom as my lips cream like a Oreo cookie lying in the beaming sun. The edges are covered in white icing. I am trying to rub my lips together with the sway of my hips to tame the itch, but it needs to be scratched. I try to distract my lustful thoughts by looking for some fashionable earrings, but my minds drifts thinking about *it* piercing my hole. *Get a grip, Avery! Grip. I want him to grip, grind, and devour my salmon croquette.*

I stop in my tracks discreetly trying to fan myself. But the heat, aaaaaaaahhhhhhh, damn, the heat is rising in higher temperatures, about 100. My forehead is moist. My body is feverish. This desire…this impulsive desire is burning in my loins. It is instigating me to be a *naughty* girl. It is driving me…ooooh, ooooh…crazy. I gotta have it. I jus' gotta.

My eyes cut to the side to see if anyone is within ears distance. I wet my bottom lip with saliva, and reach inside my denim jacket for my cellular, open my phonebook to search and find that "honeysuckle" of a man. Mmm.

Ring, ring, ring.

I get no answer so I leave a message.

"Hi. Give me a call."

I tuck my cellular back in my denim jacket and stroll through the store eagerly waiting for my phone to ring.

Ring…ring…ring.

"Hello."

"You called?" he asks in a sexy, baritone voice.

"Yes, do you have anything planned for this evening?"

"No, not that I know of."

"Well, I want you in between my legs. Is that okay with you?"

He chuckles, "Yesss."

"Okay, call me later."

There is this voice, not Avona, another—Karma—that I haven't heard in a long time blossoming inside of me. I have kept her tucked

6

away for many, many years. But I miss her. I miss her confidence to go after what she desires. Truthfully, I admire her because she is a hard cookie to crumble. She doesn't give a damn about your wants, needs, or desires. It is all about *her*. And I love her because she brings out the best and worst in me. She lives for the moment.

I doze off, but around 11:46 p.m. I roll over on my canopy bed and I view his ten digits highlighted on my cellular. I call him back and leave a message. Then I start to head downstairs to the living room, but something pulls me back to try his number again. So I do.

"Hello. Hello," he says.

"You called?"

"Yep, you didn't pick up so I was on my way home."

"Oh, well, I'm here."

"I'm on my way."

For some reason I don't have a nervous bone in my body. I am calm. Confident. Famished. There is no need to slip on anything revealing because it is just going to be coming right off. I pull my condoms from the Magnum box and slip them under the pillow, and then I wait for him to come ring my bell.

The buzzer goes off and I let him in. Three minutes later he is gently tapping my door. I open the door in the nude with my four-inch red stilettos accentuating my legs, as my eyes scroll from his Timberland boots up to his sexy face and I smirk devilishly. Then I embrace him with a hug and kiss on his neck.

My body is searing hot as his hands touch my skin. There is no time to waste so I lead him up the stairs into my bedroom. He stands on the seagrass border rug, as he lifts his muscular arms above his baldhead and pulls his green Heineken T-shirt off like he is posing for a photo shoot. All bare chest stares back at me as he draws me in with his honeyed tone. Yum. His fingers pinch my dark nipples, teasing and taunting as I lay back on the cinnabar, organic diamond-lattice duvet, parting the dark sea, waiting. Waiting for him to enter the dungeon of forgotten and come in to refresh my amnesia of what it was like having a man stroke my inner walls. The size. The width. The smell. Lord knows I can't wait to get a nibble.

His massive hands maneuver my legs above his defined shoulders. His wet tongue licks my Dove skin, as he stares deeply into my mischievous eyes. He doesn't know and I don't feel the need to share. This is my moment to feel him as real as he is. As raw as raw can be. This is *my* moment for payback. For all the times he did me wrong back in the day. For the lying and cheating and belittling me as if I was a nobody—nothing.

Now he's all grown up with a wife, a house with the white picket fence, dog, and kids. Isn't he sooooo lucky?

The lead-free wick from the scented Spa Water candle burns down into the pool of liquefied wax. Its iridescence dances in the air leaving the room pitch black. The night is young. And we are full of passion. Mmm. If sexin' him is wrong, then I don't want to be right. Not tonight. Tonight I just want to indulge in the sinful taste of a sexy, handsome, available, and willingly able man.

My finger slowly slithers underneath the pillow....

My back arches as he slips his penis in my tunnel of epidemic and strokes me with such gentleness with his young love—slow, sweet and kind. I open and invite him in deeper, as if I want him to eat me whole. Drowning in my abstinence. Having him swim for miles into the shallow waters of my lust—into the deception that has plagued me. Slowly my eyelids close, as his long tongue twirls in my mouth and pulls away with saliva drooling down his chin. I stick out my tongue and scoop it off his chin, and tongue him down. I pull away and stare into his dark eyes and tune out the truth as I indulge heavily into him, panting, squeezing, moaning, and feeling him poking me as my amnesia fades. Slipping me in and out of reality, as I feel his member thicken, body jerks, and my legs tremble as he comes and then collapses on my chest, breathing erratically. My eyes flutter as a smile spreads across my face, as I feel completely satisfied.

Isn't life grand?

Advocate for the Youth

The 250-seat auditorium is filled as Principal Knowles approaches center stage greeting students and faculty. She claps, signaling everyone to simmer down. Breathing heavily into the microphone, and a bit annoyed, her eyes burn into faces that disregard her presence. "Students, please," she says, as her tone shrieks through the microphones airwaves. Hands rush to shield ears, and teeth clench.

"Everyone settle down, please? Let's demonstrate that we can be civilized individuals," she says, in a delicate, almost Mary Poppins diplomatic voice. Her tall frame stands draped in a cherry-red Dress Barn pants suit with white-collar Ann Taylor blouse. Her soft blue eyes pierce the large audience overlooking her glasses with a hard stare.

Young, diverse, and mature faces stare back at her as she tries to get them to obey her command. Her ivory-colored hand rises as her chunky fingers rake through her thinning, dyed red hair that sweeps off her forehead, enhancing her distinguishing features of high cheekbones, and big baby doll eyes that resemble Lucille Ball. She pats her hip, waiting as she exhales for everyone to calm down.

"Attention, everyone, attention." Principal Knowles' body language begins to change. Her straight posture slouches, her right hand slithers down to her crotch. Her head tilts to the side, and her feet spread apart as her knees bend slightly. Then, out of nowhere, she yells, "Yo, I'm sayin' pipe down!" in a Brooklyn accent.

I chuckle. It is the funniest thing I've ever seen a white woman in her late-fifties do. Principal Knowles is full of surprises, and that comical display manages to catch the students completely off guard. Everyone stops and stares', thinking Principal Knowles has lost her mind.

She gracefully resumes her polished composure, tugs at her blazer, and glides her arms down as they fall to her sides.

I am impressed, still chuckling inside.

"Thank you," she says, feeling empowered. "Today we have a special guest speaker. Ms. Love is the owner of Anonymous a performance art gallery in Montclair. And she is here to enlighten us with some significant information. Please give a warm welcome to Ms. Love."

The room sounds like a concert at the Meadowlands with their palms making pop rock music. There is a lot of commotion; whispering, giggling, and snickering.

"Students, please, settle down," Principal Knowles repeats with a stern look on her face.

The chit-chattering voices begin to reduce to quiet-sounding muffles.

At that time I rise to my feet and walk on-stage in a pair of worn jeans and a lime green T-shirt with *Anonymous* inscribed on it in pink lettering. I step in front of the mike and stare out at the crowd of faces. As I gaze out a weird feeling consumes me. I feel a flutter in my stomach, but then slowly I regain myself, as well as my train of thought as to why I am here. And by doing this, I find myself becoming slightly emotional as I stare out at all the young faces. I have the jitters. So I begin to speak to draw my attention back to the reasons, the purpose of me coming in the first place. *Okay, Avery, do what you came to do. Make a difference.*

"Good afternoon, students, faculty, the Director of PCCC, Coordinator of City of Paterson Division of Health, and Principal Knowles. My name is Avery Love. I feel honored to be speaking to you all. I am so glad we were able to have you all come to Passaic County Community College: PS 5 and PS 12, PS 6, PS 4, PS 13, and Norman S. Weir seventh and eighth graders to have an open discussion about life, freedom, choices, and life changes.

"Growing up my Poppa always used to say, 'If you have something to say don't bite your tongue.' That has stayed with me, so what I am going to do is cut to the chase. Let me give you all a little history about myself. I graduated from PS 5. Had many fine teachers there. I am here to speak to you seventh and eighth graders about HIV/AIDS. But before I begin, I want to thank your parents for allowing me to come. Um, where should I start? I guess from the beginning of when my life changed."

I stand strong and erect.

"Well, I was working as a paralegal in lower Manhattan, and I loved my job. To make a long story short, I was sexually assaulted by someone I didn't know, brutally raped. It was hard dealing with it. Very hard. But the hardest of it all was being told years later that I am HIV-positive."

I can see many sympathetic faces staring back at me. My legs tremble, but I continue. "It's true. That myth you may hear about AIDS being the gay man's disease, erase it from your minds. It is everyone's disease if you don't protect yourself.

"Young ladies, I can't stress it enough, stop lowering your

standards. Stop settling for a roll in the hay just to say that you have someone in your life. Stop speaking out of context about sex. Out here prancing around like puppet dolls."

Principal Knowles scratches her throat. I ignore her 'cause I have the floor. She had her chance and it is so obvious these horny rock heads need some tough love. That nurturing, motherly side is not in me. I am my father's daughter.

"Shut up!" A young male voice yells.

"Talk dat shit to someone who cares," a squeaky female voice follows suit.

I twist my lips and snatch the microphone, "Listen, you lil' hot piss rats…."

Principal Knowles leaps to her feet and grabs the microphone and clenches her teeth straining out her words, "Ms. Love, what do you think you're doing?"

I clench my teeth back and say, "Getting through so let me do what I came here to do." I snatch her hand away from the microphone and conclude with my thoughts in a mellow tone. "Listen, sex can be a beautiful experience, but first you must be mature enough to handle it—mind, body, and soul—before you give your fishy pussies away to a total stranger."

Again, Principal Knowles jumps up in utter disgust, grabs the microphone and clenches her teeth with a vein bulging out of her left temple, "Ms. Love, have you forgotten that these are *children* you are talking to?"

"No. I know exactly what I am saying to these little rock heads. They need someone to tell it like it is instead of sugarcoating the truth. Principal Knowles, I am here to speak the truth. I speak the lingo to get through to them, anyway possible so let me do what I came do!"

"Ms. Love, you are way out of line." She squints her eyes.

"Maybe so, but I am living proof of what I speak. Can you say the same for yourself, Principal Knowles?"

"How dare you!" She snaps.

"Yes, how dare I put my life on the line to help these sex-driven kids who are practically throwing their lives away for a life-threatening hump. HOW DARE I! Do you know what it is like living my life? DO YOU?! 'Cause if you do please, take the floor. Tell these *children* how it feels to be me. Tell 'em what I endure everyday. Tell 'em how I can't seem to get a date because of what resides inside of me. Go ahead and tell 'em." I step to the side and allow Principal Knowles to have her say.

Principal Knowles doesn't move, but her hands release from the microphone and she takes a seat as her tall frame shrinks in size.

I step back in front of the mike. "Back to the issue at hand ladies and gents. Listen, you can think you know someone but how much do you really know about him? I mean, internally. Yes, you can probably run down his favorite designer: Rocawear. Favorite sneaker: Jordan. Favorite food: Chinese. Favorite basketball team: Lakers. Favorite rapper: Tupac. You can probably tell me his favorite line to get you into bed. But can you tell me his medical history? Think about it.

"Can you tell me when was the last time he was seen by a doctor? The last sexual transmitted disease he has had? The last girl he has been with without using a condom? Does he use drugs? Shoot needles. The last or first time he has ever been tested? Can you tell me that? Do you perform oral sex on him? And if you do, do you brush your teeth beforehand. Don't do it. Your teeth bleed as you brush, and there you are giving him some *head*, possibly infecting yourself. I pause.

"Now you wannabe-foot-long-wieners, I can't let you's off the hook. Can you answer any of these questions about your skank? Not your girlfriend 'cause you guys nowadays don't even have respect for the girl you are screwing. You sit up and call her degrading names…'bitch,' like that is a term of endearment. And the funny part is you girls answer to it. You giggle like it is a pet name of some sort." I roll my eyes in disgust. "You young people drive me crazy wanting to sex anything with legs, vagina, and penis."

"You suck! Get off-stage bitch," a young male voice yells from the right side of the auditorium. Followed by a spitball that lands on-stage.

My eyes squint. "Who did that?"

"Who did that?" The male voice mocks.

Everyone burst into laughter and it makes my blood boil.

I lose all cool and snatch at the microphone's stand, "Listen, you pathetic brats!"

Principal Knowles scratches her throat as if there is a hair caught in it. I ignore her trying to divert my attention.

I exhale, roll my eyes, as I pace the floor. "I am so sick of you rock heads trying to be grown! All you guys talk about is sex, sex, and sex; only it is the dirty version. I hear it everyday, everywhere I go. Instead of focusing on an *education* to make something out of your lives, you rock heads have sex on the brain. Sex to you all is like buying five-cent bubble gum. Once the sweet taste is gon', it's time to slip a new piece in your mouth."

Everyone bursts into laughter.

"You laugh, but your horny asses won't be laughing when you take yourself to the doctor and he/she tells you that you have an incurable disease. Will you be laughing then? I don't think so. I wasn't. No, I didn't ask for this to happen to me. I didn't go out and shoot needles, prostitute or have a blood transfusion. Someone attacked and raped me! He took something from me that I couldn't ever get back." I can feel the pain resurfacing. "He stole my joy and destroyed my life! Is that something to laugh about?"

Everyone quiets down.

I point my forefinger. "Lemme tell you all something, I cried like a baby. A baby. Here I am a grown woman and I cried for my parents, who are both dead. Just imagine!" I pace the stage using hand gestures to get my message across. "Here you are with a disease that folks shun you for having. You have no family, no friends, no one to confide in because you are fearful that, they too, will leave you so you hibernate behind closed doors. You are afraid...afraid of the world. You are afraid of your neighborhood. A place you've probably lived all of your life. You are afraid. You're afraid of the people, the whispers, the looks, the snickers, and the reality of your circumstance. That happened to me. Me. Look at me? Can you tell just by looking at me that I have an incurable disease? No.

"Be safe. Enjoy youth-hood 'cause if you don't, and you ignore what I am saying, and continue to grow up too fast, eventually, by your shortsightedness, Anonymous will catch you. Maybe that's what I need to do. Go out and get some T-shirts that read: Catch the "Anonymous" B4 it Catches YOU!

"Maybe that's what I need to do and charge a $1.00 and send the proceeds to one of the many foundations and charities: Keep a Child Alive. You know Alicia Keys, right? Or, maybe I should send the proceeds to A & U: *America's AIDS Magazine* in New York, or Magic Johnson's Foundation, or Iris House in Harlem for women and children who are HIV-positive. Or maybe I should take you guys on a field trip to see a one-woman show *Sometimes I Cry* and let Sheryl Lee Ralph school you guys. Maybe she can get through. I dunno.

"HIV/AIDS, trust me you will never be the same if you become another statistic. The stigma it stings. Just hearing the word ease into your ears feels like someone's stabbing you repeatedly in the back. They are trying to rid of you. That's how you feel. You feel life is over. Some people can't handle the truth and they lose their grip and go out and smoke crack, shoot heroin, sell their bodies for a hit, attempt to commit suicide, or take their anger out on an innocent bystander because they can't handle what resides in their body. Just from that one word: AIDS. It is brutal. Brutal. Your life will change instantaneously." I pace back in front of the mike and stare. "It can and will happen to you if you don't protect yourself. It can. Do you want to know what my life consists of? DO YOU!" Tears build up in my eyes as my lips tighten to hold back the pain.

"I have to take meds twice a day, every day for the rest of my life. I visit my doctor every two months. I have to watch what I eat. Exercise. Stay positive. Get rest. Basically take care of myself so that I won't be subjected to full-blown AIDS.

"You're probably wondering why am I sharing this with you all. Well, I constantly hear young ladies around your ages talking about how good it feels to be excuse my French: fucked. One talked about how big the boy's "thang" was. How it tasted. How they did it in his ride. And she was bragging like he took her to an exquisite hotel and made passionate love to her. No. He didn't make love to her. He did his business and dropped her off. But she interpreted that as being loved.

"Lemme tell you something ladies and gents, if a person that you are dating does not respect you enough to take you to a fancy place and wine and dine you, and all they offer is a backseat in his or her ride or an alleyway, basement, or park under the bleachers, in the library, in the freakin' dungeon for all I care, why in the world would you indulge in him or her? I would say that it is probably for one of the 'L' words: Loneliness. Likeness. Love.

"No. It is not worth your time, but you will probably say, I'm not your mother. Lemme tell you something you can do bad all by yourself. 'Cause if you don't the reality is that you will be suffering by yourself. You will eventually be by yourself. You will eat, sleep, and cry by yourself. And the worst of the worst is everyone dies by themselves. But just imagine if no one comes to your funeral. Why won't they come to your funeral? Because you are no longer a part of the 'ELITE' crowd. You are now a part of the 'EPIDEMIC' crowd. No one wants to be a member of your crowd. People would rather die from cancer than to say that they have any association with HIV/AIDS. Why? Because people show compassion for a disease that was not self-inflicted.

"Think about it. People talk about cancer. People hug and kiss people with cancer. They fill them with hope. Blessings. They extend a helping hand. They are not afraid of it like they are with HIV/AIDS. Young people start being afraid! Start caring about your health—your life. And STOP playing with your lives! Because sooner or later the player gets played." I stop talking because my mouth is dry. And plus, I have nothing left to say.

Principal Knowles stands and drags her feet to the microphone as I step to the side. She has a daunting look on her face but her voice remains delicate. "Let's give Ms. Love a round of applause for her straight talk." She cuts her eyes at me and I smirk.

Everyone stands to his or her feet and for a brief moment, I feel heard. I gather my things; exit the school feeling as though being a *speaker* is not for me. My approach is brazen possibly because I live the life every day. And no matter how many times I tell my story it is not a yesterday memory. It is a lifetime fact.

H-Happy

Spring is in the air as I spring-clean Anonymous. It's about noon in the quiet streets of Montclair, New Jersey. People are lounging outside eating lunch soaking up the sun. They look so damn happy. I mean everybody. So at peace. They have smiles on their faces. Their laughs expand like they love life. There are singles out, too. And they, too, look refreshed like they just stepped out of H2O Spa, down on Creston Street. What are they doing right, I wonder. And where can I go to get some of that happy?

I caress my linen dress that hugs all of my curves. It takes me back to the 60s. I love that old-fashioned look because it looks so classy enhanced with a pair of white leggings and a nice low-heeled sandal. I accentuate my look with a pair of silver, black, and white dangling earrings that plays up my sexy. I am still sporting the low-cut. It brings out my high cheekbones, eyes, and full Christian Dior glossy lips. I look refreshed. Who would ever know that I was up all night suffering from insomnia? I look well rested. The Lord just keeps blessing me and I receive.

Mmm, spring smells so sweet. The color of the sky is that pretty sky-blue. And the sun is just glowing so bright. I cross my arms about my chest and lean my back against the brick surface of Anonymous inhaling the smell of the Office special of the day. Everything smells delicious.

I resume back to my spring-cleaning. I want the artists to walk in and feel a tranquil aura. Yes, something that draws them back in again and again and again. I want Anonymous to be their spot. Like their second home—a place they can come and unwind with entertainment, appetizers, and some soothing music to touch their souls. Get on-stage and burst out of themselves. Vent. Scream. Cry. Laugh. I want them to feel welcome. So I am doing some cleaning to get Anonymous in order.

Downstairs is nearly done I just have to freshen up the bathrooms with some herbal sage. It's supposed to cleanse the atmosphere. You know, get rid of bad karma. Out where the stage resides I use my oil burner and cascade my favorite scent of tobacco flower. I dust and polish down the wood with a lemony fragrance. And run a dust mop with the scent of orange peelings over the hardwood flooring. I inhale. It smells citrusy in here. I grab all of my cleaning supplies and head upstairs to work my magic. After I finish with upstairs I go over my itinerary for the day. I am featuring Open Mike tonight, since it is Friday. I have a competition where the winner wins two hundred dollars and competes with the next poet for the title of "the Baddest Poet" in the town. Everything is done with fun in mind.

Since I finish cleaning I decide to run some errands and as I am locking up I see these two young black girls standing at a bus stop. One is skinny, light complexioned with small pimples on her face. She is wearing a pink Forever21 dress and a pair of open toe Coach sandals. Girlfriend is in dire need of a pedicure. The other is also light complexioned with smooth butter skin, a long wavy weave, and she looks a bit more mature than her friend. She has a body on her, too. And she is wearing a pair of True Religion jeans with a colorful Ed Hardy T-shirt. They are talking so loud that the whole street can hear them. Not that I am eavesdropping but I am able to catch a little of their conversation and it makes my mouth open wide.

The skinny one has a mouth like a sailor on her. She is just airing out her laundry. And lemme tell you it ain't clean. All she says is the "f" word at the end of each sentence. *Ooh, I just wanna wash her filthy mouth out with a bar of soap!* If Ma'am were here she would take that chile by the hand and quote scriptures from the Bible until her ears bleed. Skinny girl is pissed about something. Her body language shows it. You know, the twisting of the lips, maneuvering of the neck, hands on her hips, and the tapping of her feet with a stare on her face like the world owes her something.

As I am walking slowly pass the two I hear the skinny one say, "Girl, South ate me out last night!" she stomps her foot. "He tasted my shit and slurped it up!" She grins from ear to ear. "Yeah, girl, gets yours," her friend says while nodding her head wishing she got some of the action. "Last night was the bomb! It was scandalous 'cause we did it in the backseat of his ride. Girllllll, I sucked him down. Oooh, that dick tasted so good. He takes real good care of himself. And he smells soooooo fuckin' good," the skinny one says, as she closes her eyes in reminiscence. "Gurl, you'a skanky bitch," her friend says ending it with a sly chuckle. My eyes pop wide. *I cannot believe my ears.* I didn't overhear one thing about a "condom" being used during their little sex-capade. All I hear is slurping, sucking, and excuse my French...fucking. What the hell! Everything in me wants to stop in my tracks and school those little hoes. I gotta call it as I sees it. They're hoes. Out here prancing around being loose and don't even know if they have an STD or worse, HIV.

Immediately, I am pissed and it is written all over my face. They

17

are young, vibrant, beautiful black girls so full of life. And all they seem obsessed with is some…dick. Lord has mercy. I shake my head from side-to-side while cutting my eyes as I walk pass them. A big part of me wants to grab that skinny one by her hair and knock some sense into her head, but I can't do that. She is not my child. I don't even know her. But deep inside I want to just shake 'em and school 'em on my life history. I want to scare them until they shit in their panties. I start fanning myself. Woo, they done got me fired up! I wanna shake 'em and scare 'em that's what I want to do. I have to compose myself. Take some deep breaths, Avery. I can't just go around shaking kids to death. What would people think of me? There has to be another way to get through to these young girls out here just giving their pussies away. At least get paid top dollar for it. No, I am kidding. I wasn't raised that way. I had to take it there just to lighten the dark side of things.

Well, "giving their pussies away"—I meant that because that is the language they speak. Sometimes you have to come down to a person's level in order to penetrate through. If you start talking statistics with them they tune you out. It doesn't soak in as do pictures or if a person is speaking truthfully about their experiences. I just had this discussion with the students at PCCC. Where the heck were they? I tap my right foot. Someone needs to school these little heifers out here. Put some fear in their panties and maybe they will leave them up instead of dropping it like it's hot for a measly screw! I am hot under the collar because what more do I have to do to get my point across to these young people? What more….

I shake my head in disgust feeling like the little I have done means nothing. I put the key in my car door, hop in, and drive off with a grimace on my face.

***

Anonymous is full to capacity. The crowd is lively tonight. Everyone gets revved up about Open Mike Night, especially tonight because there is no theme. Anything goes. They have to come up with some fierceness tonight. Open Mike is the main attraction for the poets who are high-strung and need to burn some of their adrenaline. Things get rather hot in here. But again, it's a competition. And when money's involved people get pumped.

I step on-stage around 8:00 p.m. I always give at least an hour for everyone to wind down from a hard day's work. They get their nibble on. Guzzle down some punch and take in the newest artists hitting the scene. They pose for some pictures for my photographer, Bass. Everyone's happy.

"What's up! How my peeps doing this evening?" I project my voice over the muffle of voices to get everyone's attention. "My name is Avery. I am the owner of Anonymous for all of you who are new to this home away from home. Um, let me just add that here at Anonymous it is an open atmosphere. And with that being said I just want to tell you that I am HIV-positive. If some of you are offended or uncomfortable by this news, please you can leave, but just know that you are welcome at any time." No one moves. I clap and the audience follows my lead. "Tonight, don't take tonight personal. This is all done in fun. We have some smoking poets here. I mean, smoking so get your hoses out to cool yourselves off. Our first contestant is none other than Kharismatic."

Kharismatic glides on-stage in his dashiki with his natural tresses puffed out in an Afro. He has that blue-black complexion that is flawlessly gorgeous. About six-feet tall, medium build with piercing eyes that soak you up. And when he speaks he is fluent in his art. Fluent. His presence is known, and never forgotten. The brotha is s-e-r-i-o-u-s.

"How's my peoples doing?"

"Fine, fine!" a black, stout female in the audience shouts.

"This piece is titled, 'WORDS FROM A FLAMING BITCH!'

Sweat trickles down the sides of Kharismatic's face, dripping off his chin. That man has a tongue that spews out words like fire. Shooting some realism on your ass. All I could do after he was done was step on-stage and hand him a handkerchief to wipe some of that sweat off his face. He got the crowd jumping.

"Lets give it up for Kharismatic." Everyone applauds.

"Okay...okay. It's about to get hotter in here, y'all. With her sultry tone and her multitasking prolific tongue here's, "Drooooooooollllll."

Drool steps on-stage in a pair of Refuge wide leg jeans, an orange T-shirt, and some high heel open toe sandals.

"How's everyone doing?" she asks. "I would like to share something with you all. Um, I'm not quite myself today. I, um, I broke up with my man, and ah, I have a lot heavy on my heart this evening. If you don't mind I'd like to share it with you all. Um, excuse my French. The title of my poem is titled, 'SHIT'!"

Drool grips the mike and let the words flow from her tongue. The look on her pretty face is of a woman who is fed up with the bullshit.

"Woo, woo! Gon' girl," this slender woman shouts in the front row with long weave dangling down her back. All the women are hooting and hollering and carrying on. Drool did her thing. And all the women or at least most could relate to her feelings of being used and abused by a man.

I walk on-stage, "Damn, ladies and gents, it's getting hot in here this evening. Let's give another round of applause to Drool."

Everyone claps in unison.

"Next we have, Not-a-Seasonal Ms. C'mon up here girl!"

Everyone claps harder as they know she always comes strong with her poetry.

"Hey y'all." She sighs. "Damn, it seems like troubled relationships must be in the air and summer ain't even here yet. Well, my poem is titled, 'LOVE ME LIKE, Chardonnay.'"

Not-a-Seasonal Ms. positions her thick frame in front of the mike, tilts her head as her long tresses covers half of her face. Her right hand flings her hair out of her eye and she lets her full lips motion out what is embedded in her heart. The ladies are already revved up, but some of the men nod their heads seeing the distress on her face. She opens her mouth and pauses as tears flood her eyes, streaming fast paced down her beautiful face.

"Yeah, yeah." I am hype. "Did I lie, y'all?!"

The crowd yells, "No!"

"Did I say that it was going to be getting hot in here? Well, its no longer hot, it's smoking!"

I chuckle.

1

I've since moved to a loft, still in Paterson, New Jersey. It's a building that caters to artists: writers, musicians, sculptors, photographers, fine arts, you name it. I wanted to be around others, like myself. You know, blend those creative juices together. I wanted to be somewhere I felt I belonged. Somewhere I would fit in. Somewhere I could call home and mean it. Yes, I think I made the right choice. The place is spacious. The area is quiet. Just the way I like it. There were no special privileges getting into this building. I didn't know anyone on the committee. No. I had to fill out an application, submit it, and wait for a vacancy.

During my waiting period, I received a letter asking if I was still interested, and if I was, I had to submit a letter reaffirming that. And I played by the book. I didn't use my feminine ways to inch my name to the top of the list. Nope. I waited my turn just like everyone else. The one thing I didn't *do* was expose myself to the committee board. I guess you can say I weighed out my options. Stopped to think, first. You have to understand it is like truth or dare, living with HIV. Truth you tell and you dare if no one else will. What are the chances of someone keeping my "status" confidential? Slim. It is no different than being a child molester living in a quiet area around children. Once the word is out, oh damn.

Oh, I understand that everyone is not as embracing as they may say they are or would be in that situation. People try to show compassion, but underneath all of that niceness they are shitting bricks hoping you don't hug or kiss them on the cheek. Oh, damn! God forbid you do that without them seeing it coming. You might as well hand them a bar of soap in your presence to wash your poison off of them. I am telling you, when you are confronted by someone who has it flowing through their bloodstream things change so drastically. I become invisible to the naked eye. I become a face without my birth name. I become "Oh, that *black* woman with HIV." Truth hurts those who have brittle bones. I may have an incurable illness (knock on wood that that changes), but I am not living in denial. The reactions in the past have mended me into who I am today. A black woman on a mission of awareness and I am truly blessed to be able to give back to those who have given to me. It only takes one person to step out of bounds to create a frenzy for more to step out and inspire.

Since I've been here I find myself writing more and more these days. If the days are tranquil I'll take a stroll up to the park and sit on the bench staring out at the murky waters with my pad and pen in hand and my thoughts floating in the cottony clouds. Sometimes I lose myself in my surroundings: the trees, the spotted grass, the dirt, birds chirping, squirrels running amuck, water brushing against the rocks, ants, and flies and bees buzzing. It all becomes my painted canvas in Spoken Word. I sit back and take it all in. Yes, cherish the quiet moments of life while I still can appreciate the wonderful things that God blesses us with. I take nothing for granted and everything for face value. Just like with poetry. Poetry is genuine. It's profound. It's loud, soft, contradicting, funny, sad, loving, mad, sweet, nasty, humble, and hostile. Poetry is real. It digs deep down into the hollowness of one's soul and lifts all of that stuff up and out for others to relate to. It pierces your heart and makes you weep in your seat. It makes you make love to your mind with each stroke of word. It makes you listen and untwist the messages that are inscribed in black ink and felt in red grief. Poetry is strong and fearless. It is a warrior in my eyes—a black, gray, and white warrior.

Poetry has become my survival. And the arts are my reason for living. I truly believe this. Not only because of Anonymous, but because it gives me a way of sharing a pastime with my beloved father, Poppa. Knowing that he had a way with words leads me to believe this "voice" is where it resonates. Poppa. So much I didn't know. I still have Poppa's poem in its special frame, but now it hangs in my living room. Every time I read it I yearn to know certain things, things that he could never answer or just chose not to. It helps me heal, slowly; because I now know he had the best intentions for me. But it takes time for flesh wounds to close. And I am not forcing a thing. When it is time it shall be done.

I realize over the years that it is difficult for *men* to express themselves and I think that was what I had forgotten about Poppa. Poppa was a man first, husband second, father third. I guess I assumed that he would know how to nurture me, but that wasn't the case. Until—

Well, you know the story. And those of you who don't, well, you have to crawl before you can walk. Basically, what I am saying is there is another part of me floating around out in the world. If you look and inquire you will find me. Word of mouth is like a mother. Mama always knows.

***

I am truly blessed! That was the afterthought after exposing to Anonymous that I was raped and as a result contracted HIV. I thought eyes would roll and heads would turn. I never thought in a million years that those folks would embrace me. Not after Tyde Jobar Graham, a.k.a. Storyteller, got on-stage to recite his poetry. God rest his soul. I thought they would boo me right off-stage and the doors to Anonymous would have been shut. To my surprise, the outcome was just the opposite. I was elated. We, my extended family gave a vigil at Anonymous for Storyteller. It was Tyde's home away from home so I felt it best to send my brotha off right. Now, he's with his mother. Storyteller stays in my thoughts and I appreciate my life more and more because of him and Johnnie. I miss Johnnie. It's been like forever with him vacationing in the afterlife. I still don't believe that he died. I've been keeping track and I keep telling myself that he is vacationing somewhere in the Virgin Islands. I know it's not good to be living in partial denial, but losing someone so dear to you is not easy to ingest. I know it in my head, but tell that to my heart 'cause it is not trying to hear it. Even after holding his urn in my bare hands. After sprinkling his ashes out of the helicopter and letting him dance on air falling to his favorite place of serenity, Central Park. In my heart, Johnnie will always be alive. I guess that's why I am still seeing my therapist, Dr. Cristal, because I know I have plenty of unresolved issues. I guess that's why Dr. Cristal makes the mega-bucks—because of people like me.

I am *now* considered a veteran at Red Alert. I didn't think that Xavier Combs III would want someone like me still working for him. I mean a thief. He took me by the side that evening at Anonymous and gave me the biggest hug I could ever imagine getting from anyone. In the back of my mind I thought he was setting me up for the kill, but he wasn't. He let bygones be bygones. I broke the rules of his confidentiality agreement, but I was helping those like me and I guess he saw the message that I was trying to deliver. We are the best of friends so I kept the position at Red Alert to help those like me. Still today, I have good and bad days, but I am making a difference because *now* I let them know that we are in the same damn boat. And their voices light up like they are talking to flesh and blood. It is hard to describe, you have to be there.

My co-workers, Rae, Horace, Khalis, they were my phone buddies when I first started at Red Alert. Well, the word got out about my status. 'Ey, I wasn't a bit surprised. I was paranoid. I kept seeing myself walking into the office and all eyes were planted on me. Their hands hid their mouths as they whispered among themselves right in front of my face. Talk about harsh. Uh, I had bad dreams about returning to work, but once I stepped foot back in everyone treated me as normal—at least most. Now, they don't have a problem with what I carry around inside of me. Nope. They say, "Avery, you all right." And we laughed 'cause that's how it should've been.

Now, the rest of 'em, for instance, Careen Walker, my manager, oh, she had a different outlook on the whole deception as she put it thing. Some people got to blow things way out of proportion. She called me every derogatory name she could muster up, but the one name she dared to call me the "N" word. Oh, she would have gotten a foot planted right up her flat ass.

Well, Careen resigned from her position because of stupidity, ignorance, prejudice, and fear. Actually, it was because she was a racist. She didn't consider Xavier black because of his lighter skin tone. I found that out later, and the two combined bare bone facts: Black + HIV-positive= Avery. Oh, she was fit-to-be-tied. She told Xavier to take that job and shove it up his sell-out ass. So unappreciative, I thought. She was there since the birth of Red Alert, but that's her hang up, not mine. People fake the funk all the time, especially when reality smacks 'em in the face. But that's water under the bridge.

Speaking of water under the bridge, I haven't bumped into Blu McDowell, lately. He must've moved or got married to that skank he was slobbering all over. I wasn't jealous just a little livid by his actions. I mean, I came clean and the brother went ballistic. Practically threw me out of his car. It hurt like hell when he said that he should piss on me. Talk about harsh that was brutal. I had never been treated that way, and I must say his words dug deep into the white meat of me.

Now, Travar Atkin, I've seen him one other time at the His and Her Incense Boutique here in Montclair, and we were cordial. I must admit it felt pretty awkward. I still had feelings for him, but what we tried to share was now a past memory.

I heard through the grapevine that Zaelyn Homes reconciled with his wife. She knew nothing about the reconciliation because she assumed their marriage was fine. Having an exhilarating night with me made him decide to do right by her and his children. I was the bigger woman even though I didn't want to be. I was head-over-heels for that man. He hurt me deeply. He played me emotionally and I felt like a complete idiot because I let him woo me right out of my thong. As I recall, I initiated it because I truly thought that he had deep feelings for me. That he cared for me even after telling him about my status. He chose to have protective sex. I gave him options. Why couldn't he give me the same? I thought he was the one. I coulda loved him so unconditionally. If only. My body was hungry and he fed me plenty, but it came with consequences. Yes, I was heartbroken. De-va-stated. Letting him go nearly ate me up. Day after day, I cried like a small child. Yes, it was hard. It took me about a month to get over him because of the night we shared. Oh, I wanted more, but. It meant something to me because I hadn't been made love to in soooooooo long that I savored that moment in time. It coulda been special. The thought did cross my mind to take the little I could get and be satisfied. But I felt I was worth much more than a night of unimaginative passion. I wanted many nights of passion with a one-woman man. Call me old fashion I really don't care. I want what I want and I am never gonna short change myself ever again.

Time. All I do work, work, work my fingers to the bone. Success comes with an understanding that you won't have much time for pleasure. I am everyone when it comes to keeping Anonymous together. Sometimes I wish I had a partner. And I know if Johnnie were here, he would be. Being a proprietor becomes demanding, frustrating, and smothering a majority of the time. Sometimes I feel like I can't breathe. A social life. What's that? It had never really entered my mind because my time is limited. And then the process of divulging my status comes into play. Sometimes I get discouraged and would rather be alone, than hurt. Relationships are hard work. And honestly, I have enough food on my plate. I am not expecting to meet anyone, anytime soon. Dating and I don't seem to mix so I consume myself in work. It is easier this way. My feelings can't get hurt from work. Work won't purposely make me cry. Work won't purposely disappoint me unless *I* do something wrong. Work is a sure win to being content, at least for me. No drama, droopy eyes, or droppin' of the panties and that is how I like it. Or so I thought.

***

The end of November of '08, somehow companionship snuck up on me. Clever little rascal. I saw this chestnut-brown complected fellah, about 5'10", stout with a potbelly and one slouchy eye all up in the crack of my rump-pa-dump. Literally speaking. Brother had no type of refinement to him. I can't stress it enough. Ghet-to. It was that obvious. But he was a smooth dresser in his five-hundred-dollar-suit, three-hundred-dollar square-toe-shoes, and a brim hat with a sly grin on his face. Like he knew that he was going to snatch me up. Uh-huh. I could see the spit drooling down the corners of his mouth like a pit-bull. I sensed bullshit a mile away. He was most definitely rough around the edges. There was no way in hell I was going to give him the time of day. No way Jose!

First of all, there was no physical attraction on my part. I couldn't see past the ghetto-ness. Whatever. Yes, to all of you twisting your lips up. I'm me. And being upfront is a part of my makeup. Okay, now untwists those lips.

Listen, I wouldn't be mean if the man spoke to me. There was no need to come off shallow. Dating him. Now, now, that was another story. "Class" and "Ghetto" were like oil and water. We didn't have anything in common. Nothing. Zilch. Nada.

Well, to my surprise this man kept nagging the hell out of me.

"Woon't you take my number," he stuttered.

"No, thank you."

"You might wanna call me," he insisted.

"I don't think soooo." The grimace on my face was a dead giveaway to stop while he was ahead.

"Well, here take it anyway. You never know," he insisted, again.

I sighed.

Then he stuck a pen and a piece of paper in my face. And I left his hand dangling.

Then he proceeded to write down his phone number and placed it gently in my lap.

I looked at him like he had a screw loose as he walked away with that damn sly grin plastered on his face. Oooh. I could tell 'cause his chunky cheeks spread like he had buttermilk biscuits stuffed in his mouth.

His persistence started wearing me down. And my ears began to open to hear what this man by the name of Brick Sumpton had to say. Ooh, this fellah stunk with drama. It was a bit overwhelming. I could smell liar, liar, and liar all over his person. And it smelled like a landfill. Yep, that foul. I was neither amused nor impressed by him or his embellishments of himself. Puuleeeeasse *say something intelligent. Let me know that you are not a complete dickhead,* I thought to myself. That was wishful thinking on my part. I had high hopes for this fellah. But I realized you couldn't turn a "Low-down-Dirty Hustler" into a "Gentle-man Thug." Why? I asked myself that very same question. There are no feelings inside of his callous shell. It's like his insides are made of bricks. Go figure? The only complete sentence that escaped from his Ebonics-speaking tongue was, "Ms., you gots some fuckin' pretty toes. Damn! Where you get dem feets from?"

Where'd you get that foul mouth? 'Cause I know dang well your mama taught you how to speak to a woman properly. Why'd I bother? Don't ask and I won't have to tell you no lies. What happened? I haven't got a clue.

It seemed my toes captivated him and he wanted to *suck* them. No man has ever said that to me before. Somehow, that broke the awkward feeling I had about him. And it opened me up to something different. I had never dated a *hustler* type before. No. My preference was clean, polished, and successful white men, at least that was until I met Blu, Travar, and Zaelyn. Brick's occupation: street-hustler. A high school dropout. A felon. God only knows how many times he had seen the inside of a jail cell. He was separated, not divorced. And he has crumb snatchers. Snotty-nose-brats! Clearly, I was delusional. There was no foundation to provide the stable lifestyle that I was accustomed to. The man still resided with his momma. His mammy! Practically pushing his late forties and still pulling on his momma's skirt tail. That right there was strikes one—no independence.

Let me just go down the lists: No driver's license. Did he think I was going to be chauffeuring him around? I thought not! No cushion setup in the bank for a rainy day. He only had that gift of gab to make his hustle and his money, which he either squandered himself to the poorhouse by gambling, drinking it up because he was also an alcoholic+, the + being a casual cokehead. He splurged on the latest fashions and finest restaurants—tried to dress to impress. His survival skills were no different than living from paycheck to paycheck. And he was making tax-free money. He had no investments—nada. He definitely wasn't the suave debonair type. Not one ounce of him. But he pretended to be charismatic. And once his mouth opened…the truth was leaked out because the ghetto-ness came spewing out a mile a minute. And he wasn't intellectual enough to clean it up. So basically, he worked with what he had, which wasn't much. He accomplished his goals of making money, but just as fast as he made it, it was gone even faster. Nothing was learned from his mistakes because an alcoholic or rather an *addict* can't see his mistakes. He thought he was superior. Brotha-man had been living a façade for a long time. And *I*, for the life of me, could not see the attraction until he spoke of his *deceased father*. Damn. We, at that point, had something in common.

At a time in my life I resented my father with a passion and so did Brick. I mean my bitterness was strong enough to cough phlegm in my own daddy's face. He hurt me deep. And it took years to come to the realization of wanting to know why he hurt me. It never was told until I found that one poem. And I guess in some small way Brick was experiencing the same thing of wanting to know, why, but never being told. So he was left to pick up the pieces and I think it made him feel inadequate most of his life. The pain. The pain was that controlling and inside he would break down, but outside he would rob and steal to fill the void. I was able to hear the little boy in him and it saddened me. Somehow that brought us closer.

***

Looking at Brick I see something I never thought I would see from his hardcore shell. Compassion. Shit, a conscience. But it would only last for a hot minute until his mood swings kicked in. I keep thinking that the brotha suffers from bipolar disorder. He goes from up to down in a matter of seconds. I never know how he's gonna be by the time he sits down on the clay-colored sofa. Yes, just that quickly he starts to sink in depression. But he doesn't seem to notice. Some people block things out because they don't want to be "classified" as having an ailment. Shit, I'd rather know than walk around like a freakin' time bomb. But that's him and only he can help himself.

I never confided in him about my status. Why? Well, constantly I heard him use a derogatory word: *faggot*. I told him he shouldn't judge because most folks he's around are probably gay. It made me think about how he would look at me. What would he call me: Death. Poison. Silent Killer. Yeah, that marinated in my head a lot. With that being said, I didn't feel the need to tell him. The chemistry between us is at a simmer, anyway, and plus, he is very self-centered. Everything is about him, him, and him. That alone leaves me to believe that he is not the reliable type. Not when it comes down to being a shoulder to lean on.

Under pressure, I see him showing me his back with a smug look on his face, and me picking up the pieces alone. But even still, I sense something spiritual from him. Maybe I'm fooling myself to believe that there is some good in him. I mean there have been a few people who have approached me about him and nothing good was said about the man. Nothing. It made me wonder can someone really be that bad. That piqued my curiosity. Yep. I had the weirdest feeling about him.

Now I feel like there is something hiding underneath all that imitation thick skin. The man is empty and seeking acceptance from damn near anywhere he can find it. That is the only thing that is real about him. I am able to break down those barriers as Zaelyn had with me and I see a wounded soul. Like, I used to be. And I see what I think is a good man with a bunch of baggage wearing him down to think small and live even smaller within the walls of pain.

2

Elementary.

When I was little I attended PS No. 5 in Paterson. During the spring and summer break I hung with a clique: Shortbread, who had a steel plate in his head. He was always having seizures. And he loved to talk junk for a short guy. Greasy and Hi-C were brothers, Hi-C, being the oldest. Actually, Hi-C was in my eighth-grade class with Mrs. R. Then there's Drip, he was the slick talker who always stirred up trouble, but then tried that gift of gab to grab the ladies. His brother, T-bone, was no different. T-bone was skinnier than a toothpick but walked around like he was a muscular bodybuilder. All the girls thought he was butt-ugly and he looked like he stank. Dimples was always horse playing and laughing over simple stuff. Method was the pretty-boy. He looked biracial, but I am not 100% sure. He was the finest one out of the bunch, though. He loved his crease-stitched Lee jeans with his nameplate belt buckle. And then there was Sin and Stretchy, those two hung pretty tight. Stretchy seemed a little sly. Out of us girls, there was Wisdom, who had the biggest crush on Hi-C, but unfortunately he wasn't into meaty girls. Then there was Meechy, Booty, Jelly; I called her Jelly 'cause she jiggled when she walked. Oh, she had it bad for Method. Girlfriend changed her 'do from natural to perm to catch his attention.

Then there's Toothy; he was so mouthy that his teeth just beamed like the sun. With all that yellow skin just shining likes a streetlight. And his older brother, Left-Foot, came aroun' to shoot some hoops and hung with Sin and Stretchy.

Then Toothy and Left-Foot sisters joined in from time to time. Their mouth-o-mighty sister, Bootsey, would come sashaying around the corner with her wide hips and her watered-down-fake-good-hair-wearing self. Everybody knew she had a perm. Or their sister Juicy, who had a body like a woman, high yellow skin, short ash-brown hair that she laid the edges down with baby oil or Vaseline to make it look like baby hair, and legs that would track yo' every move. Her legs were toned and flawless. She was like all the boys' goddess, all of 'em. Boy she made them *hard* all the time. And trust me, she knew it. That head wasn't raised high, those hips weren't swayin', and that booty wasn't shakin' for nothin'.

In spite of our differences we all hung pretty tight. We met on

North Eighth Street at Commons Park or the basketball court, which was right across the street, just hanging out. It was a different mixture of personalities. A lot of the times the boys would try to talk to us girls and some of us just weren't interested. Of course, no one likes rejection and that led to the name-calling to cover their soft spot that had been bruised. Most of the boys picked on me because I was an easy target. Some of the boys called me mean names like, "stick," "bag of bones," "bony," "skinny," which manifested as lower self-esteem for me. They called me "baldhead," and I just smirked trying to hide the pain. My body ached most of the time. The name-calling continued with "bird chest" and the names branded my skin. I didn't have a tablespoon of cute in me. Boy did they have a good ol' time stomping me down with their harsh words. I figured if I acted like them, by being a "tomboy" by playing basketball, hopping fences, doing belly flips on the swings, that they would befriend me, but it didn't matter much. The name-calling remained and I never really had any comebacks to wound them with. So I suffered in my skin.

During the summertime it was even more difficult because the name-calling only worsened. Either you did the "nasty" with one of those boys to shut them the hell up and ended up with a reputation or you continued to hear the name-calling. I preferred to hear the name-calling. Those boys seemed childish, anyway. I believed they were being someone they weren't. They really didn't know how to approach a girl properly. I could only assume that they thought you had to be hardcore to impress a girl. It didn't impress me. Butt-ugly or not I still had options. I wanted a boy who was polite, trusting, and a dreamer. I craved a boy with thick skin, not a wimp. Heck, it didn't make sense for both of us to be cowards. I just desired a nice boy. Just the thought made me nod my head and smile like I was floating on a natural high. I was not a daredevil, but I wanted someone who was spontaneous. Thinking it might add some oomph to my life, to my spirit, and somehow build my confidence up. I wanted someone understanding, too. I felt I needed nurturing and love in my life. Not pain. I wanted no more pain. Sometimes I got tired of watching 'pain' sitting on the stoop, hugging its love handles, damn near slaughtering me from laughter. Son-of-a-bitch!

Out of the bunch, Wisdom Sparks and I were real close, almost like blood-sisters. It seemed all the boys in the neighborhood picked on us the most 'cause we stood out like two sore thumbs. We were just two odd balls to the world, but the best of friends to us. We desperately tried to not let them get the better of us. I mean, figuring they always nit picked and clowned jokes about us told me it must be something about us worth talking about. Nevertheless, their words did cut through my skin.

Wisdom lived around the corner from me on North Eighth Street. I could see her sage-colored house through the wired fence of my backyard. At times, I'd hop the fence instead of walking around the block to visit her. Wisdom was the total opposite of me. She was high yellow with big breasts and smart as a whip. She wore her hair in a low Afro, until she eventually got a straight perm. She attended Catholic school and engrossed her eyes in Nancy Drew books. She was hungry for knowledge. That's how her mother and father raised her. We seemed alike, meaning, she had two parents living under one roof, but soon after they separated and later divorced. Neither one of us had ever lived in the projects.

***

I was twelve years old when my eyes laid upon this oatmeal-complected boy who resided on North First Street. I always saw him when I walked with Wisdom to her cousin Meechy's house. I never knew his name so I made one up for him: "Dream-Boy," and I gazed at him like he was a superstar. He had eyes that were round and filled with bronze tone, and a sweetness that gave me a sugar rush. Yes, Lord, that boy had me sunk. I mean I was drowning in puppy love. And he was none the wiser.

I was paranoid to utter a word, thinking that it may come out all tangled. Or I may start stuttering from nervousness. In my mind, the thought of him being taken by me was such a far-fetched idea that I tried to downplay what I was feeling internally for him. This warmth, this churning in my tummy, tingles in my feet and toes, smirks that wanted to expand into big smiles, eyes that craved to cry for I was experiencing my first real crush. He moved me. I was smitten like a shy girl. If only he could see me, not the outer of me, but the inner. *Then maybe, just maybe I have a shot at winning his heart*, I thought. I inhaled each time I saw him and he simply took my breath away. I was in silent love and it hurt so badly because I didn't give myself the benefit of the doubt to trust in me and speak from my heart of how I felt for Dream-Boy. He was a rarity, compared to the boys in my neighborhood. He was a different boy of quiet and proper manners, not obnoxiousness or ill manners. He was my dream boy.

In my dreams I felt him embracing me. Of him piercing my eyes and touching my hand and making me full with his trustworthy words of how much he worshiped the ground I walked on. Oh, I was exaggerating with particulars and I was most enchanted by my creativity. Still, I yearned for him. My skin glistened and exuded a glow to my less-desirable face. Deep in the pit of my stomach I knew that he was meant to be mine, but I was too embarrassed, afraid to be rejected with harshness that I admired him from a distance. Still, loving him with respect, but in my mind I felt one day we shall meet again, so hopeful that I would have blossomed by that time, shedding the ugly duckling into an exhibit of natural beauty.

***

I met a girl named Bitty Greene. She was brown-skinned, with a droopy bottom lip from sucking her thumb. She had a pudgy nose, and a petite frame with wide hips for a slender girl. And she had long, black, thick hair. She lived up the street on Jane around the corner from me. She went to a Catholic school, too, like Wisdom. Her parents owned a big white house that took up most of the corner. Her mother was from the Carolinas and sounded like it, too. She was a hardworking woman, a foreman at Nabisco. She seemed to value quality time with her daughter. I valued quality time with *her* 'cause I didn't get it from Ma'am. So I visited quite frequently.

Bitty seemed to have the good life because she had a mother and a father all living under one roof. She had her own bedroom with a canopy bed like a princess. Her mother paid attention to her, bought her nice clothes, shoes, and talked to her. She included Bitty in her life. That intrigued me and I always wanted to be around her. Her mother fed me home cooked meals and complimented me. I was not used to compliments. Though, it made me feel good inside. Like, she cared.

Bitty's mother always wanted the best for her, but sometimes Bitty came off a little shallow. Bitty was a spoiled brat! At times her mother would ask her to do little things for her and Bitty would give her attitude. Like, for instance, if she wanted her scalp scratched (scratchin' her dandruff before she washed her hair), with a small-tooth comb. It seemed that relaxed her mother's nerves. Bitty would whine 'cause she didn't want to do it and would give her mother back talk. (Any other mother would have slapped the shit outta her.) So I volunteered 'cause it didn't seem like much to ask for. Her mother complimented me, "You like my second daughter." Wow, I thought. She soothed my insides with kind words. At times I felt guilty and discouraged because I dreaded leaving her home, but I had my own home. It just wasn't as inviting.

Things gradually changed with Wisdom and me 'cause her and Bitty didn't see eye to eye. I liked them both as friends. I mean, Wisdom and I had more in common. We were not spoiled rotten. We had to grow up faster than our years. But for some reason I clung more towards Bitty 'cause of her mother. Her mother saw something in me and she expressed that I was a good girl. *Finally! Someone sees it*, I thought. That mattered a great deal to me. I never wanted anyone to think negatively about me. Bitty's mother didn't know a lot about Ma'am and me. But she based things off of the way I acted. I had matured in more ways than one psychologically, but I was not all put together like she thought. If anything, I lived in disarray. My outside was a toasted marshmallow, but on the inside I was not sweet like candy. I was broken like glass.

***

What is love?
Love: to feel tender affection for somebody.
Is this love?
Girl-to-Girl…

It was a hot Saturday. Ma'am was going to work to put in some overtime and she had asked one of the member's daughters from her sewing club to watch over me. I was fourteen, at the time. I was old enough to care for myself. I was a latchkey kid. Ma'am felt the need to protect me from harms way. Little did she know?

Persian was pretty. All smothered in mocha skin. She was tall and slender with a slick back ponytail. She was a polished kind of girl. You know uppity. We talked little. And somehow we ended up in my parents' bedroom. Persian laid me down on the bed, ever so gently. She kissed me with those pouting lips, ever so gently. And she lay on top of me, ever so gently. But inside I felt nauseated. I felt trapped. I felt like I was suffocating as she gyrated my terry cloth shorts with the feel of her denim jeans. Her fingers eased down into my shorts and inched them down to my buttocks as her zipper slithered down and her jeans wrapped her thighs. Around and around her body movement flowed as if she was dirty dancing against my innocence. And her movement became intense, not hurtful, but intense as if something was building inside of her. I was unaware of that feeling. I was still pure.

The baffling thing about this was that Persian had an admirer. It was one of my relatives. He was salivating for her in his boyish way of salivating. Extending her a box of Valentine's Day candy and card and possibly a stuffed animal—I'm not certain about the stuffed animal. But I didn't know what the outcome was on that February day. Obviously she had a liking for the kitty. But her liking was not my cup of tea. I preferred something manly when that time approached.

Her scent of delicate, of soft, and subtle was a memory I chose to forget, but as always some things never die. Nightmares tend to invite themselves and mope around in your presence like a temple-throbbing hangover. I had many uninvited hangovers and this particular one affected me in more ways than one because it involved a *she*.

As I got older I became paranoid like I had this 'thing.' This seed planted inside of me that was different. I wondered if I was living in the wrong body. I wondered if I had this scent that triggered pretty pussies to be fiend for me. I became confused about me. But a woman never turned on my eyes. I considered women beautiful and I would voice it out without hesitation because I felt comfortable enough. But that explosive thought of connecting intimately with a woman never dazzled my mind. Never tingled me to seek. Never challenged me even with white, Asian, and Black women who had boldly and intentionally come on to me. I would simply be polite, not even engaging in the thought of 'us' being in lust. Let alone love.

I hadn't seen Persian for some time. The last time I saw her she was married with children. Perhaps she was going through a phase. Or perhaps that gyrating pretty pussy still lives inside of her famished for the delicacies of the cat.

***

What's come over me?
I had this one boy on the brain.
Yep, Sin.
And I questioned would he *hurt* me or not.

Liking Sin seemed so weird because the more I watched him the more I realized he seemed to absorb trouble. After a while I couldn't stand his black ass. He was not the ideal boy for me as I had hoped. Even though I was butt-ugly I felt I still had options. I wanted someone laid back and slow-paced. Sin was most definitely the opposite of that. Truthfully, I didn't know what changed the colors of my eyes.

Sin and I gradually talked. He wasn't a complete bore, as I had perceived. The brotha' actually had a good head on his shoulders. He was articulate, smooth, and he displayed this confidence about himself. Hmm. That must've been what grasped my attention.

The other thing that wooed me was the fact that he accepted my ugliness. I didn't have to duck, dodge, or explain why God made me so damn hideous. That was a load off of me. I sensed empathy from him. After that, I was hypnotized. I was under this spell of comfort because I felt he understood me. That he could literally look me in the eyes and see all of my baggage. He consoled me. He listened to me. He touched me in a way I had never been touched before. He held my petite frame in his arms. He sniffed me. I could finally breathe.

I emptied myself out to Sin. I felt myself opening more and more. And the more I opened the more attentive he became. We spent much time together after the clique left to go home. We stayed behind and smooched in the dugout of the baseball field. He kissed me. Me! His hands caressed my body and squeezed my butt as he let out a moan, "Damn, you feel so soft." I wrapped my thin arms around his neck and held him so close to my heart. I stared into his eyes and I kissed him with a peck, then we both opened our mouth and our tongues greeted spiraling recklessly in our mouths. I felt a slight tingle and I knew that the love bug had bitten me. I had this energy. I dreamt of him. I doodled his name on my notebooks with little hearts. I whispered his name just because. I wanted to live with this boy. Grow old with this boy. My mind was racing with thoughts of him. I was experiencing my first love.

Eventually Sin would lead in discussion of wanting to go to the next level. You know, first, second, and third base. I was hesitant. Marriage, I'm saving myself for marriage. Mr. Right might come my way and sweep me off my feet. You never know, I thought to myself. But Sin had a way with words, and kisses, and hugs, and I felt that we would be together long-term. I was fourteen. What did I really know? Nothing.

This little voice started dissecting me down to a crumb. This was the first boy who had ever acknowledged me. He was the first who had kissed me intimately. Not a peck. He was the first who had listened to me and gave me advice. He showed compassion. He made me feel like he cared about me. Then my mind had me thinking that he was the best I could and would do. Honestly, who would want to be with me, someone so ugly? Who would want a ugly girl? I was batting a thousand, no one. So that made my final decision to give myself to Sin.

I had it played out in my head. This first time was going to be so romantic with candles lit, soft music playing, food (hamburgers or T-bone steak) and drinks (Kool-Aid or iced tea), and flowers (preferably long-stemmed red roses). Yeah, I was dreaming, all right. I just knew that he was going to sweep me off my feet as my negligee flowed in the breeze, as he carried me to the bedroom and laid me down gently admiring my beauty. Desiring me. Again, I was dreaming.

The reality of my first time was just the opposite of that.

Our first time was in the basement of his parents' home. It smelled like bleach and other household products. He held my hand in the dark and led me into this room where there was a couch. He laid me down and I heard the couch squeak. Off came our clothes and I covered my small breasts. My body shivered because there was a chill in the air. His lips caressed my nipples, making them harden. His hand eased down to my "yum-yum" and he massaged it gently. I felt his penis enlarge and I swallowed hard. Deep inside I don't think I was actually ready to give up the most precious thing I had preserved, but as his body gyrated his breath grazed my earlobe and his thoughts of me sang in my ears. I let go of all of my fears and insecurities and I exhaled still with that hardened lump in my throat.

"Damn, you are sooooo soft. Damn." He said.

I tried to get into it by moving my hands down his smooth back and easing down to his buttocks. I felt the tightness in his muscles. All that black skin was hidden in the dark, but in my mind I'd imagined what he looked like in the nude. I closed my eyes and opened my legs as he had asked and my body flinched as he tried to enter me. It was the worst feeling in the world.

"Relax." He spoke gently.

I tried so hard to, but the feeling was not pleasurable, as I had imagined. There was no romance to comfort my anxiety. No music to distract my thoughts. No candles burning with fragrant scent soothing me. No flowers in a vase gazing at me. No brightness. I felt duped. But then he whispered something in my ears that led me to believe that I could follow through.

"Trust me," eased out of his mouth as he stopped and I gazed into the whites of his eyes. And I had asked myself at that moment, did I trust him. And my answer was yes. I trusted him with personal information. I trusted him by allowing our tongues to greet. I trusted him with my body and my mind. But this trust came with trusting him with my 'soul'. Yes, once I gave myself to him I felt I was giving of myself completely. Freely and endearingly. If I followed through I would be giving him a precious part of me and I could only hope that he would cherish and savor the experience.

I opened my legs wider and he tried again, and again I flinched as my eyes squinted.

"Relax your body. I won't hurt you."

And I believed his words. I believed that he wouldn't intentionally hurt me like others had. So by the third attempt I braced myself and tried to clear my mind. I took a deep breath and opened my legs even wider and he entered me slowly not to have me go into major shock.

"Stop!" I shrieked, tapping his back like a ghost had spooked me. The feeling was most unpleasant and I wanted to stop and get dressed and go home. I didn't want it because I felt like it would rip me open. I didn't want to feel pain. I wanted no more pain. Sin assured me that he would be gentle. I sighed. And we tried it for the last time. I felt the door to me opening as he slowly eased himself in. My eyes squinted as my fingers dug in his back. His body had a rhythm and I opened wider and wider and wider. His breathing grew as moans and groans were like music. I'd imagine soft music in my head. His body began to rattle silently through his skin and I felt the warmth of our bodies and I heard the sound of wetness oozing and I felt it drooling from me. Sin collapsed on my small breasts with his heart pounding rapidly through my skin. I felt what I thought was his "love" for me. Even though he never uttered the word.

After I got dressed and went home. I never said anything to Ma'am. I kept my secret buried in my chest.

The next day was like nothing ever took place and I was somewhat baffled. *This is not how it is on the soap operas*, I thought. I guess I assumed that Sin would be sniffing me like the boys did to the girls at school. I was wrong. There was no special treatment. His demeanor was completely the same as before. But somewhere between that prior evening and the next day, my feelings had changed dramatically. I had fallen in love.

I would hear someone's car radio playing "Always and Forever" or "Magic Man" and I was swimming in thoughts of Sin. And anytime thereafter, when he wanted to indulge in my "yum-yum" I never deprived him. I fed him breakfast, lunch, and dinner if he wanted it. I was wide-open. I couldn't believe that I could feel something for someone else with all the baggage that bled inside of me. I simply couldn't believe that I had found someone who was delighted with me. Who wanted to share my space, not just my body? But then reality hit me over the head with a two-by-four. BAMM!

I saw Sin walking down the street with another girl. I was devastated. It hit me hard. I felt sooooooo stupid. So clueless. Naïve. Gullible.

It was evident that Sin was not thinking about meeeeeeeeeeeee. He was merely interested in wetting his *lust* tool. And I allowed him to indulge in me plenty. He never missed a meal. *Why couldn't he see that I was a good girl who had been deprived? Love* was a necessity in my life. I was starving for it. My head felt like it was going to burst. I was heartbroken. I cried so grievingly like someone had just died. Someone had. Me.

To make my heartache worse I noticed changes in me: sleepiness, fatigue, I felt lousy most of the time. Why? I wasn't sure, but with all the lack of protection it could only be one thing.

Hello. My name is Avery. I am fourteen and, and, and, I am pregnant.

Talk about petrified. I was beyond petrified. How did this happen? It was simple to answer. I let my guard down and I was swept into this fantasy that Sin simply adored me. I was duped. So I weighed out my options after taking a home pregnancy test. Tell Sin or not? I needed his help so I decided to tell him. Until—

"I'm leaving for the Navy." Sin said.

"When?" I asked.

"Today."

WHAT! BUT...BUT... I HAVE SOMETHING TO TELL YOU. I'M...I'M...PREGNANT.

As you've guessed I never told him. I tried to carry the weight on my shoulders. My life was crumbling right before my eyes. *What am I gonna do?* That thought ran through my mind quite often. I hadn't a clue.

Deep down I wanted to divulge my secret to someone I could trust. There weren't very many options. Wisdom. Bitty. But they wouldn't be able to help me. I needed an adult because this was an adult issue. I wanted to divulge the news to Ma'am but I didn't know how too. Many thoughts ran through my head: She's gonna hate me. She's gonna judge me. She's gonna punish me. She's gonna...so many different thoughts scattered through my head and I was flustered as to what to do. I didn't have to do anything. Why?

Because Ma'am was very perceptive and she sensed that something was wrong and took me to the doctor. I tried to be shrewd in thinking of ways to dupe her. I felt ashamed and I didn't want the doctor telling her about what I had done, and as a result of my carelessness I was pregnant. It mattered how and what she thought of me.

Let the role-play begin!

Actually I had learned from her so I added a pinch of confidence in my tone and told her that I was feeling much better. She wasn't trying to hear it. I scratched my scalp. Okay, let's try this again with a little more conviction, shall we. Time was money. And I didn't want her spending her hard earned money on me. I was scared. Panicky. You name it. So I gave it one last shot, and low and behold it worked. Hurray, I'm off the hook! No, no, no! I felt even worse because I had twisted the truth to momma to save myself the embarrassed of her finding out that her fourteen-year-old daughter was knocked up by a nappy-headed boy, who mind you was eighteen years old.

The day had finally come when I felt I had no choice but to spill the beans to Ma'am. I was experiencing nausea and there was no way I was going to be able to continue to hide my secret. I gained some strength from somewhere and confessed. Ma'am was quiet. And then she walked into the living room and told Poppa. And he immediately told me to c'mon and took me to our family doctor.

This nice white doctor gave me a blood test and told Poppa that he would call with the results. On our way back home there was silence in the car. Poppa was quiet. In my mind I was thinking this silent treatment is not helping me. I need to be talked to. I had many, many thoughts racing through:

Say something for goodness sakes! This silence is killing me, Pop-pa! (I started scratching my scalp like I had fleas) Okay, enough already! Open your mouth and ask! Ask me something, Pop-pa! Ask who's the nappy-headed boy who knocked you up! Where does he live? What's his mama's name? Who's his daddy? Ask me something so that I can lift this burden off of my chest. I am sinking, Pop-pa, sinking! Help me, Pop-pa? Help save me?

Poppa remained quiet.

He couldn't even look at me. I was devastated.

The phone rang.

"Yes, this is she."

"Oh…."

Silence.

Click.

It was confirmed that I was indeed pregnant.

For the first time there was silence in the house. I could actually hear myself think, cry, whimper, and scream in my head. I had made a mistake and now I had to suffer the consequences of my actions—alone.

I kid you not, that silent treatment was the worst punishment of all punishments I had ever experienced. I was expecting to be seated down by both of my parents and talked to in a way that made me feel valued. It made me feel like they were going to be there for me. I thought *we* would see it through together. But it wasn't like that. I guess they were numb, but so was I. *And* I had to weather the storm all by my lonesome while Sin sailed to different countries, exploring the world. It didn't seem fair. But when was life ever fair to me? Touché.

There was a lot to swallow with having a seed inside of me. My mind was cluttered, confused, overwhelmed. What am I going to do? How will I care for this seed? Who will help me? What choices do I have? I haven't even finished school, yet. Will I still be able to finish school? How can I do both? Where will I get money? Blah, blah, blah, blah.

My brain was fried.

The decision making was left in my premature hands. My parents still hadn't sat me down to discuss the matter with the both of them together. Ma'am asked and she relayed the message to Poppa and off we went to Beth Israel Hospital in Passaic to carry out my plan. There was no way I could have a baby with no education, other than elementary school, no financial support, no stability, and no baby father to depend on to help care for our child. No. Understand *I* helped create this catastrophe and I was doing my best to make it right. And quite frankly, I needed a grown-up's help, but that wasn't the case. So I had to woman up and fly right.

After the one-day procedure I went home to recuperate. Still, no one really talked to me. Ma'am came into my room days later and handed me a box of contraceptives and walked out of the room. She didn't even explain how to use them. Nothing.

The after-effects of my decision grew heavy on my heart. I felt like I wanted to hibernate within. To never come out of hiding because I was ashamed, angry, bewildered, belligerent with thoughts of Sin, tired, and so so very lonely.

That experience changed me. I had shut down. Became

withdrawn and I felt like I was aching all over my body. There was this continuous pain that circulated throughout. It was hard to accept my choice and it made me feel very, very bad about myself. I had matured into this wounded individual and I was consumed with grief. I was drowning in it. Yes, I transformed seemingly overnight. From sneakers to heels, make-up, but I still was in a underdeveloped body. But my intellect seemed beyond my years. I hated having to grow up so fast. Time never stood still for me to live out my teen years. I had developed this persona of "woman" even though I had no idea of what made a full-fledged woman.

***

By sophomore year things were calmer, at least in school. Nothing really changed at the house. I started doing more things for myself like shopping for clothes. Wisdom and I or Bitty and I would go shopping in downtown Paterson at Jacobs, Meyer Brothers, Woolworth's, and around Thanksgiving we would go to the movies at the Fabian Theatre. I was becoming more independent. But I was suffering. My past history started to haunt me in my sleep. I began to write out my feelings with such brutal honesty. I seemed mad and I needed to address my anger.

"GOD, I HATE YOU! I HATE MY PARENTS! I HATE MY FACE, BODY, MIND! I HATE SIN, SIN, SIN! I HATE ME, ME, ME, ME, ME!!!"

Sometime after this meltdown I got word from Stretchy that Sin was coming home to visit from Norfolk, Virginia. I shrugged my shoulders as if to say, "So what." What was done was done. I was making strides alone to bring balance back to my life. And I wasn't interested in seeing him. That's what my mind was saying, but my heart was speaking some real talk. *Girl, who you think you're fooling. YOU know damn well you want to tell that man that he hurt you so deep that you lost pieces of yourself. You need to tell him how you feel, how much you felt for him, how losing your virginity was a big deal for you, and on and on and on.*
There was so much to say, but just the thought of seeing him in the flesh made my stomach bubble like I was bloated. And how I was left with all this "stuff" that I couldn't get rid of. For some reason, I mentioned to Ma'am that Sin was coming home. I don't know why. I think it was a slip of the tongue. Well, she took me by

42

surprise when she said that she wanted to see him. Why? I thought. *If I don't care to see him, why do you?* I never asked her that question because I felt she had her reasons.

"Okay, Ma'am, when I see him I'll be sure to tell him." I said, as I walked out the door to return back to the park.

Unfortunately, the *day* had finally presented itself....

I was gazing out of my living room window when I saw him in his white sailor suit, cap, and shiny black shoes. He was be-bopping down North Seventh Street. I didn't want to utter his name, thinking I might split my lip and bleed. His face glowed as the sun beamed on him. Shiny blue-black skin, hands extended into hugs to greet his second family who lived across the street. A fiery sensation zoomed through so quickly that I removed myself from the window. My heart sunk and saltwater ran down my face as the wounds had opened. I wiped them with the back of my quivering hand and entered my room, and pondered. Why did he come home? I don't want to see him. Why does momma need to see him? It would only make matters worse for me. I don't want to face him. I want to forget and move forward, but I couldn't because of the residue that had already settled within my flesh.

Weeks had past and yet the words when I did see Sin never was released from me. But one day I thought of Ma'am, so I had finally addressed him with a hello. We chitchatted briefly and I eased it in the conversation.

"Okay, what time should I come by?" he asked staring deep into my eyes.

I looked away. "I don't know. Whenever you can, I guess," I said.

Before the day had ended there was a ring at the door. And as I went to open it there stood Sin on the front porch. I took a deep breath before letting him in. Ma'am was sitting in the living room on the loveseat watching TV. We entered the apartment and I introduced him to momma.

Ma'am's eyes bulged, "Baby, who in God's name named you that awful name?"

"My dad, ma'am."

"Well, is it okay if I call you Solomon?"

"Yes, ma'am." He smiled.

I rolled my eyes. *Let's get this over with*, I thought.

Sin sat down on the sofa as did I. Ma'am raised her body off the loveseat and walked away. Within seconds she returned with paperwork in her hands. Sweat was scrolling down my armpits. I glanced over to Sin and he looked cool, calm, and collected.

43

Ma'am stood in front of Sin and said, "I just want you to know that my daughter was pregnant."

Sin nodded his head up and down to acknowledge what she had said.

"You can look at this paperwork to see that she later had an abortion." Ma'am said with watery eyes as she lowered her head.

And again, Sin nodded his head and reached in for the paperwork. He looked over the paperwork and handed it back to her. Ma'am sat back down on the loveseat and they engaged in conversation. I couldn't believe how quickly the conversation had changed with them laughing like things were just yummy. I couldn't understand why. *This is no laughing matter*, I thought. I was angered by the outcome. He wasn't scolded, threatened, or shaking in his shoes. Ma'am was too damn nice to him and I was a girl's wrath. *This is not going the way I pictured it*, I thought. *How come he gets to laugh and smile? Where are the tears that are supposed to be running down his face? What happened to the tough love strategy? What happened to putting fear in his heart? Ma'am, make him pay! Ma'am, make him shit in his pants.* I got nothing. No type of satisfaction. I was infuriated.

Soon Sin stood to get ready to leave and I stood to show him out. But what really ruffled my feathers was when Sin said, "...it was nice meeting you," and called Ma'am by her first name. How dare *he* use her name that was printed on the mailbox? My eyes spread so wide. It angered me because Ma'am never corrected him to say, "It's Mrs. ...." No, she let it slide. I kept my composure in front of Sin but I was stewed inside. Stewed. I walked Sin to the door and as I walked back into the house I had a tight face and walked passed momma in a heated rage. I plopped on my bed and let the tears have their say. It was too much for me to bear.

***

I couldn't let bygones be bygones right away. That was the stubbornness in me holding a grudge. I was hurt. It only escalated from past inflictions of hurt and I think I wanted to make this last hurt an example of what I would no longer stand for. Of course, things didn't go as planned.

I rehearsed the conversation between Sin and Ma'am and immediately I felt my lips pressing together and a wrinkle rolled on my forehead like dominos. I felt like he came and went with no words to comfort me. It made me feel like I meant nothing to him.

That I was just a piece of virgin pussy. Yeah, I was keeping it real with myself. That's exactly how I felt. But I knew there was more to me than that. I guess I needed and wanted confirmation that he knew it too. If Sin would have displayed compassion towards me I think it would have made a world of difference. I felt disregarded. Dismissed.

When he left for the Navy. Tears began to build and I just let them roll down my distressed face. I lay across my bed so distant. Those who had hurt me seemed to get off with no scrapes or bruises. I received no apologies. Things were easy going for them so it seemed, and yet I suffered. I'd taken partial blame for the pregnancy. I'd taken all the responsibility for the abortion and he'd taken none of the responsibility. I didn't understand how a man could know that his seed was aborted and show no type of emotion. It left me wondering if I had decided to keep the baby and had had a miscarriage would his reaction have been the same. That question goes unanswered.

I realized I had a steep mountain to climb to get myself back on track. I started thinking about after I graduate what I wanted to do with my life. Where did I want to go? Cosmetology was my trade in school, but I also had an interest in interior design so I decided that New York would kill two birds with one stone. Often, the thought of being a lawyer crossed my mind because of how my childhood affected me. I thought heavily about becoming a lawyer to defend sexually abused children and teens. Children in broken black family homes. Children whose mothers might have suffered from a form of mental illness. Children who parents were divorced. Children who felt unaccepted and unloved by their parents' significant other. Children going through different forms of abuse or worse. I wanted to have an impact on their lives. To let them know that I truly understood because I, too, had walked in their shoes. But just the thought stirred up too much emotion in me. That was a clear indication that maybe it was too close to home and maybe I needed to rethink that career choice. I cried many a nights for the ones who were too tiny to defend themselves. It touched the depths of me. Children needed a warrior, someone who could take the blows and still stand firmly on their feet. They needed a fighter and I was neither.

***

Sin.

There were many times when I would see him and my body and mind would freeze in time. There inside me lingered a small piece of him. I could still feel his touch. Hear him moan and groan. Feel him entering me, inward and outward. Hear his breathing so heavily and perverted. We didn't share lovemaking. I had to be honest. Lovemaking was two souls as one, a rhythm of body motion, of minds uncluttered with only the image reflecting that moment in time. A climaxing moment, a pausing to share a moment of silence still connected as one. One mind. One body. One soul. That to me was lovemaking. I had never experienced that nor felt that kind of love with a man, but I had more experiences to come. I just had to remain patient.

Gradually I felt stronger. Capable of seeing Sin and it not wear me down. Often I would bump into him. Sin and I would chat little. Then times we'd set a time to meet. I didn't know why I was putting myself through this. What was I looking for from him? A lot, I guess. There was this enormous amount of guilt, anguish, resentment, that I needed to release. That moment was my opportunity to shed some weight off of me. I wanted to feel like I mattered. That I wasn't *trash* that was discarded and dumped in a landfill to rot away. I had to be more than trash. I just had to be.

During one of our conversations, I heard this smoothness in Sin's voice. He had this young man's charisma that would pull you in and make you devour his every word. He was too calm, confident about himself. And deep down I was intrigued with him. And then it turned to sorrow for him. I felt this wall was being built up to shadow what was really the man in him. I believe someone he was infatuated with had hurt him. Possibly, I was his rebound. And possibly whoever came about after her, he would feel no pain. I felt great pain and I expressed how I felt to Sin. He did not interrupt my train of thought. He merely sat and listened or he appeared to be listening. "You hurt me. I needed you. It was difficult for me. I had no one to turn to. You left me hanging. I had to make the decision on my own. I was scared. I was frightened to tell my parents. I hated you. I hated myself for even getting involved. I, I, killed our baby. I did it, not you, me. You don't know how it hurts me so…so deep it hurts me."

Sin remained silent.

It seemed surreal because I pictured him scrambling for the right words to say, stuttering, or suddenly develop amnesia about what we shared. But his dark eyes connected with mine. Face-to-face he greeted me and he spoke softly about his feelings. After I had gained more respect for him, than before. I didn't want to fall for him again, but it was too late. I had already fallen.

I thought the time apart had given us time to grow, mature, and it turned us into wanting to be around each other more and more. Or it could've been that I thought we were on the same page of wanting to soak up each other's company. Which, I was not certain. My guard was up high because I wasn't sure what to expect from Sin. Here we decided to have a long-distance relationship. I still loved him and I had hoped that he would grow to love me back. Sixteen. I was so vulnerable. We decided before he left to go back to the Navy that we would be exclusive. I was elated. I wanted it to work. All I wanted for and from him was to love me unconditionally and appreciate the little I had to give.

Sin would come home once a month or every three months. I missed him and we wrote every chance we could get. I was looking forward to when he'd come home and we made the best of the little time we had. We had lots and lots of "yum-yum" and during one of those times Sin expressed, "I love you," and my insides were swimming with this man. This man who uttered the words I had longed to hear. I was in heaven. But heaven transformed so quickly to hell. With our inconsistent use of contraceptives and condoms the end result was me being pregnant again. And my unborn baby's father was not enthused. No. I don't think he wanted me to have the child, but I was adamant about my decision. I would suffer the consequences of my actions. I decided to go to Sin's house to speak with his mother face-to-face before she heard it traveling through the neighborhood. This was going to be my first stand at being responsible. I tell you I never thought things could get so ugly.

I rang the doorbell to the yellow house on West Broadway and waited patiently for Mrs. Grayson to come downstairs. When she opened the door just the look on her face told all. *This woman can't stand me,* I thought. Mrs. Grayson stood tall with her jet-black hair gleaming in loose curls. Her raisin-colored skin flawlessly bold, and her eyes burning with fury through my imitation thick skin. I hadn't even said a word, as of yet. She placed her hand on her waist and continued to bleed my eyeballs with a stern look on her face. And then the rippling of her words soared out of her mouth with ease and execution.

"Whachu tryna do, ruin my son's life?" she snapped.

Her words burst my eardrums. She seemed taller after she spoke with a face of disgust that glared. Then she bashed me inch by inch and until I shrunk down in my shoes.

"If you had kept your legs closed none of this would have

happened!" she snapped again and her bloody red eyes pierced mine.

I was at a loss for words. I stammered, not wanting to give back talk. And then I turned around and walked away. *She hates me*, I thought. Tears eased out of my eyes and I wiped them away. I realized I was in this all alone. Mrs. Grayson would not lend me a helping hand, motherly advice, comfort, or compassion. No. She would rather see me fail so that she can remind me of the decision I made to carry this child. She would rather punish me with her way of thinking. *I'm gonna prove her wrong,* I thought.

Unfortunately, I never got a chance to prove anything because later that evening I ended up having a miscarriage. Life sucked.

***

In my senior year, September of '85, it was a shock to all that *I* was actually blossoming into a beautiful swan. A few of my peers would gradually stir up small talk to find out "what did you do this summer" and others would just stare me down. I loved the attention. I was still in my relationship with Sin. But Sin and I had to get to know each other; even though we knew each other it was as if we didn't. I don't know if that makes sense to you, but that was how I saw it. With him overseas I really hadn't spent enough time with him to know his likes and dislikes, and neither did he with me. Sometimes I felt like I had rushed things again. I let my heart lead instead of my intuition. Don't get me wrong—there were times when I thought about what others would think about me having a baby and not being married. But realistically, it was not about them, it was about me. I had to concern myself with finishing school, first and foremost.

Eventually eyes were no longer admiring my newfound beauty as I sashayed through the halls.

In my economics class, Doug P. was one of my classmates and the brother was comical. Our seven-foot economics teacher used to constantly have to speak to him. But Doug did not care. Doug always made me feel special because he would take time out of his prankster mode to tell me how beautiful he thought I was. He would extend his butterscotch-colored hand like he was going to caress my face. Quite often I wished he were Sin because he seemed gentle.

Our economics teacher used to give him a dead stare, and Doug would turn his slender frame around in his seat and have his glasses hanging off his nose with his feet pigeon-toed in his suede Pumas.

His long arms glued to his sides, and one balled fist sitting on his lap with his back hunched over looking like a nerd to make light of the situation. And his laugh, oh his laugh sounded like soothing music to my ears. Brotha' was fun-ny. Little did Doug know he really made my day in high school. Without him, laughter would have never entered my life.

***

Often I talked to Sin through letters and over the phone. I stressed the happenings at the house and he would just listen. He never suggested that we get a place of our own. He started coming home on the weekends and we spent lots of time together. Sometime after his departure back to Norfolk, Virginia, I began experiencing some pains in my abdomen. I went to the clinic. I was examined and it was determined that I had an STD that was treatable. What! Oooh, I was faithful to him. It hit me hard to know that he cared so little for me. While I was dealing with bullshit in that house, he was out screwing around with some cheap thriller. My heart was crushed.

During my recovery period, Sin was supposed to be coming home to visit but he never did. Uh-huh. That seemed so weird to me. So when he phoned I explained my situation. He denied having anything wrong with him. Liar. Yeah, he was indeed the liar but I had to put blame where it really belonged. I knew that I had not been with anyone, but him. I loved him to death—more than life itself. I shoulda broke things off then especially knowing that he cared little about my well-being. But I didn't. I stayed. I was young and dumb and so very naïve about love.

3

As adults I saw him…Dream-Boy…a.k.a Mr. Jordan Seymour in the Foodtown supermarket. There he was in a navy-blue uniform, about 6'1" and chiseled down to the bone with light facial hair, low haircut, and my man was looking…yum-yum.

Jordan stood in one of the aisles lookin' all eat 'em up as I had to persuade myself to get some backbone and go over and lay some "sugar and spice with a teaspoon of vanilla extract" on him. I was stalling. Scared out of my mind. Then my inner voice, Avona, stuck her two cents in, Look I am tired of you acting like a wimpy bitch. If you want the man, dammit, go and get the man! She was screaming at me like I was some child. I was definitely trying to talk myself out of it. Until I took another glance and all I thought was, damn, he still is fine as ever. Somewhere I gained some confidence. I think it came from my big toe.

I took small steps until I shadowed his back. He turned around and I introduced myself. And he instantly remembered me. How? I didn't know. I wasn't an eye full, back then. We chitchatted as I gazed into his brown eyes that made me melt in my heels. I tried to compose myself but it was most difficult. My panties were soaking wet. But that was my opportunity to try to give him my phone number, especially after finding out that he was single with two children, a boy and a girl. He lived not too far from me. He gave me his number and I waited a couple of days before I called him. Then, one day, I got bold and thought, Listen, you have been smitten with this man since you were a kid. Now is the time for you to act on your plan of making that young man, your man. So I picked up the phone and called and that was how things ignited as close friends between us.

We stayed on the phone for hours reminiscing about our lives. We laughed. I missed laughing. Well, things progressed in our friendship and I finally had the opportunity of sitting in his home. We talked in his kitchen after many, many conversations over the phone. Jordan had been living in his home for several years. He lived there with only a kitchen set and his bedroom set. The rest of the house was empty. I didn't care about him not having a fully furnished house. Material things didn't matter to me. He had a roof over his head. He was a homeowner. His relationship with his ex, a

Caucasian, deteriorated after possibly twelve years. He never married, either. It felt good to see him in the flesh, alone just us two, and at that moment I knew that I wanted him—all of him. Oooooooooooh. If I could have had my wish our bodies would have been heated bodies of erotica. I closed my eyes. What I would give to have all this come true. I bowed my head, feeling a blanket of gloom shield my shoulders. I loved him and, yet, I couldn't love him internally. I ached hard. This nauseating pain clung to my flesh. I wanted so desperately to taste him. But I could only taste him in my vivid imagination and our "yum-yum" was the fuckin' bomb! I felt as I had prior with a little more oomph after our imaginary night of ecstasy. Deep down I knew the possibilities of us being intimate were slim. What I have to lose by telling him, I thought to myself. That evening I exposed myself to Jordan. And it was the most frightening thing I'd ever had to do. More so than with Blu, Travar, and Zaelyn, reason being was because I was deeply in love with him. Still am.

Jordan was quiet at first. My feet started moving back because I didn't know what to expect. My prior experiences led me to believe that a Negro might freak the hell out. He might even try to beat a sista down just for the hell of it. Not again, I thought. But as I stood there I felt a sense of peace with him. I guess he was taking it all in. I didn't want to wait because my feelings have not changed. If anything they had grown. I needed to tell him and face the consequences. In that moment, Jordan did the unthinkable. He reached in and gave me a loving hug and kissed me so softly on the neck and forehead. I savored it. The feel of him. The smell of his mint breath. His warmth. I soaked in him in that moment. He gave me intimacy for the very first time.

When I left his home I wasn't sure what would occur. I mean, I didn't know if he would call the next day, if we would see each other again. I didn't know what to expect.

Well, he did call, and we did continue to see each other, but I had one problem, Brick was still coming around, calling, and I didn't know how things were going be with Jordan and me. It had finally taken me all these years to get him and I surely didn't want to lose him because of Brick.

Jordan makes me feel powerless. He makes me feel safe. A feeling I have never encountered from a man in my entire life. He makes me feel wanted and I know that by the way he holds me in his masculine arms. He cradles my heart. I inhale him and I feel so full for life. God, I love me some him. This is the first time the word "love" has ever parted from my lips for the male species, other than for Johnnie. But this love is not a brotherly love. It is an emotional feeling that has consumed me wholeheartedly. I've never experienced this in my entire life. Never was open to it. But I am now. The way I feel it is contagiously driving me over the edge of losing the man in me. That masculine side that is fixated on power. Somehow, I've become submissive, vulnerable, and delusional about the realities of true love. Yes, I have transformed into a woman. Every fiber in me has converted without my full knowledge. I am in love! I chuckle. Where did the man in me go? The powersuit? Where has this sensitive creature come from? I shake my head. I don't want to be her, I say to myself, matter-of-factly. I don't know how to be her. A huge smile is painted on my face. I want the old Avery Love back. The sassy, difficult, and standoffish woman who gave mixed signals. Not this woman who knows who she wants. And why she wants him. Who is this woman who cries at the drop of a hat. What is her freakin' problem? Where has all her testosterone gone? Where has the man in her gone? Where is the male figure that would give a rat's ass about folk's feelings? Yes, the self-absorbed, tyrant who loved to have her way. This isn't fair! I burst into smiles. All I am left with is estrogen that makes my hormones get all crazy. I've become this woman who has found it within to fall in love with a man. Me. Avona intervenes with her twenty-cents: No, no, no, this is how you got hurt with Zaelyn by letting your soul open only for him to crush it to dust. That love shit will do you dirty and all you will have left is a wilt of woman. God, I don't want to travel down that road again, I say to myself. Jordan. So quickly he slips in my mind. I can't allow this one to pass me up. I just can't. I shake my head. He means too much to me. Is it worth getting hurt over? "Avona, shut up!" I scream. I take a minute to ponder. And everything in me says, yes, he is worth pain and more.

I never thought I would be the woman saying this, but I love him enough to take the risk. My only wish is that he reciprocates the same. And if not, I guess I'll be performing a rendition of that movie *Something's Gotta Give* with me bawling my eyes out everywhere I turn simply because I let my guard down and fell in love with a man who has never traveled the journey of my internal walls. That is my only regret. Flesh never met flesh. I sigh. I wished I had spoken up sooner before my life became a billboard: www.AveryLovehiv.org.

Ring…ring…ring.
"Hello, Anonymous, Avery speaking."

"Oh, so you are there. Ms. Early Bird, as usual."

I smile. Hearing Jordan's voice just does me good.

"Hi. How's your morning, thus far?"

"Oh, I can't complain. I'm actually off from the firehouse so that leaves my day open. How 'bout taking a day off?"

"Hmmmmmmm, I don't think I can do that on short notice. I have a meeting with some artists around noon."

"Okay, the busy woman never takes a moment to breathe."

"Yes, I do. It's just that I don't like to say I'm going to do something and not do it. It's bad for business. Surely you can understand that, Jordan."

"Yes. Why'd you have to be so damn independent?"

I chuckle.

"I thought that's what you liked about me."

"Yes, but sometimes...."

"Sometimes, what?"

"Never mind."

"Are you okay?"

"Yes, just...."

"Just what?!" *If this man doesn't complete a sentence I am going to scream.*

"I was just looking forward to seeing you. With all the hours at the firehouse and the ruckus with my kids I barely have—a man needs *me* time too. I just prefer not to be alone during my 'me' time."

"Well, rain check?" My brows rise, waiting for his response.

"Uh-huhhhhhh." He kinda sings it, out of disappointment.

After we hang up waltzing in the door is Brick. My eyes widen, a bit surprised. Normally he is still in the bed sleep until about noonish. That's what happens when you have so much time on your hands. If he doesn't get a hustle, he gets bored. So I guess that explains why he's here. He must be bored to death.

"What's up?" Brick asks standing in front of the register dressed in some rust-colored Timberland boots, slouchy jeans, and a black hoodie with white lettering advertising his cleanup business with his baseball cap snug tightly on his head. He's gnawing on a toothpick with his crooked teeth and it is annoying the hell out of me.

"When are you going to get some new shirts made? That one still has your old cell phone number on it. How are folks supposed to get in contact with you, if they happen to see you walking around and jot down your number?"

"My man, he's printing up some more business cards for me."

I shake my head because he just doesn't get it. *Why wear the shirt*, that's my point.

"How'd you get over here?" I ask.

"Caught a cab."

"You caught a cab from Paterson to Montclair?"

"Yeah…what?" His forehead crumples.

Oh boy, I feel a mood swing coming on.

"That costs a lot of money."

His shoulders bounce up and down. "So! It's only money."

"Say no more." I raise my hands. I keep my mouth shut because his poor money management skills are his problem. *Doesn't he know that money doesn't grow on trees?*

"What brings you here?" I ask, while vigorously wiping down the counter and straightening up odds and ends.

"I, I, I, wanted to see my Baby Gurl."

I stop what I am doing just to set the record straight.

I look him directly in his eyes. "My name is Avery, not Baby Gurl, save that for those chicks out on the block, okay."

"Aiight, aiight, my bad. You so sentimental."

My eyes greet the ceiling 'cause he is starting to get under my skin.

Brick paces the floor until he finally takes a seat. He becomes fidgety like he has ants in his pants.

"You want somethin' from the store?"

That money just burns in his pockets, I think.

"No. Thanks."

"Aiight, I'll be back."

My lips press together and ease out, "Hmmmhum."

Ring…ring…ri—

"Hello, Anonymous, Avery speaking."

"I can't relax. Have dinner with me tonight?"

"Jordan, find something to do. Go to the spa, go for a drive or go to the gym." A girly grin displays on my face. "What time do you want me to be ready?"

I can tell that he has a smile on his face by his voice.

"Seven-ish."

"Okay. Don't call me anymore. Get out of the house."

He starts laughing.

As I am putting the phone in its cradle Brick enters the door with a small cup of coffee in hand and a newspaper under his armpit.

"Who was that?" he asks.

My eyes spread. "Excuse you?"

"Oh, oh, my bad. This is your…." He throws up both of his hands as if to say, "don't shoot a brotha", dropping his newspaper. He kneels down to pick it up as my eyes pierce his back.

The wrinkles in my forehead say it all. It takes every ounce of humbleness not to put him in his place. The thought of coming to see me was nice, but I come to work to relax and unwind. Not to get all tense. He could've called me instead of wasting his money if he's gonna bring this crap in here. I don't need the negative energy floating around. This is a place of tranquility.

"So, what's up?" He leans back in the chair.

At that moment I lose complete coolness, "Don't lean back in that chair! What is wrong with you? You think I have money to be constantly replenishing furniture up in here, huh? You might spend your money like it's water, but I don't!"

Brick looks at me blankly. I get a grip and continue wiping down the counter and then stroll over to the tables. I light some scented Country Dreams mulberry candles and take a seat. Brick slurps the coffee lid and then takes the lid off and sips his coffee while reading the local newspaper. I sit, thinking about what I will be wearing for my date with Jordan this evening. I walk over to the counter and pull out a piece of 8 ½ x 11 papers to jot down a poem I wrote the other night about Jordan and me. I thought I might share it with the crowd, Thursday when I host Open Mike.

"Whachu writing *me* a poem?" Brick takes another slurping sip of his coffee.

Why does everything have to be about him? What he thinks he's God's gift to women?

"No."

"Whachu writing?"

"Just jotting some things down, do you mind?" I snap.

"Wha' the fuck is wrong wit' you? You got an attitude. You're so fuckin' ungrateful."

Okay, this must be mood swing number five since he has been here. Stop drinking and getting high jackass because your brain cells are useless. Where did "ungrateful" come into play?

He hit a nerve in me. I stop writing, lay my pen on the table and let it rip.

"How am I fuckin' ungrateful because I am working, unlike you? I don't have time on my hands like yourself to just sit around at my leisure just twiddling my thumbs waiting for my boy, Sticky-Fingers to come ringing my bell!"

Brick's face completely droops and his eyes darken.

"So what you sayin', Avery?" His arms spread wide totally confused.

"Like I said, nothing registers with you! You don't listen, but you expect everyone else to listen to you! You want everyone to hear you speak, but yet, you tune everyone else out because what they have to say and how they feel means nothing to a selfish bastard like yourself!"

"Who you callin' a selfish bastard!"

"If the shoe fits, wear it." My stance says it all.

Brick's feet plant the hardwood floor and he heads towards the door.

My chest rise and falls full of fury. And the burning desire that festers inside of me needs to be released before I blow a gasket and take it out on an innocent victim. My hands clench my waist and I spew out words like a mad black woman with each step Brick takes: "AND that's the other thing!" My head is swaying from side to side. Brick's pace slow motions. As I pour out my emotions. "I am so tired of seeing your *back* every time something is said that you don't like. Grow up! Every five seconds it seems you're having a freakin' mood swing. Are you suffering from bipolar disorder…seriously?"

"What's bipula?"

"Bipolar! Damn, get a dictionary and look it up. Better yet, go to the doctor and find out." I stand looking piercingly into his one insensitive eye. "When are you gonna play the role of the *man* in this…this?" Both of my arms rise in the air trying to figure out what *this* is. My elbows point outward as my hands land on the top of my baldhead, quite disgusted.

Brick's footsteps are still making their way towards the door and then the door slams behind him. I stand still for a brief second to bounce back. I breathe back in the positive energy, take a seat and restore my thoughts. A smile emerges across my face just by the thought of Jordan. Suddenly, my smile turns into a frown as I am distracted by Brick's image. He puts me in mind of some of the men I used to date when I was just a naïve little pussy.

4

Arriving home I take a shower and sit down on my mocha leather armchair to relax and engross my mind in *Black Pain* by Terrie M. Williams. Quickly I am distracted by Brick's image. I try to remember where things started off with us. Then it hits me, his deceased father. The man Brick yearned to receive love from. I shake my head from side to side remembering how it was with Poppa. How I yearned. My lips press together, head dangles, eyes weaken, feeling as though Brick doesn't know any better, like he is a child or something. But he's not. He's a grown man who has not grown up since his childhood. I raise my body and walk over to my desk and pull out good ole Sis, my journal. I feel the tattered edges thinking that I've gotten my money's worth outta her. I nod, as I read passages about my best friend Johnnie.

Then the phone rings, distracting my train of thought.

"Hello."

"I'll be there on time so be ready."

"I will, Jordan." I smirk.

I start to get ready for my date with the man of my dreams. After I am done I stare in the rustic wood mirror on my bedroom wall and smile. Then I walk over to the window and gaze out as I take in the wintry scenery. I spot Jordan's shiny black Ford Escalade. He double-parks in front of the building at 6:58 p.m. He buzzes the intercom and I buzz him in. By the time he pushes the elevator button to the first floor, I grab my keys, coat, purse, and hat and head downstairs. And by the time he reaches my front door I am ready at 7:00 for a night on the town. I open the door and just the look on his face makes me feel good. He is pleased with the outcome of my ensemble and I with his.

Jordan and I dine at popular spot in Clifton Commons, The Kake House. He has to get up pretty early so that's why he chose somewhere close. The one thing I like about Jordan is that he is very practical about his money, but tasteful too. There is an oil spill around the parking space so Jordan helps me out of the SUV like a true gentleman. I feel like a complete ditz because I have on pea-green four-inch high-heeled Paolini boots that I can barely walk in. And plus, there is a bit of snow on the ground. Duh, it's December. I couldn't find the right pair of shoes to go with these Paris Blue bootleg cut jeans and Marc Jacobs' pea-green sweater. We enter the restaurant. I hang my camel-colored cashmere pea coat on the coat rack. And unravel my handmade silk woven magenta scarf and stick my Anne Klein burnt-rust leather gloves in my coat pocket, as well as my hat. Jordan sports a thick Armani sweater and baseball cap with his faded Old Navy jeans on and a pair of black Kenneth Cole boots.

As soon as we enter the restaurant we are escorted to our seats. The inviting music lingers above our heads. The ambience of white china, crystal wine glasses, polished utensils, fancy napkins and amber-colored tablecloths and fine window drapery accentuates the room. Menus are placed in front of us as well as glasses of ice-cold water. We take glimpses at each other and smile. Deep down I am ecstatic that he asked me out.

"So, busy woman, how was your day?" Jordan asks.

"Fine…just fine."

"How did your meeting go? Meet any interesting people?" He takes a sip of his water.

"That's always. I met an aspiring writer named Travesty."

Jordan burst out into laughter almost spitting water in my face. "TTravesty…what kinda name is that?"

"Exactly. It makes you ask questions. That's the very reason she named herself Travesty. I'm going to have her read excerpts from her book, *Close-knit*.

Jordan chuckles so loudly that heads turn in our direction. I put the menu in my face because it is somewhat embarrassing. He massages his tight stomach because he is hysterical with his watery eyes staring at me. I shake my head because it is not that damn funny.

"You okay?"

"Yeah, yeah, oh man, that hit my funny bone. When is she going to be appearing I have to mark that day on my calendar?"

"Thursday. Enough about her," I say a little annoyed that he isn't into me.

"Do I detect a hint of jealousy?" He cuts his dreamy eyes at me.

"Noooo," I smirk.

Jordan nods his head and strokes his lips with three of his fingers.

Seconds later the waiter greets us with a pleasant smile.

"Hello. My name is Vladimir. I will be your waiter. Would you care to order now or do you need more time?" he asks in a very sexy voice. His dark hair and his honey-toned skin with his medium build are definitely attractive.

I take a sip of water because my mouth is dry.

"I think we're ready." Jordan looks at me to confirm and I nod my head.

"For starters, we'll have the shrimp scampi as an appetizer."

"Would you like salad? Caesar or toss?"

I pipe in, "Yes, Caesar salad."

"Very well, madam. Sir, what would you like?"

"I'll have the same as the missus. And we'll have a pitcher of red sangria."

"Sure."

I love a man who knows what I like.

Just before we order dinner and as we are engaging in conversation this ivory-colored woman with size double D cups, a flapjack backside, and an overkill of bright red tresses comes sashaying towards our table in a cozy gray Mossimo sweater dress. I must admit she has legs to die for. I twist my lips. *Skank.*

Avery! Yes, I surprised myself. But if you could see what I have sitting before me, giirrrrlllll, you'd react the same damn way.

"Jordan, is that you! Oh, I thought that was you." Miss Redhead practically ignores me sitting here. I scratch my throat using it as a decoy to say, "Ah, get rid of this huzzy." But Jordan doesn't catch on. For him to be so damn smart he is dumb as hell all of a sudden. *Can't she see that we are on a date!* I try to keep a pleasant look on my face, but underneath I am a heifer in heat with eagerness to slap this floozy. I can't believe she is trying to steal my man right from under my nose. In my face. Ooh, ooh, ooh, I am hot under this skin of mine.

Calm yourself, I say to myself. My legs crisscross at the calves, shaking like a leaf underneath the table. My hands meet my thighs and I try to control my fidgetiness, but I am about to burst.

One Mississippi, two Mississippi, three Mississippi....

I have never felt like this before. Truly this man means the world to me. I exhale out of my nose not to draw attention to myself. *Don't show your insecurity. Don't let her see that she can whisk him away from you. Don't you even think of shedding one tear! Stay calm. Poised. Confident.*

Jordan is racking his brain trying to remember this woman. His eyes widen. I guess it finally registers, "Dolce...Dolce Spellman. It has been what...years?" He reaches out his hand to shake hers. And she quickly embraces him as their hands connect in a tight clench.

I grit my teeth.

"Yessss, I'm surprised you remember my last name." Her sea-blue eyes sparkle.

"Oh, oh, where are my manners...Dolce, this is Avery. Avery...Dolce."

"Nice to meet you," I say dryly.

Okay, now move it along.

"Sooo, what's going on? Um, what do you do for a living?" she asks, striking a seductive pose with those legs to die for.

"Firefighter."

I catch Jordan's eyes scrolling her discreetly and it infuriates me.

"Really!"

Really, Bitch, now scram.

"Any kids?"

What is this, questionnaire day?

My eyes pierce the ceiling. *Am I not sitting here!*

"Yes. Two. How about you?" Jordan says.

"Oh, I'm a registered nurse/entrepreneur of a day spa. I have a daughter. Single mother. Married three times. Divorce...three times."

"Sorry to hear that."

Dolce bats her long fake lashes and waves her freshly French manicured nails. "Non-sense, it was for the best," she says, as she dangles her hand showing off this big ass rock on her middle finger.

Dammmmmmmnnnnn, I had to take a second glance.

Okay. Now that you've done questions and answers how 'bout you beat it!

My eyes cut from side to side. I pinch myself to make sure this is not a damn dream. And it's not, I am sitting here.

Dolce pulls out a card from her oversized Mossimo hobo and hands it to Jordan, as she accentuates her deep cleavage. "Call me sometime."

My mouth opens. *Oh, no, she didn't!*

Miss Prima Donna sashays away with her hair sailing in the breeze while I have a look on my face that could beat a sista down.

"Avery, are you okay?" Jordan asks.

"Am I okay?!" My head bobs up and down. "That's all you have to say? Am I not sitting here? Are *we* not on a date, please let me know?"

"Yes, why? You're upset; please tell me you are not one of *them*."

"One of what?!"

"One of *them* insecure women. All I was doing was engaging in small talk. It was harmless."

"I wonder how you would feel if I pulled a stunt like that." I give him the evil eye.

"It wouldn't matter to me. I'm secure with mine."

A wrinkle stretches across my forehead as one brow rises, "Oh, really?" I raise my forefinger, "Waiter, check please?" I say in the pleasantest tone I can muster up.

Jordan shakes his head as he pulls out his Visa credit card. "Women," he mumbles. I push myself away from the table, stand to gather my things and stand by the door tapping my feet three times. That Bitch, Bitch, Bitch!

I guess when I get home I might as well spend the rest of my evening watching, *Something's Gotta Give* 'cause Avona hit the nail on the head with this love shit. Dating sucks! Love is definitely over-rated.

5

My eyes open around 9-ish and admire my limited edition print of Sarah Kay Anderson's *Reminiscence* on the center wall of my bedroom. I stretch and jump out of bed. I grab my candleholders and sweet mango scented candles head straight downstairs and place them on the coffee table, then enter the white and soft green bathroom. After freshening up, I get dressed in some sweats, and head down the hallway to the elevator. I land on the lobby to check my mailbox.

As I am heading out of the lobby, I bump into an old acquaintance that lives in the building, Teka Miller. She's a nudist who models for a living. I try to avoid her, but she has spotted me so I have no choice but to play the role of long-time-no-see.

"Hi Avery, how's things?" Teka asks, fumbling for something in her pink duffel bag. She looks like she just came from the gym with her headband pushing back her thick, natural twist, spandex shorts that are stuck up her crack, and a sweaty tank top that looks like she bought it from the junior department at the Rainbow Shop. She smells rather funky, too. But you ain't hear that from me.

I smirk, just to be friendly, but really, if truth need be told, I can't stand Teka. Why? Because she makes me gag by the way she flaunts her Tiffany & Co diamond ring in my face. No, she hasn't done it today, but in the past it was every time I bumped into her size 0 frame. She just annoys me something awful. I mean, when I first heard I was happy for her, but damn, it was a bit too much hearing it all the time. I wanted to say, "Damn, Teka, I get it. You're engaged! Congratulations!" But I didn't.

I swallowed my words for the sake of not showing the fact that I was a tad bit envious. I think every woman goes through that phase at least once in her lifetime with a girlfriend. And even though Teka and I were never close it still gets under my skin. And I have held this grudge for a while. I guess it is time to get over it. I know. I know. So by me acting like I am glad to see her is definitely a start on my part. I'ma phony, but it's a start. I might as well be the bigger woman.

I put my key in the box and twist it open. "Oh, Teka, things are good. I just came down to pick up my mail," I say, as I pull out a bundle of mail and tuck it under my left armpit.

Teka stands in the doorway as her cell phone rings with a ring tone of "Bleeding Love" by Leona Lewis.

"Well, Avery, you have a nice day," she says, and answers her phone as she pulls the door to the stairway.

I have a delayed response. "Yeah, you too." My mind seems preoccupied in thought. I step back in the lobby and take the elevator to the second floor.

As I am opening my door, I make a mistake and drop a letter on the floor addressed to Jewell Love. This is the second letter I received from Garden State Life Insurance. This time I get a little annoyed so I close the door, drop my mail on the saffron storage coffee table and decide to give Garden State Life Insurance a call to let them know that Jewell Love does not reside here. I don't even have a relative named Jewell.

I pick up the phone in the living room, while pacing the saffron/ivory tile rug, and press the 1-800 number as I hear a recording asking me to hold for the next available representative. So I hold.

"Thank you for calling Garden State Life Insurance, this is Pauline, how may I help you."

"Hello, Pauline, my name is Avery Love. Well, Pauline the reason why I am calling is because your company keeps sending me someone else's mail...a Jewell Love. This is the second time this month I received her mail."

"Ms. Love, may I have the policy number on the top of the form, please?"

"Well, I haven't opened her mail, ma'am."

"No problem. Let me look her up by last name. May I put you on hold so that I can check our system?"

"Sure."

"Thank you."

I hold for a few seconds staring out of my high-rise window watching the cars passing.

"Thanks for holding Ms. Love. Well, I don't seem to have a Jewell Love in our system."

"Are you sure?"

"Yes, ma'am."

"That's strange."

"Is there anything else I can help you with?"

"No, thank you."

"Well, thank you for calling Garden State Life Insurance. Have a great day."

I hang up.

Okay, that's taken care of, I say to myself.

I go into the kitchen and toss the letter in the garbage, open the silver/black Maytag refrigerator for a peach-flavored LaYogurt, grab a spoon out of the drainer, and return back to the living room to engross myself in Lifetime.

After watching TV for a couple of hours I inadvertently pick up the phone and dial Johnnie's number. But then it hits me like a bolt of lightening. Johnnie's dead. How quickly it slipped my mind. It is hard trying to get over someone you've loved. Memories take me back so I climb the stairs to my bedroom and pull out Sis from my nightstand drawer, grab my favorite writing pen, and sit on my saffron-colored futon and start to babble about back in the day.

6

I cannot get over the things I've endured. I can't even laugh at some of the stuff because it seems so out of my character. But I have to remember I was not always like I am now. Actually, I was worse after the episode with Poppa.

I open the refrigerator for the spring water, tilt my head back and take my meds. Then I go into the bedroom chuckling about back in the day. I pull out my journal, turn on my wire-base lamp, and sprawl across my bed.

My fingers are cramped so I massage them. Then I lay my lethargic body across my bed to take a load off. I realize I had been through a lot as a young girl. But the relationships I was in never amounted too much. It almost felt like I was destined to be alone. Men. I really haven't experienced the inner warmth of a man. I am not referring to intimacy; I'm referring to love. I wonder what is wrong with me. Sometimes my thoughts pulls me back as to how I got this way. I say *this* because it is still who I am underneath many layers of progression.

November '86

I could feel my bones chattering that November. It was 20 below. The kind of cold that damn near froze my eardrums. I tighten my lips. I remember. Quarter-sized snowflakes were smacking me in the face and melting into my heated skin. Each step I took I mumbled a cuss word under my breath. Only God knows what I said. I rarely used words like those, but I was beyond livid.

The wind was howling a shrieking howl as my full-length pink-and-white-polka-dot bathrobe soared in the air. It was the wee hours of the morning. Dark. Quiet. Desolate. But it was real, as my name was Avery. It was all too real. I was homeless. First, by the hands of the man I called Poppa, back in June. Secondly, by the young black man, Grand, who took me in and claimed to always love me. He even said that he would wait until I was ready to give up my yum-yum because he was just that kind of fellah. He always used to say, "Avery, you'a good girl. Kind. Special. You sweet. Different from any chick I had ever been wit'. You my buddy." And me being so gullible, I believed that nineteen-year-old equivalent of a boy, not man. That was the same boy who used and abused me for his own selfish reasons, because he felt he could. He had that power to deceive with a straight face. Cold-blooded. And at the time of being heartbroken about my circumstances, I felt I needed someone, anyone. I was in dire need and he used that against me. He'd manipulate and compulsively lie to have his way. Treated me like a slave because he paid my way by feeding me, clothing me, sheltering me. And everything that he had done for me, which I thought was out of the goodness of his heart was thrown in my face like piss. As if he'd said, "Here, Bitch, take this and this and this, now get the fuck outta my face." He would tell me that he loved me and five minutes later eat his words by doing something to make me feel small. And I always felt like things could be worse, and at that time it was, but I was in a sticky situation, what could I possibly do? I thought he really cared about me, but I was highly mistaken. It was just false statements made to gain access to my yum-yum, which by no means had he ever had the pleasure. I tried to make him happy. To express my appreciation, but it didn't seem like what he was looking for. Grand took my kindness for its weakness and basically farted in my face. And he never said, "Excuse me." He uncaringly put others before me, made plans with me only to call to break them. And his favorite reminder was that he didn't see any of my family helping me out.

That was a low blow, but unfortunately he was right.

And all it did was make me try harder to please him, but underneath I was spiritually dying. The worst of the worse was when he disregarded my feelings by making me retrieve his key from the mailbox. Day in and day out I did this because he wasn't willing to give me a key of my own. He wanted control. So I was humiliated as folks, his friends, his family used to see me inching my fingers into the mailbox, unlocking the sticky lock that I had to jiggle for at least five minutes, then make my way up to the attic where I had another key lock that I had to unlock in order to get into his room. There were many nights when he "supposedly" forgot to put the key in the mailbox and would make me wait until he got home to let me in. I was in a bad way, and he made me feel like I wasn't worth the shit a dog pooted out.

That evening, we yelled at each other all because.... I rationalized. He pushed me first as he clenched onto his glass of vodka. I confirmed. I had no alternative but to call the police. I nodded. He cheated and then had the audacity to have her out in the open in his bedroom. I sneered. I'm only seventeen; I shared with the two police officers. To them I am an adult, I thought. And to him, I was a cock-blocker.

"Man, she gotta go! Yo, I want her outta my house," he said adamantly while standing in the entranceway.

"Ms., he wants you out. You have to leave," the white officer acknowledged.

"I have nowhere to go," I said standing a few feet behind Grand. "I'm not even working, yet," I said. "I just graduated in June of this year," I said, because I thought they would feel empathy for me.

"Ma'am, this is his house and if he wants you out, you have to go. Get your stuff," the white officer said defiantly, while his brown-eyed partner remained silent.

I entered the small dimly lit bedroom as the silhouette of chocolaty legs sat smugly on the bed cocked open exposing her bush. Grand stared at me with darkened eyes. I never thought I would cry, but the tears eased out and slowly dripped, splashing into the stained, once light-blue carpet. I quickly packed, not having enough time to change my clothes. I needed to be heard, but no one was listening to a seventeen-year-old. I wrapped myself up as the two officers watched me trample through the five feet of hardened snow. The bag upon my shoulder was wearing me down, along with the pressure that cooked within the residences on the east side of town in Paterson, New Jersey. All the drama started because I had come home a little too early from job hunting. All because he had an itch for someone new, and didn't have the balls to tell me. He'd rather sneak a hussy in behind my back. Well, in front of my face like I was nothing. I meant nothing. No. All because of the hard liquor that lit him up and slurred his tongue. No. All because of that slithering python that shared his bed. All I heard was the crunching of snow underneath my feet. The night whistled as the streetlights paved a way as I made a right hook onto Broadway, and a left into an unfamiliar world of loneliness, liars, and life lessons. From that day forward I promised to change my ways. To not be submissive to a low-life who had an unstable dick.

This was not the beginning of my hardships for I had experienced more than one could bear. The mental and emotional abuse was another cycle that I had to overcome.

I discovered a hideaway two houses down from where my parents lived. I wanted to be close to them, even though their love for me seemed afar. I slept sitting up in a stairwell with my arms crossed about my chest, pleading before God to hear my cries.

During the wee hours of the morning, I felt, knew, and had accepted the fact that I was compromised for the sake of a smelly pussy. No matter what others might have thought, I felt swindled because I was faithful. His skank could not stand the sight of me. And he could not see what was transpiring because he was emphatically an "alcoholic" who complied with getting drunk within the walls of his home. To him it was okay because he worked Monday-Friday, and the weekend was his time.

I sought out for shelter by going to a friend's house and explaining my circumstances to her mother. She allowed me to stay until daybreak, and then I was left to wander back into obscurity. I reached out to some family, but no one wanted to get involved. I tried to seek help from the Board of Social Services, but I did not meet the qualifications because I had no children and no permanent address so the much needed help was denied. So back to the streets I'd returned. Until an old friend, Derwood Hamilton, embraced my circumstances and took it upon his shoulders to help a sista out. He used to sneak me into his parents basement to shield me from the blistering cold. Other times I would sleep in the backseat of his Grand Am because I was afraid I might get caught from his mother in the basement. I did not want to split hairs. I just wanted to get my life back in order. And through all of this I held on dearly to the thousand dollars Poppa had given me. It was all that I had.

As I roll over I feel a sense of relief that I made it through the storms that could've destroyed my life. It was hard facing being homeless. It was hard being thrown to the wolves by my own daddy. It was hard dealing with men who didn't give a rat's ass about my well-being. I lower my head. Huh, life was simply hard.

7

SUNDAY, December 16th 2008...

As I am towel drying a Williams-Sonoma baking utensil my cell phone rings.

"Hello," I say in my soft-spoken voice.

"Avery, hey, girl!"

"Never?"

"Yes, girl, it's me."

I hadn't heard from my long lost first cousin in God knows how long. The woman with dark evenly toned skin, big bright eyes and medium frame with a strut the oozed confidence. She ate, slept, and breathed the aspiration of becoming a doctor. All of her hard work paid off and eventually she was living the American dream. She was married with two beautiful boys, a house, cars, handsome husband, and a career that she had longed to have. I wondered why she was reaching out to me. I hadn't heard from anyone since my parents died.

"Damn, a hurricane must be coming if you're calling me," I say.

Never laughs and then her laughter drifts and somberness sneaks in her voice.

Never takes deep breaths that mimic a soaring wind in my ear. For some unknown reason, I immediately feel my heart flutter as a rush of blood surfs through my tiny veins. I feel so sick like something is terribly wrong. It is damn near whispering in my ears, but the words would not leap out to ask. I lean the end tail of my spine against the kitchen sink and stare at the glass table full with cinnamon, nutmeg, walnuts, wax paper, cake pans, carrots, flour, and sugar because I was just about to blend the mixture for the carrot cake with cream cheese frosting when the phone rang. My mouth had been craving something sweet for days. Never's voice simmers but then it slightly changes and it is keen to my ears. My slender body trembles and arch brows rise as my brown eyes aimlessly wanders the fleshly painted off-white kitchen walls, ceiling, and cut to the side to glance out of dusty film window.

"Are you sitting down?" Never asks.

"No. Why?"

There is a pause that seems longing.

Last I heard Never was a best-selling author for her self-help book for young adults. It runs fast through my mind like whiplash. I faked a smirk in hopes that it was so. I am bursting with excitement waiting for her to spill the beans. But, again, Never's pause is too damn long to be of good news. I know she would have blurted it out by now.

A hot flash zooms through me as if a warning to prepare me to hear something that would tear into me so razor-sharp. *God, what is it? C'mon, Never, spill the beans so that I can jump up and down, twirl my body around, kick my heels, and bounce my shoulders until I break a sweat. C'mon, now stop toying with me 'cause I can't take the suspense. What's going on?*

My body seems unbalanced turning from hot to cold, cold to hot. Then an eerie chill slowly slithers my curved spine. I flinch. Shivering a kind of shiver that seems everlasting like the temperature has decreased to zero below. My eyelids close for what seems a split second. There is this tone in Never's voice that changes again. It is delicate as if she is speaking to a child who has lost something so precious, like a lucky charm. Yes, a soft, fuzzy, purple rabbit's foot.

I am eager to know, even though my gut is forewarning me. It warns me with a feeling like seasickness in my belly. It warns me with the fine prickles of ash brown hair that stand boldly on its ends. It warns me by me welling up for no apparent reason other than the tone in Never's voice. And I inhale to bone-dry my eyes. *Tell me, Never? Tell me?* I bubbled up trying to overshadow what I am really feeling. I am anxious. My soft palms start to itch and tingle. I rub them together like I am hoping to win at the slot machines in Atlantic City. The itching of my palms stops, but not the mild breathing of Never. *Okay, I'm ready. C'mon, now, let it rip? Stop stalling. I can't take it anymore. Just tell me?!*

I sense something is terribly wrong. What? I still don't know.

If Never, the woman who always knows what, how, and when to speak is at a loss for words and pauses too many times, it is evident that something dreadful has happened. I am overzealous with curiosity as it plummets from hyped to hanging near the edge of a cliff. *I'm waiting.* Subconsciously, I tap my long fingers against my thigh. Then suddenly I change my mind. *No, no, I don't....* It is too late.

There is a grayish film circulating around me, but then the cloudy film slowly dissipates and all that is left is a black backdrop. *Hit the cradle and click.* My conscience speaks with authority, but my index finger does not oblige. Never's calm but shattering breathing is disturbing my train of thought. I pant. *Let me guess. Don't utter a word. Let me guess.*

"What happened?" I say in a low crackling voice.

My knees buckle.

"What happened?!" There is hysteria in my voice as I stand in place, still leaning against the kitchen sink.

Never pauses.

"Jewell."

Why does that name ring a bell, I think to myself.

"Who's Jewell? Is she a relative of ours?"

Never pauses, again.

"You don't know?"

"Know what, Never? What are you talking about?" A frown appears on my face.

"Avery, Jewell is your sister."

I literally drop the phone.

There is inaudible silence.

I stammer for what seems like a second, "W-W-W-What! I have a sister that I don't even know! Where is this so-called sister of mine? How come I've never met her? Why am I hearing this for the first time?"

"It's complicated."

"COMPLICATED!"

My body grows limp and it trembles. My long fingers rise to my narrow face and smack it unintentionally, and then my hands glide down in slow motion smearing the tears that pour out of me like a heavy rainstorm. I black out and come to. Not ready to hear what is about to be said next.

"Avery, please, calm down?"

"CALM DOWN! You want me to calm down after you tell me some shit like this?! Are you serious?!"

"Listen, there's more."

I roll my eyes and stare at the ceiling. I swallow hard.

"What, Never! When do I get to meet this sister of mine, huh? Where is this mystery woman? Who screwed up?"

"What do you mean, who?"

"Is this sister from Poppa or Ma'am?"

Silence.

I hear Never breathing softly afraid to answer my question.

"LOOK, DAMMIT! I need to know. Who screwed up?!"

Silence.

"Your…your mother."

I stare wide-eyed at the receiver astounded.

There are moments of silence as I try to collect my thoughts.

"When can I meet this woman…Jewell? Where does she live? Is she older or younger?" My hands grip my flustered face.

"Um…um…." Never stammers.

"Speak DAMMIT!"

"Um…she's younger. Um, Jewell was killed in a car accident."

The phone crashes to the floor.

"No, No, No!" I scream and hard cries intertwine. I jump in place indecisive of how to cope, which way to run, with no arms to console me so I plant my vibrating hand against the wall. I am contemplating to jump out of my window, but I live on the second floor, too close to the ground. I want to be on the sixth floor where I would possibly die from the impact of the fall. I want to die because all these years I never knew I had blood roaming around out in this world. Oh, it is the worst feeling I'd ever felt. Pain is already an unwanted associate in my life. But it had come undefeated in taking this woman named Jewell. My…s,s,s,sister.

I run throughout the apartment in hysterics. I fall to my knees and scrape the hardwood floor in the living room with my nails like a kitty cat. I raise my wounded body and plop down on the sofa and slide off falling back down to the hardwood floor. Ball my fists pounding them against a hardcover book making sounds of beats of grievance. I stagger to stand and drop backs down to the hard floor like a rag doll still holding the phone cord in my hand. Never is still on the phone listening to me wail so loudly. So uncontrollably, that I hear her weeping as well.

I tightly ball my achy palms.

Why did Ma'am keep this from me? A longwinded scream releases from me so full of anguish,

"Noooooooooooooooooooo. Nooooooooooooo!" My breathing skips. Heart pounds heavy beats. Eyes flood with much emotion. Tears drool down my face. Hands run across my natural crown and back in a flustered state. Lips quiver pain-stricken. I am so lost. My hands touch my chest. Legs grow weak feeling like lead. Vision blurs. Voice echoes. Feet run…stop. Run…stop. Run…stop. I am exhausted. Screams roar from me. I start to hyperventilate. I pant with such bitterness stewing inside of me. I scream some more. It all seems surreal. I cry so sincerely for this sister I never knew—my baby sister. My inner strength has dissolved. I am deliriously broken. Weaken beyond what I've known to be weak. My wails are loud, loud, and louder as if I am being bludgeoned with the sharp edge of a machete slicing my heart into small pieces. Oh, Lord the pain is too great. I plop on the sofa again and try to catch my breath while Never listens and cries simultaneously. I am so empty, so very alone.

We hang up.

Five minutes later the phone rings.

"Hello," I say in a crackling voice.

"Baby Gurl, are you okay. You sound down."

"Um…Brick, can I talk to you later? I'm kinda having a breakdown."

"I'm, I'm, I'm…coming over."

We hang up.

I sit in darkness waiting for Brick to arrive. Unfortunately, he leaves me hanging by a thread, as usual.

8

I have never been to Clarkton, North Carolina. But I know I have to pay my respects in person to this young woman I never had the pleasure of meeting. I have to gulp down my pride and be there for my little sister. Never spoke of her stepmother, Jo-Ruthie and Sisal. Sisal was Ma'am's old flame. I never knew. Poppa never spoke of this child. And neither did Ma'am. Tears were purged from my eyes.

Brick generously insists on traveling the distance with me. I didn't expect him to volunteer so unselfishly. I call to make hotel arrangements at the Best Western in Whiteville, North Carolina. Brick and I make plans to leave for North Carolina on Wednesday, December 19th around 1:30 a.m. We head out onto Parkway South and the twelve-hour journey is placed upon my shoulders. I, being a novice at traveling had to reassure myself that I could do it. That I could drive long distance into a town I had never even heard of.

During our journey an officer who has no legitimate reason for stopping us stops us in Virginia. He stopped us due to the fact that both of us are black, driving in a rental Ford Five Hundred with New Jersey plates. The white officer asks me for my driver's license and states that if he finds no points on my license that he will let us go. I reach into my handbag and open my red Kenneth Cole Reaction wallet and pull out my license and hand it to him. Brick asks the officer if I was speeding.

"No, she's not in a heap of trouble," the officer says as he looks at my driver's license and then proceeds to ask, "Where you going?"

"Clarkton, North Carolina."

"That's a bad neighborhood. Where are you from?"

"Paterson…New Jersey."

"That's a bad neighborhood," he says repeatedly as he grips my driver's license with his index finger and thumb. He looks at the photo and then at me.

Enough already! It's hot as hell in this heat, I think.

"Look, sir, I don't know the area here. I'm driving to North Carolina because my sister was killed. We are trying to get there for the funeral."

The officer never checks my license. He hands it back to me and sends us on our way. Brick and I both know that we were stopped because of the Jersey plates. The officer was suspicious thinking that we were possibly smuggling drugs, but he was way off base.

When we arrive in Lumberton, North Carolina, I call Sisal and Jo-Ruthie to meet us at the Comfort Inn parking lot because I am exhausted. My legs are sore and heavy, palms ache underneath the skin, eyes are tired and droopy, buttocks are numb, and my feet tingle. We head off exit 20 and flag Sisal down in his white van. I pull into a gas station and Sisal follows. He drives the rest of the way to his home getting on Highway 222, Clarkton, North Carolina.

Arriving at Sisal's home is eerie for me because the whole situation is surreal. I never knew of Sisal and my mother being an item. Poppa never mentioned a thing. I walk into Sisal's home and immediately feel a weird sensation all throughout my body. It is the most uncomfortable feeling seeping through my pores. Brick and I sit down among all the others that were already at the house. Jo-Ruthie and Sisal talk to us about what had happened. A tall, slender, brown-skinned woman named Fever, who is Jewell's youngest sister gets up off the sofa to get some pictures and hands them to me as I view the smashed Mountaineer SUV. In the pictures there is lots of blood on the inside roof of the car. Jo-Ruthie describes in graphic detail what occurred with Jewell.

Fever hands me the article in the paper while Jo-Ruthie explains that Jewell was driving from a girlfriend's house around five in the morning. I read the article and it states that Jewell was coming up to a curve on Silver Spoon Road in the Western Prong community. She was traveling east at an estimated 50 mph and had veered off the road to the right, she lost control of the car as she came back onto the road, her car skidded sideways on the highway, slid off onto the right shoulder again and overturned onto the road. It was noted that the car slid thirty-five feet on its top. Jewell was wearing her shoulder strap and lap seat belt, which trapped her in the car. She died at the scene from head trauma at the age of thirty-one-years old leaving behind her two sons, six-year-old Antwone and eight-year-old Tyree.

My eyes mourn from the viewing of the pictures and story. Soon after, Brick and I decide to head to the hotel to rest up for Thursday. Traveling so far makes me fatigued and I need to relax my mind. We get settled in at the Best Western Hotel and just watch television for the rest of the evening. We eat. Take our showers and relax some more until our eyes grow heavy. I can't believe that I am actually in North Carolina for a funeral for people I had no knowledge of.

After Brick dozes off I go on the balcony and call Jordan. God I miss him. I need to talk and I know that he will listen. I didn't call him before I left to say that I had to leave town on an emergency. I shoulda told him maybe he would have come with me. But it was such short notice, and plus, he has duty at the firehouse. It woulda been too much of a hassle.

"Hello."

"Hi."

"Avery. Woman, where are you? I've been calling and calling you."

"I'm out of town."

"Is everything all right? You sound out-of-it."

"No. Jordan, things are not all right, but I just...."

"What, sweetie?"

I smirk.

"I just wanted to hear your voice. I'll see you when I get back. Bye."

I push the 'end' button on my cell phone. My fingers meet my eyes to wipe away the tears.

The next day, Sisal and I take a moment to get acquainted. I've never felt so out of the loop before in my life. There is so much I want to know. Why keep Jewell a secret from me? There is so much Sisal says I need to know so we sit in the heated gazebo as he reminisces about the woman he called Cashmere, but I knew as Ma'am.

"Cashmere and I courted. I can't even recall how long? Not too long after, we joined in holy matrimony, June 22, 1963." He smiles.

"You two were married?!" I say, wide-eyed.

"Sho'. We met on Bergen Street. Yessum, Bergen was known fuh flooding and finding drowned bodies in the murky waters of the Passaic River. Cashmere was home with hur mama, Mrs. Ella, and hur two brothers, Billy and Diggs. Dat's what she wanted. Anything she wanted I tried to provide." He smirks. "Miss Lad-dy, we got our first apartment on Fair Street. Yes, siree, we believed in family. Swore we were gonna grow old together. I wanted to give hur the world." He nods his head up and down as I hear his neck crack.

"Cashmere was twenty-four when you was born. Poppa was, um." He pauses and scratches the nape of his neck. "Oh, he was twenty-six."

I am still in awe looking at Sisal like this is too surreal.

He seems to be entranced with back in the day.

"Avery, I 'member sumptin so terrifying about Cashmere."

This captures my attention.

"Sumptin in me nudged me in the wee hours to get up. I keep thinking it wassa spirit or sumptin. My limp body rose from the dead sleep. I glimpsed at the window and saw dat the sky was still dark, glowing a purtty indigo blue. I dragged my feet across the carpet 'cause I was dead tired and entered through to the kitchen. I 'member hearing a humming sound coming from the refrigerator and little creaks here and there, probably from the old pipes. The linoleum floor had glittered specks of red, blue, green, and yella shaped like flowers all splattered upon. It reminded me of the colors of a rainbow. I headed towards the door and wit' my forefinger I gave it a slight push and walked in.

I 'member the bathroom light was off. I took care of my business and as I turned around. *Jesus!* It was Cashmere. She stood still as a tree trunk in the bathtub fully dressed with a glazed look in hur eyes. A look I had never seent befuh. Frozen ice bits surrounded hur—ice dat had come from hur defrosting the freezer, just yesturday. She seemed okay yesturday mornin', as she'd thrown all the ice bits into the tub to melt, but I saw dat it hadn't. She had a flustered look upon hur face as I reached my hand out fuh hur, but she hadn't reached back. She just stood lost in a world of hur own."

"I don't understand." I say, full of frustration in my tone.

He raises his large hands. "Just listen," he says in his baritone scratchy voice and then releases a deep sigh.

"Cashmere did not resemble the womans I knew hur to be. It was distressing seeing hur dat way. My nerves were rattled. Heavy heartbeats pounded so strongly through my skin. My breathing hissed like a mist comin' outta the radiator. Through the inaudible silence in the small bathroom I heard the fear in each breath dat I took. It was too real…too spooky.

"Cashmere's eyes were dead. And hur body was stiff as a board. Almost as if she mocked a mannequin in one of those windows display. Hur scalp was freshly cut crystal bald like she was inflicted wit' a form of cancer. Hur skin was dat ashy gray color. My big eyes were stuck wide on hur as a gulp of spittle slithered slowly down my throat. I had to call someone fuh help. It could've been a half hour dat had passed and then the doorbell rang. I took long strides and rushed to open the door and welcomed these two white men into us home.

"The two men in white uniforms entered us home and spoke wit' me. Then, the men pulled out an off-white colored jacket that buckled from the back. Goodness. Cashmere looked like a mummy in dat jacket. Dey strapped hur in." His big hands rose and glided across his coiled silver hair. "I said Father God, please…why?" Sisal eyes are weak and glossy looking.

Sisal's voice grows hoarse. "Cashmere stood still while the men fitted it, sliding in one arm at a time. The men fastened the buckles on the jacket. I was beside myself. I literally felt like I had failed hur. I stood quiet in the hallway watching wit' weakened eyes. I couldn't go wit' hur. I wanted to, but I couldn't stands to sees hur like dat. So I watched from the hallway. I didn't want to miss a glimpse of seeing hur ashy gray face, possibly fuh the last time.

"One man opened the door to the white paddy wagon, as the other man entered from the driver's side. The door closed. The man assisted hur into the backseat. The door closed. I could see hur side profile as she stared straight ahead. The knot twisted tighter in my stomach. It ached. My head hung low, eyes full of saltwater trying to weather the storm dat had overcast us home. My daddy always taught us boys dat mens don't cry. He used to say mens show no weakness and no misery, and especially no emotions in front of dey womens. Lemme tell you sumptin, I cried fuh yo momma. I cried like I was an infant chile. I love-ed dat woman wit' every ounce of man in me, from my feet to the pit of my soul. You hears me?"

I nod my head.

Sisal sniffs as he wipes his eyes with the back of his hands. I guess the pain is too great even for him. I remain silent.

"The other man entered on the passenger side. The door closed. The man behind the steering wheel started the engine. And wit'in a flash of a second, dey drove off. I remained silent in my cloud of thought. I was shaken up purtty badly. My sunken heart was cowering as tears instantaneously freed from my old soul. Tears were running freely down my worn face. I love-ed dat woman wit' all of my heart. God knows it's true. The mens took hur to Greystone Psychiatric Facility."

Sisal turns and looks me in my face. His eyes look like glass marbles and I swear I could see Ma'am's reflection.

"Cashmere, your momma had several nervous breakdowns." He lowers his head. I swallow hard and reach my hand out to pat him on his back. I am at a loss for words.

"Ms. Lady, your momma, Cashmere was purtty. All dat beauty all smothered in cocoa powdery skin and almond-shaped eyes dat were brighter than watt light bulbs. Hur lips arched in the middle with fullness on the bottom. Oh, she was as radiant as a sunrise and as quiet as a mouse, but hur brain…hur brain was so thunderously full of noise. Hur onyx-colored hair swooped off hur forehead not to smear shine from the pomade dat glistened in hur loose curls. Hur cheekbones high wit' rouge tone. She looked like a fifty-cent piece.

Yes, Lord, Cashmere had class. She tried." He wipes the sweat beads off his forehead. "Oh, yes, she tried wit' all hur might to take those meds." He lowers his head for a minute then he lifts it back up. "My heart was heavy fuh hur. It was a rough road traveling wit' yo' momma. She had an illness called schiz…" He pauses straining his brain. "…called um, schizophrenia. Some folks said 'mentally disturbed.' There were other harsh names, but I never cared fuh dem."

I remain silent ingesting all that he shares.

"Cashmere began to display her rendition of 'the voices within the woman, multiple personalities' on the outside. I was humiliated. She would come out of the house just strutting around the streets of Paterson. Dem voices took a hold of Cashmere and she traveled their journey of influence by their floozy personalities: one shorthaired redhead I called Lacey. Oh, Lacey was loose wit' hur tongue. Then the medium-length brunette I called Coffee. Coffee was a sly fox who took risks. Then there was the pin-curled blonde I called Fairy. Oh, Fairy love-ed to dress in inappropriate attire fuh a lady. She love-ed attention. There was the longhaired Cher who was adventurous with hur sports. And then, the natural-haired Cashmere who was more reserved. All of 'em wassa handful. Cashmere's many personalities displayed on the outside of hur off Broadway renditions.

"She would come out in dem skimpy mini-skirts thinking dat she wassa tennis player. You 'member dat womens Billie Jean King the professional tennis player?"

"Ah, I recall hearing about her," I say.

"Yessum, she dang near showing all hur goodies. She would come out going to play softball wit' hur glove and all. She would come out and sits on the porch in hur bathing suit; hosing hurself down with the hose hooked on the side of the house like she was at the beach somewhere. She would come out roller-skating around the corner, where everyone could see hur. She had dat ho-hum attitude. She'd just skate aroun' wit' hur long wig dangling downs hur back wit'out a care in the world. I constantly asked myself, *why is she doing this?* Boy, she wassa sight to be seent. She would come out being whoever she thought she was from the voices in hur head. Whatever those voices dictated, she would do. It was bothersome time fuh the both of us. I guess you can say I wasn't man enough to stay so I left and took Jewell. Jewell was jus' a baby."

No wonder I always felt motherless.

"This doesn't make sense. I'm the oldest. You're not my father, right?" I say, with a perplexing look upon my face.

"Right. Yo' momma met Poppa way befuh me. She got pregnant wit' you unintentionally and Poppa wasn't so pleased."

My heart sinks when he says that. I lower my head.

Sisal lifts up my chin and eases out his words with compassion.

"Pumpkin, Cashmere, she love-ed you wit' all of hur heart. Poppa left hur and you so I picked up the slack of taking care of you two, but when things got hot and heavy wit' her mental illness, l left and took Jewell wit' me. Poppa later came back and took care of y'all. I never intervened because I felt ashamed. He became the bigger man. Dey were never married; just what some would call 'common law,' I's sorry."

"But...but." I stop because I don't know what to say. This is too much to bear. I sprint out of the gazebo and slips down the stairs scraping my knee. I sit there with my hands covering my face in such distress. Sisal comes to the screen door to make sure I am okay, but I don't respond. I leap to my feet and run to find Brick.

Brick and I leave to go back to the hotel. We snuggle in bed as he holds me within his lead arms. It is difficult for me to rest because I have so much on my mind and heavy on my heart. I am unsure of how to handle this 'heavy burden' that has been bestowed upon me. I look over at Brick and he handles his stress by drinking Heinekens. And I indulge in having one to get some sleep. With my eyes wide open I wonder how my life came to this. I feel betrayed by my parents. I feel inadequate. I feel lied to. At Sisal's home I felt so out of place it wasn't funny. Regardless of how I feel, I'm here and I will pay my respects wholeheartedly to this young woman named Jewell.

Thursday, December 20th, the sky is blue. The sun heats the pavement and warms my trembling skin. Brick and I go to the Waffle House and have breakfast before going to Sisal's home. And as we are leaving out of the restaurant Brick's face frowns like he's in pain.

"What's wrong?" I ask, with concern in my voice.

"My chest," he says, as his hands grip his shirt.

I grow wary.

There is this spa near the hotel so I say, "Why don't you relax yourself with a pedicure." For once he doesn't hesitate and we go into Tiff's Spa and Salon to get his feet pampered. I know exactly what I am doing. I need him to be able to hold me up in my time of need. It doesn't make sense for both of us to be stressed. Brick comes out of the spa feeling and looking refreshed.

Once we arrive at Sisal's home we go inside and greet everyone, "Good morning." We sit down and stare at the TV screen. We both sign the guest book that is near the front door, and we greet visitors, family, and friends. Later we head outside in the backyard and sit and feed our stomachs with salted shell peanuts and Powerade drink. As folks come to pay their respects we greet, smile, and remain humble to these strangers. We sit in the gazebo that is like Sisal's bachelor pad; it is comfy and cozy away from the ruckus of voices high and low.

As the day eases into the afternoon I overhear someone say that the wake is today, and it would end around eight o'clock should anyone want to view Jewell before Friday. I start shaking just from knowing that her wake is today, and I hyperventilate within for fear of viewing her. I suddenly feel sick inside. My stomach feels queasy. I am so full of uncertainty that I don't want to step foot in Grassroots Funeral Home in Whiteville, North Carolina. Lordy be, I am petrified. I have to somehow build my nerve up by talking to my uncle Billy, Brick, and some other folks who basically tell me to go ahead and get it over with. That I will make it easier for myself come Friday. I decide to go.

Once we arrive at Grassroots Funeral Home my heart is thumping through my skin. When we step foot inside the lobby of the funeral home, I pant. My feet feel glued to the carpet. My body feels wobbly. I put my hands up to my mouth feeling like I am about to gag. It is too much for me to bear. I can't step one foot in the room where Jewell is. I can't figure out how to walk. I am vegetated.

Brick tries to help by pushing me but that instigates the soreness in my heart. Finally, I step foot into the room, but I can't bring myself to look toward Jewell. I am under a spell of grief that is so strong. I cry full of hysteria as some of the guests stand watching, figuring that I am the *other* sister from Jersey. My face crumbles. I panic. I scream with saliva drooling from my mouth. Brick picks me up off the floor but I fight him because I am afraid of heights. My arms swing at him to put me down still screaming at the top of my lungs. Everyone else stands back and lets me fight the air. My legs are kicking and pedaling to feel the earth. My stomach is in knots. Brick puts me down and I cry on his shoulder. As he moves away, I stand still. Brick walks up towards Jewell and touches her hands and turns to me and says, "She has a smile on her face." Still, I can't look toward her. I put my hands back up to my mouth, crying with my mouth hanging open. I take baby steps toward the lavender casket and quickly take a glance of her, but it is quick. I can't remember what her face looks like. Did she really have a smile or not. I ball my tissue and cry a cry of pain. I sit down and cry on the arm of the loveseat. My chest tightens and I fall to the floor. I faint. I lay on the floor until I feel a cold compress upon my forehead. Lord. Yes. I need the Lord to help me. I am broken as I lay here and my heart is twisting like a piece of licorice. Brick helps me stand and still I can't look. Then I hear singing from behind me. I hear my uncle Billy say, "Let her go. Let her get it out." Brick lets my hand go. And at that moment I build up whatever strength I can muster up and I make my lead feet move slowly towards the casket and I cry with such dismay. I stop. Move forward. Stop. Move forward. Stop. The pain increases to the point where I sprint out of the room, toward the lobby entrance, and storm out of the door, and take deep, deep, deep breaths. Brick follows me outside and grabs me and holds me tightly in his arms and says, "You did good." I continue to cry so full of mourning for Jewell. It is worse than I anticipate. My nerves are in a frenzy and I am uncertain if I can bear it come Friday. I am more afraid than I'd thought. I am literally shocked outside of my brown skin and back in.

Jewell's death triggers so much emotion that I can't grasp the loss of her. It is surreal, but real in the sense that I will never know her or see her again. Even with the quick glimpse it was not enough for me to put an image of her in my head.

On Friday, December 21st, Brick and I watch a church program on television. The "I can do anything" attitude hits my spirit. I am feeling on top of the world. I actually have an appetite. Brick lay in bed resting quite nicely as I reach in my luggage bag for my undergarments. I go take a shower, lotion my body down, and Brick is still sound asleep. Finally I say, "Brick, time to get up." I walk toward the window and it is a gloriously beautiful day. I reach for my black silk blouse, black pin-stripe trousers, black boots, and black with white and beige embroidery suede three quarter jacket. Brick finally gets out of bed, takes a shower, and gets dressed in his black suit, gold dress shirt, and black square toe shoes. He puts on his shades, dabs some cologne on, grabs the hotel keys and we head out the door.

We arrive at Sisal's home early, possibly around 11:30 a.m., and most of the folks there aren't even dressed yet. It is hot outside. The temperature is in the 80's. Most of the folks still have on their lounge clothes. Brick and I sit and rest our feet, nibble on some salted shell peanuts, and just relax. The funeral is not supposed to start until 2:00 p.m. Soon more relatives are arriving and the backyard, gazebo, and house is flooded with folks. There are so many cars parked on Sisal's property you would think there is a car auction going on.

Time starts creeping by and a thin layer of wetness forms on my forehead. I massage my hands and Brick massages my back reassuring me that I will be okay. I see a van and black limo pulling up. There is a police car to escort us to Pleasantry Mission Baptist Church. Everyone moves around like fire ants. We are led into prayer by the pastor, and then our names are called to enter the limo. I exhale heavily as I hear, "Avery Love." My eyes flood with emotion. My toes curl in my boots. My armpits moisten. My mind is flustered. My heart pounds out of control. My nephew, Antwone, turns to look at me and I force a smile to hide my anguish. I am deeply troubled and I know that it shows on my face. Brick rides with my uncle Billy and his wife, aunt Haylene.

Everyone arrives at the church. We wait for a few minutes in the hot limo, and then exit in a line. There are so many folks, a crowd of unknowns to me. Butterflies flutter in my stomach. I rest my hands upon my stomach, hoping the unsettledness will cease. But it doesn't. It gets worse. Brick finds me in the crowd and stands by me. Fever hands me a program of our sister. And tears stream slowly down my wary face, as I wail internally.

It is time to move forward inside the church and I am paralyzed. Tears streak my face. My chest and heart hurt. My eyes hurt. My body hurts. Moans of mourning are released from me and Brick touches my shoulder pulling me closer towards him. Folks are telling me that I can do it, but I can't move. My vision is blurry. I take one step and then another as Brick holds my hand.

We sit in the second row on the right side of the church. I make sounds of sorrow, loud, louder, pressing my hands upon my mouth trying to muffle the mournful cries. Brick puts his hand on my knee, patting it. I keep my head down and then raise it hoping that the casket is closed and I feel relieved that it is, but would it remain is what I question. The church is packed. Soft music plays. I find myself constantly turning around looking to see if Never has arrived. I wonder if she is still coming. She is traveling by plane. I look to my left and I spot Never's sister, cousin Skye, with her long salt-n-pepper dreadlocks sitting beside her daughters and granddaughter.

Around 2:20 p.m. Never arrives. She sits next to our cousin Nigel. I feel at little at ease with all the solid rocks by my side: Brick, Never, and Nigel. The choir sings. A cousin and uncle read the scriptures, Old and New Testament. Prayer of Comfort follows. A solo is sung. Acknowledgement and Obituary follows. Remarks. My uncle Hawk sings a solo in acappella. Special Prayer. And then a stout, mocha-complected, round bellied, full of anointing, soulful man sings another solo that shakes everyone in the church. The eulogy follows by the Reverend, which I personally feel awakens a lot of folks, especially me.

The slender, caramel-complected Reverend preaches, "Time, when it is time it comes when God wants it to. We don't have any say so in what God chooses for us, we just betta' be ready when or if He calls." The Reverend speaks in words that are of truth and conviction. And during my emotional state I understand as if he is speaking directly to me, especially when he speaks on "ideas." That it's best to follow what your instincts say to you and not waste time procrastinating. To do and work with what God has blessed you with because "time" may be running out. I muffle moans and groans of anguish trying not to outburst over his sermon. Pain seeps in every particle of my being.

During the Reverends sermon Never nudges her elbow into my side and asks, "Are they going to open the casket." I shrug my shoulders. But honestly, I don't want them to. I tap Sisal on his right shoulder and ask him and he says, "They will open it at the door." *No, no, no!* I close my eyes, swallow, and turn to Never to tell her that they are going to open it at the door and she says, "Okay." I am not ready. I panic inside. The look of fear must show on my face because Brick pats my knee again.

As the service is coming to an end, my body feels clammy. I keep looking back at the rows to see how many more are left before our row is to head up. It is time. Our row stands, and I can't move. I take a deep breath. Still my legs will not move. Brick stands and waits for me. No one rushes me. Never stands behind Nigel. Brick takes me by the hand and leads the way, but I stop. My throat is dry and sore. Then it is watery. I want to vomit. My stomach hurts like I have drunk sour milk. My feet tingle and I feel lightheaded.

Brick continues to walk up the aisle. I feel my feet wanting to give way but I remain standing. We are getting closer to the casket and I stop in my tracks. I stomp in place. Then my legs feel like I have shackles around my ankles and the weight holds me down. Each step grows harder and harder as if I have to leap over a five-foot fence. My body shakes. My arms tighten. My fists ball tightly. My vision blurs, again. My head pounds like I'm being hammered over the head. My lips quiver. Tears run fast, fast, faster. I back up. I can't move forward. I see my cousin, Cirk, who is one of Never's brothers. The dark-skinned, doe-eyed minister with a humorous

84

disposition and business savvy is telling me to "C'mon," his hand movement speaks without words. He moves his lips but I can't comprehend. But I stare at his hands. I am frightened. I am weakened. I am wounded. I am slashed, cut, burnt, and shocked with extreme fear. My eyes close, as I get closer to the casket. Others coach me by saying, "Avery, c'mon sugar, you can do it."

Oh Lord. I can't move. Lord, I can't move.

We get closer to the casket, and everything in my being fights not to go past. My will fails and I faint into the arms of a stranger, and Brick takes me in his arms and carries me. My eyes are open but I can't comprehend. My mind grows blank. I go into shock. My body is limp. A bunch of folks come to help me. I've lost my grip. I fade in and out. I am losing me. Folks are talking. Folks are trying to keep my eyes open. Then my nephew, Antwone, comes and hugs me. The six year-old tries to help hold me up. I fade out again.

My feet drag as Brick tries to make me walk. He carries me. I come to, and then go back out. Brick carries me again. Nigel rushes to pick me up and carry me as if he is carrying a sack of potatoes on his back, and he puts me in my Uncle Billy's car. I feel coldness touch my face and forehead. I see my cousin Skye touch my wrist. My eyes are open but I am numb. Brick gets into the car and sits next to me. I hear his voice. I see his face. I see the fear in his eyes. I see his lips move and I hear words coming out of his mouth. I hear fear. I hear him speak in tongues. I feel his hand on mine. I hear him speak clearly, "… please don't do this to me, please!" He shuts his eyes and sighs deeply.

The car starts to move and soon we are back at Sisal's home, while everyone goes to the cemetery. I sit in the gazebo because I don't want to go into the house. Tears form in my eyes. I try to speak, but nothing comes out. I've lost my voice from my nerves being so traumatized. No sound will come out. I lower my head in sorrow. Everyone is alarmed—my uncle Billy and aunt Haylene, aunt Marge, cousin Nellie, cousin Skye and her daughters Kayla, Toni, and granddaughter Kenya, and Brick. No one knows what to do, except wait. We wait but no sound comes out. Brick feeds me chicken while he pours himself a glass of wine. I try to speak and nothing comes out. Aunt Haylene gives me a glass of wine. And nothing comes out. Brick feeds me more chicken, and pours himself another glass of wine. Then he drinks a beer and then more wine. And nothing comes out. We continue to wait.

Monday, December 22nd, Brick and I stay to celebrate my nephew, Antwone's seventh birthday. It is a difficult time of burying his mom the day before and then celebrating the birth of him the day after but if Jewell were here she would probably have had a birthday party for her son. To me, she was here—just not in the physical sense.

9

My journey back to Paterson is stressful with Brick constantly complaining. *Shut the hell up backseat driver!* That's right; I have to get me together enough to drive us back home. He can't do it! I have to drive twelve or more hours back and I don't care to hear his bullshit! My nerves are already shot from the wake and funeral and I don't need any more added to my pain. I am trying to remain focused on getting us home in one piece. My hands shake at the steering wheel. My vision is fuzzy. And my mind keeps rewinding back to Jewell. I need comfort on my drive back and Brick is not accommodating me. I sigh. He keeps telling me to get off on exits that continuously get us lost and he gets hostile with me. I have to stop the car because my nerves are getting the best of me. And I fear if I keep on driving that I might kill us both. We stop at a Super 8 Motel in Maryland.

Come morning we get back on the road. I can't wait until I drop his annoying ass off because my brain is fried with hearing his mouth. I drop him off as soon as we get back to Jersey. I drive home and then take the car back to the rental agency.

Once I get home all day and night I agonize over my sister. Brick is nowhere to found. He doesn't call to make sure I am okay. I call him and he never answers his phone. I leave messages stating that I need his help, but he never returns my calls. I am sinking deeper in my hole and the pain is so overpowering.

My mind starts drifting back to when I was a child. *Why am I thinking about this? Why are the memories resurfacing?* I start to remember more than I bargain for. I cry so full of resentment, realizing so much has been blocked for so many years. Why now, I question. Sisal. His image appears in my head as bits and pieces come through. I don't want to relive the traumatic stages in my life. Please, Lord, don't let me remember. I kneel on my knees pleading to have mercy on my soul.

***

Early '70s…Paterson, New Jersey

I could hear the songstress voice of Natalie Cole singing "I Got Love on My Mind," as a woman's voice background sings off-key. Her unpolished toes are exposed, as her ashy bare feet, two-step scraping the blue tweed carpet with the soles of her feet as if she had a partner motioning along. A smoky fume crowded the living room illuminating a smelly haze. My teen body fought its way through, not welcoming the secondhand smoke to invade my lungs. As it made her cough, gag, almost regurgitate its poison from within. Her lungs must've screamed to be saved but she kept chaining them one by one like a fiend. As if she wanted to get hooked on its taste that fouls her tongue, lips, and fingertips. Its residue lingered within the sofa, loveseat, walls, and carpet, into the dining room, kitchen, and her four cornrows that lay neatly against her scalp as a familiarity of its existence. There was a carton of Marlboro's resting on the end table as the 60-watt bulb gave light to the misty room. There was a glass ashtray with overlapping buds toppling over each other. I wondered, why she is doing this to herself, to me, but I didn't have the gall to ask. I merely listened to her cackle and sass talk at the walls as each voice came out to play. There were many who came to play. So many that we couldn't keep up with who was who. I was only familiar with one that spoke softly as a child. The woman whose nerves shook like a shiver ran through her spine. The woman who shied behind closed doors and cried within her skin. Wondering where had *she* roamed and would she ever come back to visit, not as someone else, but as the one she was most familiar with—herself. The woman I called Ma'am.

Christmas was big in our home with wicker buckets of sweet bubble gum, large round oranges, tangerines, grapes, apples, nuts, especially Brazilian and pecan 'cause these were my favorite. Ma'am, Poppa, and I would unwrap gifts and smile and laugh. Goodness. We had us a jovial time. We'd listen to Christmas carols like those by Nat King Cole, Johnnie Mathis, Lou Rawls, Diana Ross, the Jackson Five, and watched *Miracle on 34th Street*. But this particular Christmas the phone rang. Poppa looked to be getting ready to leave and he took me with him.

Poppa drove us in his pickup truck to Park Ave; Eastside High School was across the street. (Yes. The same school where the movie *Lean On Me* was made.) There stood a yellow aluminum-sided house and Poppa rang the doorbell. This woman with smooth brown skin, a permanent smirk, with long black Indian-like hair opened the door. She welcomed us into her first floor apartment. My eyes wandered around at the unfamiliar place. My eyes scrolled this unknown woman. *Who is she?* I gaped at baby pictures of a little girl on the mantle thinking that she was as cute as one of my black bald-headed baby dolls, if not cuter. This unknown woman had Christmas at her home, too. It was decorated with color and trimmings and presents displayed underneath. My ears eavesdropped and I found out the unknown woman's name was Verdi-Dee Briggs.

Stepping out of Verdi-Dee's spacious living room was a little girl who was her daughter named Nana. She was a lanky ole child with legs that looked like two hockey sticks, chestnut-brown-colored with long hair, too. Poppa seemed friendly towards 'em. A little too friendly if you asked me. Then unexpectedly, Poppa added to my already flustered state as he leaned in and kissed Verdi-Dee right in front of my face. My eyes bulged. My forehead crumpled. *Ooooooh, I's tellin' mommee!* My tummy grumbled. It was obvious that Verdi-Dee and Nana was no kin to me. Oh, how I sopped in sadness. *Mommee.* I *had* no choice in the matter. I had to tell her hopin' she wouldn't cry a river.

From that day forward, Christmas was just an ordinary day. There wasn't nothin' special 'bout gift givin' 'cause at the end of the day the lights flickered off, and after I raised up from saying my prayers and fussing Poppa out in my little head, I lay in pitch blackness and all I saw was *that* kiss on another mommee's lips.

***

Tillery, North Carolina mid-'70s

I had an imagination that ran wild. I loved to pretend. I pretended that I was a cake baker, a baby doll, a beautician, a broken toy, a doctor, a model, a mother, a nurse, a teacher, a towel-wearing-long-haired white girl, a singer, a break-dancer, a track runner, a ballerina, a princess, but I'd never pretended to be an "abused child."

Poppa towed me in his truck to his hometown to visit his sister, Aunty Bitch. He said we just visitin', but for some reason he left me visitin'. I cried out for mommee. "I want my mommee!" But mommee was nowhere in plain view. Mommee was up in Jersey, my home far away from here.

Mommee was very ill. Her face was in mourning. Skin was ashen—not mocha-latte brown. Eyes sulked in deep misery for her indiscretions. Her voice scatted when she spoke. I *saw* her look. I see her look like she's sittin' right in front of me. *Mommee's tummy hurts*, I thought. My tummy hurts. I was three, four or five. This many, I lifted my hand up and spread my lil' fingers like a Chinese fan. I'm four.

I bowed my little head and looked up with the whites of my eyes and the pupils beamed into the sun. Its rays blinded me. I couldn't see any rainbows. My feet swung and my legs dangled offa the chair. I was small, thin, and I could tie my own shoes. I smelled pig and they stink. I smelled chickens and they stink too. And they clucked all day long. Cussin' and fussin' up a storm. I covered my ears to tune 'em out. I heard roosters crowin' making all that ruckus. I saw a dingy dog fanning its tail swattin' flies. Trailers, there were many stretched out on land like chewy sweet bubble gum across shades of tall, fearless trees. I scratched 'cause the mosquitoes kept nagging me. And I thought the dog might have fleas. I sniffed in the clean air that smelled like fresh laundry with a pinch of vanilla extract from someone baking sweet potato pie. I smelled stinky mud. The ground was scolding hot. My feet blistered from its mean streak. My body was clammy as I wiped the wetness offa my forehead with my bony wrist. *It is some kinda hot!*

I heard the door squeak. I turned slightly. I saw *her* eyes. They stared little at me. I turned back around and gazed at the sky; it painted a pretty picture in my head. I veered slightly as I felt heated eyes soaking in my back. Those eyes mysteriously disappeared. I exhaled the fear out and sucked it backs in. I wiped the sweat offa my face with the tail end of my T-shirt. I scratched the plaits 'cause they itched. I sniffed my fingertips and they smelled sour from the sweat and dirt. I felt sticky like lollipop candy. I heard water flowing through the stream. I saw dust tagging behind cars and its smoky cloud flowed and evaporated. I spread out my arms, flap, flap, flap. I saw a colorful butterfly. I wanted to fly like the colorful butterfly. I shooed a fly away with my hand. "Get outta heres," I said. I saw a yellow bumblebee hovering over the tin can of black spit tobacco from Aunty Bitch's snuffing. I heard the door squeak open. My heart was burning rubber. I didn't turn to look. My eyes cut from side to side as my two fingers eased into my moist mouth and I bit down on my itty-bitty fingernails. I bit down till there's no mo' nail. I lowered my head and wrapped my little arms around my tummy and rocked back and forth. I missed my mommee. I missed my home. I wanted to cry, but I feared *her* voice.

I lived in the boonies where the streets were dirt roads. In front of the dwelling lied a ditch with wanderin' water. I wanted to stick my head in the ditch and drown in its peace. Stream me away from this shabby old place for good. Across the road were a trillion cotton fields. I smelled misty mornin' rain almost every mornin'. And the sky glowed powdery sky-blue with white fluffy clouds that danced in slow motion. I sat inside the screened-in porch hearing the flies buzz and green hornets harmonize. There was an outhouse in the backyard. I saw the door was ajar and led into the living room, straight ahead was the kitchen with a back door exit, towards the left was a bedroom (more than two), and a sharp turn towards the right led to the narrow bathroom. This was my home away from home. I dreaded every wakin' moment.

I need Jesus like I never needed Him before.

"Help me, Jesus," I said. "Helps for the snakes rattle me outta my good senses."

My mind was distorted. There was a blackout of my memory and the light bulb flickers, but there was nothin' there. I tapped the crown of my head. Many nights I whimpered myself to sleep 'cause I felt helpless. I was disfigured with a bunch of emotional rubbish. And mountains of resentment climbed upon my scrawny chest. I heaved, startled by the sight of her—tall, obese, scary woman. I saw her sketch in my head. Ole grumpy woman. She was always spitting venom like she was mad at the world. "Take it up wit' Je-sus," I'd whisper in my head. I whispered for my mommee. I savored her beauty in my palm and stroked the lines that looked like small veins with subtly. Saltwater leaked from my eyelids and cast away within my ashen skin. I gripped my skin, tugged, and yanked, pinched, *this is not reality*, I said to myself. My lids peeked. They slowly closed motherly hugging my weak, red eyes. I turned slightly. Chaos moved behind *that* door. Swept cluttered debris in my face and dust mopped vague memories away. I inhaled and embraced death. Life was too high maintenance for a thin-blooded child like me, I thought. I thirst for mommee as my brain dehydrated memories. My mouth dried with no taste. And my airway pretended to play possum with my life. I wished to sing, but there was no music in my soul. There was no beauty or laughter or smiles. I was witnessing with my own eyes my demise, yet still breathed in that country air. My ears sharpened to the scraping of hard soles. The smell of sweet honey lingered in the air to distract the sounds. I heard the door squeak. I clenched my knees to stop the shake. I rocked to relax my fear. My tummy hurt.

It saddened me by not havin' a "normal" mother, or what one would consider to be a normal mother. A mother who talked to you, spent quality time with you, kissed your boo-boos when you fell and hurt yourself, took you out, took you shopping, and did cool things with you. As a child that's all you're hungry for. I lowered my head. At least, that's all I was hungry for. *Enough*! I thought. What could I possibly do being so far away from mommee? Nothin'! But my insides burned so hot that I balled my fists, stomped my feet, and squeezed my eyes so tightly trying to make 'em bleed.

I was pretty fed up and my mind got the best of me and my imagination took control. I pretended to mask my face with petroleum jelly and put my little dukes up, instigating a fight to beat down the Voice. Somehow I got bold, maybe 'cause it was all imaginary to me mainly because I couldn't physically see the Voice only except through the affected behavior of mommee. Nevertheless, I stood my pint-sized ground and asked the Voice some questions: "Why are you taking my mommee from me?" I rolled my big eyes. "You stay all up in my business with this foolishness. I want my mommee! Give me back my mommee! And I want the real mommee to so we can play with Barbie. I meant it. You take all of our time for your selfish reasons." I stomped my feet with my hands on my halfa pint hips. "I need my mommee! Now, give her back!" Squeezing my eyes tight trying to stop the flood of tears from fallen. "I NEED MY MOMMEE!" I ranted. "Why did you take her from me? Huh? Why can't I have a mommee like all the other children? I'm worthy. My spirit tells me so." There was continuous silence. "Mommee, I NEED MY MOMMEE!" I demanded. Then the real me came crawling out and I got all sensitive and emotional. Dang. My head hung low like sand was weighing it down; my big eyes looked up and a sourpuss look spread upon my face. "Please, leave my mommee 'lone? Pleasssssssse? I promise to behave. You have to believe me. I'll be a good lil' girl. Pinky swear. Pretty please? Just leave my mommee 'lone, 'kay?" I bowed my head feeling beaten. The Voice was a quack. It didn't seem like mommee stood a chance in hot fire hell making it out sane. Why her? Why me? I wondered. I missed out on having a relationship with mommee. Who? When? Why? It was obvious that some monster came and kidnapped my real mommee. And nobody called the police to catch the bad, bad man. Nope. He out here runnin' loose stealin' mommee's away from lil' children. When they find him I hope mommee kicks him where it hurts. "I neeeeds my mommmmeeeee!" I screamed out loud for the last time. Tears leaked from my eyes and formed a puddle at my feet as my bones crumbled like saltine crackers.

Aunt Bitch overpowered with a stern stare. She swallowed me whole and fed my innocence to the devil. I was growin' faster than the delicate summery breeze that wrapped around my body. I was growin' faster than the storms that poured out their misery so they wouldn't go stir crazy. Yet, I was small in a borrowed temple that crackled brittle bone. Constantly, Aunt Bitch humiliated and insulted my quick wit. I had no protection from her. Where was Superman when you need him, I questioned.

At times, I developed strength to uncoil out of my shell clenching of my palms, grittin' of teeth, squinting eyes that pierced at the back of her, and cussed with rage. I cussed and fought in whispers. I pleaded for freedom of my thoughts. Let them flourish and grow like head cabbage. My palms balled, head bowed, prayed to not discard who I was. I begged of thee, God. I had to be mindful of what I thought. Aunt Bitch was not godly for she had the power to deceive. I smelled her dark side; foulness that made eyes cut red onions, burn unsightliness into my skin. I used to be adorable, but then I was just a glow in the dark light bug whose mind flickered on and off.

Poppa called and Aunt Bitch shadowed my thin frame. She hovered to listen to my private conversations. I literally felt her breath scuffmark my earlobes. My voice trembled, often. Poppa never picked up on the tremors in my voice and I knew why. He wouldn't conceive of the thought nor did he detect that anything was wrong because he trusted his sister. She was *his* family. She nurtured him. Fed him, clothed him, when their parents shut their eyes.

His mommee, Fate, had a heap of children. She died giving birth to a stillborn. His poppa, Payne, was a womanizer, mean, and stubborn. He drank himself to death. All together there were nine of 'em clinching like glue to a mousetrap. Some were unleashed from the trap and roamed in others home—Poppa, being one. All I wanted was for Poppa to come and whisk me away from the blasphemous hands of Aunt Bitch, but I thought I was wishing for too much.

Poppa wasn't very observant. He didn't listen to the beat of his heart 'cause it was hardened, sweat from his glands were like ice cubes, or the soreness in his throat 'cause he drenched it with hard liquor. His eyes ignored the signs of agony as he gaped at my face that was shrinking along with my frame. Things were rather bleak. Verdi-Dee, oh, she was a heifer who wanted what she wanted when she wanted it. So acceptance of me was neither fathomed nor worth negotiation. I was a "black sheep." And I heaved a slothful sigh for the dislikes of her. I rolled the balls of my eyes and sucked my vulnerable teeth in disgust. Somewhere my parents' marriage became mangled, peculiar, and pain-stricken, way before Verdi-Dee foxtrotted into the wounded heart and arduous southern arms of Poppa. This was the lesser of my woes. I was wilting by the day. Like a flower that had not been watered so it dried and crumbled and died. Underneath its earth of soil was a dead root. I, at that particular time, was as such. I questioned, is there really a God in the heavens?

Aunt Bitch's home was not invitin'. Naw. She was belligerent toward me. Not so much with words, but more so by her treatment. Her greed confessed by actions and stole my prized possessions: birthday cards, clothes, and money, seems it all had disappeared. Aunt Bitch was a bloodthirsty demon. I couldn't fight her with my mind. I pleaded for the ability to inject fatty tissue into my flesh and prayed by sunup to have a thicker layer of skin. To stand tall with an arched back and gracefully hold my head high protecting the innocence of me. I wallowed in this life of captivity as my promise dwindled into a dysfunctional small being that stood no chance at life. And as a result I adopted nervous symptoms: nail biting, jitters, and teardrops. I was a pint-sized frail being slowly diminished with time. Time was depleting with every minute in the presence of Aunt Bitch. But images gave me hope, many false at times. I missed my parents. I missed my freedom, sherbet ice cream, cracker jacks, animal crackers, and paddleball to laugh and smile and play. To hug my mommee's long legs and scrape her pantyhose with my fingertips, feelin' the silk-like texture. Or stare into her eyes that looked like brown marbles. To whiff her sweet scent called "Mammy" a very popular perfume that only true mothers would sell by the hug full. Mommee's fragrance lingered as I pretended to inhale a profound sniff and blatantly accept her elixir of adulterer between her mind and herself.

Suppertime was an unappealing menu of grits and fatback. I could hear Aunty Bitch yellin', "Naw, y'all fixin' tuh eats so go wash y'all hands," to whomever was in the house. I despised the look, taste, wit' a passion. Just the thought of being fed the two made me wanna puke in my plate. It was like being force-fed iodine salt and snot balls. Lawd have mercy. My eyes watered losing hope. I watched with fiend eyes Aunt Bitch indulge her hefty hand into a bucket of fried chicken and help herself to an overbite of succulence. My mouth watered for a sliver of white meat, but I could only dream of indulging in the seasoned poultry that smelled so heavenly. I sniffed to savor the aroma like it was a gift from the Tooth Fairy.

I knew not of another and hoped to never, as Aunt Bitch was the evilest blood aunty I had ever come to known. Within my small being I hated her with a vengeance, wished death on her sour soul, and wished flies eat her flabby skin, and hornets poke holes in her unfeeling heart so that she could bleed to death. And those beady eyes, I wished to gouge them out of their sockets and douse gasoline and strike a match and set them ablaze and watch with a devious grin upon my face her singe to dust. And then set the rest of her ablaze, then stomp on her ashes and sweep them in a dustpan and flush her mean ass down in the outhouse. She was not even privileged 'nough to be flushed down the toilet bowl inside of the house. No, no, no. I smirked sinisterly jus' by the deviant thoughts.

My little palms clasped together and I prayed to my understanding spirit, to Jesus, to Heaven, to Saturn, Venus, Mercury, Mars, Jupiter, Pluto, to have mercy on my soul. Physically I was wilting like a raisin in the sun. Emotionally I was salty as hard-shell peanuts. My mind dissipated within those walls of abuse. Where is this spirit call Faith, I questioned. *I sho' liked to meet her*, I thought. I wanted to give *her* a piece of my mind. My faith had been compromised. I no longer believed that there was a light at the end of a tunnel. I had yet to feel the softness for of life and laughter. What was in remembrance of me? I saw a shell of a child, Black in ethnicity, fine hair, and mocha-latte brown skin with big saucer eyes, wide nose, full lips, and lil' ears that heard whip lashing actions that burst out louder than words, and macheted into my thin skin, as I profusely bled sparkling red. Blood ties were not thicker than water with aunty. Heavens, no! I wished that to be an illusion, but the contusions that befriended were real, mental black and blues.

I missed my mommee. Unbeknownst to me, someone in the family became the stool pigeon and advised her of my whereabouts. Ma'am packed a bag and hopped on the next Greyhound bus smoking to Tillery to come and get her baby. There was a knock at Aunt Bitch's door. And Aunt Bitch or her daughter, Nellie opened the door and there stood this woman. I stared in awe. Oh, she was an angel from the heavens. But I couldn't piece together how she looked, what she was wearing, how long we stayed after she arrived, I was in shock. And my shock extended up till the day we got on a Greyhound bus and headed back to Paterson. So full I didn't keep track of how long it took to get home, if we talked, how she acted on the bus, did I cry, I stayed in shock not wanting to come out of unconsciousness.

Being back in Paterson, my teeth beamed, eyes glowed, skin

warmed to the sweet freedom, but it only lasted temporarily as distilled vinegar turned it bittersweet by Poppa. There was a court order for me being in Poppa's custody, so he relied on his sister Aunt Bitch to be my caretaker, and within days I was heading back to her unloving home. *God, why don't you just let the bogeyman eats me, huh? Why do I have to go back to this mean lady's house? If I had an ice pop stick I would gag myself to death. By the time daddy reaches her home I'll already be dead*, I thought to myself.

I felt the heartburn building in me as I was being chauffeured back to Aunt Bitch. I imagined mommee's tummy hurting, again. I imagined it killing mommee. Almost like she was being punctured in the back with a pitchfork. Ouuuuuuuuuch! Going through the court system did nothin' but make me a hateful chile.

***

Tillery, North Carolina

When I saw the house of Aunt Bitch and smelled the scent in the air—my body quivered as my fingers eased into my wet mouth. I was back in hell. The six-foot long-legged man who sat nonchalantly on the driver's side with his arm resting on his lap, as the other hand, the size of a catcher's mitt, clasped the steering wheel. His dark eyes steadied the road, as he hummed some hillbilly tunes. I slouched down in the backseat in gloom playing spider web with my fingers.

Aunt Bitch was an actress. Uh-huh. She knew how to fold in and out of character. The Southern Belle was a performer and she saturated that southern hospitality on thick, but at the stroke of twelve she changed back into her evil self. I watched this heathen in action and it made me want to doo-doo in her pocketbook. Then I wanted to gag and vomit in her granny drawers' drawer. I was disgusted with Poppa that I said nothing because he was just inexperienced. It was hard to swallow seeing my own daddy not noticing a difference in his big-boned sister or me. It stung me like a Queen Bee. Ow!

Sometimes I sat with both elbows planted on my knees, lost in thought about if Poppa made visits to see mommee. I felt that she was back after my leaving. How was she gonna function without her child, I wondered. I felt sad most of the time 'cause I couldn't extend my arms out to rub her back and say, "Shhh, mommee, don't cry. M-o-m-m-e-e, don't cry." When she was afraid of the bogeyman I couldn't say, "Mommee, just turn the light on and he will disappear." I couldn't wipe her snotty nose with Kleenex and dry her tears that streaked her worn face. I couldn't stop her from whimpering in her bed sheets. I wondered if Poppa cared for her. Did the vows they shared mean anything? Through sickness and in health mean anything to him in their times of crisis? I hoped so. I wondered if he was sticking by her side or did he leave her high and dry to pick up the pieces alone. I wondered, does love evaporate so quickly that it was inconceivable of him morally supporting her in her times of distress? Or were the wounds so hollow that he couldn't begin to repair what burdened him for the sake of rebuilding her back into the woman he knew her to be? I wondered, but I had no one to ask. So I blocked the thoughts out of my mind.

Everything resurfaced in the household of Aunt Bitch. It immediately wore me down. Ma'am phoned frequently. And as Aunt Bitch's normal routine, she'd shadow my body with her obese frame, squint those beady little possum eyes; and made sure I didn't say anything that would snuff her out, if my parents found out the truth. Oh, Lawd, Poppa might've whooped her something good. I grinned to the thought.

Within weeks my weight dwindled down to a twig. I was already a pint-sized scrawny ole child. I looked dreadful. Cambodian-like. And I was not even taken to the doctor or to the hospital while livin' there. Things worsened because I caught a case of the worst ringworms, a contagious skin disease caused by fungi and marked by ring-shaped discolored patches. My hair was dry as dirt. Her chunky daughter, Nellie, washed my hair with Octagon soap. That soap was mostly used for laundry because of its harshness. I didn't know if this was an old-fashioned remedy to use hoping it would cure it. All I knew was that it made my hair brittle and coarse. Scalp was scaly white with dandruff- like flakes. Patches of hair disappeared. Still. I was not taken to the doctor or to the hospital in Aunt Bitch's care. That heathen was unmoved as she eyeballed my emaciated frame unconcerned whether I lived or died. It was evident that I was soon to die unless the Man Upstairs granted me a miracle.

***

Paterson, New Jersey

It was February of 1975 and the news of a court order from the Judge for Poppa to bring me back to Paterson filled my emptiness. In ten days I'd be with my mommee. It was a blissful moment, but a devastating one all in the same. Poppa came to get me and we returned back to Paterson. Unfortunately, I was taken to the hospital and I was diagnosed as malnourished. Bones poked out of my thin skin. I was an innocent child who was abused by her aunt. *Why didn't she like me? Why did she want to get rid of me? What did I do? Where de hell was Division of Youth & Family Services?* My body slouched, wanting to hide.

Everyday I had to drink a powdered supplement that came in a blue and yellow can, after each meal to gain weight. I was a sight. I was ingesting medication and using medicated shampoo, creams on my scalp to clear up the infection, EVERYDAY! Poppa caught the ringworms because of me. All of my hair had to be cut off to a baldy. I mean crystal. I had to wear a stocking cap on my head to support the wig that I *had* to wear to elementary school, ELEMENTARY! EVERYDAY!

There was a time when I visited Ma'am on the weekends and I had visited and old schoolmate who lived down the street. Well, a gush of wind came out of nowhere nearly knocked me on my butt. I managed to hold my balance but that wig didn't. It flew off my head like Superman and tumbled down the sidewalk like it was taking a stroll in the park. There I was running after it, trying to snatch it from the wind and place it back on top of my stocking cap. But that wind was strong and the wig just kept tumbling. I was humiliated but I managed to catch it before anyone saw me. That wig and I became instant enemies. I hated that curly-ass wig.

I attended PS No. 14 during my ordeal with Poppa as my shadow. Ma'am eventually started washing the little new growth I had and greased my scalp with blue grease. It was a mournful time for me. Any type of confidence I had must've dwindled down and embedded itself in the soles of my feet. I walked over my confidence, will, and strength so much that it weakened me into a useless soul.

***

I sob so full of grievance. My body slides off the sofa onto the floor. Why, why, why? I pounce my hand against the hardwood floor begging to know. I have so many questions to ask and the main two to answer are dead. They're dead! Why would they do this to me?!

My eyes cut up at the ceiling and I sneer at it and tighten my lips as my eyes darken black. "I hate you both and I wish you's rot in hell!" Just the words I scream make my stomach ache as I stagger to my feet and make my way to the toilet bowl to vomit out my pain.

I have to hug my own skin. I have to comfort myself and it is most difficult. I start talking to God, Jewell, Johnnie, and Storyteller, asking them to help me out because I cannot function with normalcy. I cry every single day, all throughout the day. I pray for me. I reach out to some acquaintances, but no one seems to have the time to talk. It discourages me and I sink deeper. I cannot believe that Brick has abandoned me. I cannot believe that he would allow me to grieve alone. As a result, I grow strong and then fall crumbling weakened by Jewell's death.

It is an emotional roller coaster that I am on. Up and down, down and up. I feel so lost within. I feel neglected like Brick never gave a damn about me. Knowing how distraught my state of mind was when we were in North Carolina. He is cold-blooded. I assumed too much of him thinking that he would be there to help hold me up since he traveled the journey with me. I assumed that he cared for me. I assumed that he really had strong feelings for me, and all his actions were confirmation that he was ruthless. He cared about no one but himself. I don't know why I am surprised because I knew all of this from day one. But somehow I believed that people could change, the part that I seemed to have forgotten was that he or she actually has to want to change.

It is a Thursday and I am home as I hear the fire alarm sounding off. I am not cooking anything. I stand on a chair to press the button to turn it off, and every time I turn to walk away from it, it blurts that annoying beeping sound again. It irks my last nerve. Some days it doesn't go off at all, but then I realize most of the time when it does go off is when I'm distressed. Then is when it hits me that its Johnnie letting me know that he is in arm's reach even though I can't see him. He is here. I can hear Johnnie telling me without words that I have to keep going, no matter what. That I don't need Brick because he has shown me what he is made of, and he knows that I can do badly all by myself. I smile because I feel his presence. I feel the warmth of him surround me. Then I fall short and start bawling into my palms because I miss him so much. Tears pour up out of me and I lay fetal on the sofa.

I decide to go back to an old manuscript I started writing after I disclosed my status to Anonymous titled, *To Love Him Is To Leave H.Y.M.* I want to dedicate it to my sister. A woman I never knew.

Each morning I awake, I turn on my computer and start to write. I want this first novel to be a compelling story. I want it to be a meaningful story about a woman's loneliness and how with the help of a special love she is able to accomplish greatness. I work day and night, night and day, just to keep my mind preoccupied until I become obsessed with the character and her journey of healing. I push myself daily. Feeling her anguish. Feeling her emotions for this man. Feeling her frustrations. I want her to struggle as I have. I want her to be haunted by her past as I have. I need to be able to relate to the character in all phases of her life.

During my pursuit of getting Brick out of my system, he calls me from a payphone. My heart literally stops. His voice penetrates inside of me and I grow numb.

"Avery."

I remain silent as my eyes wander the ceiling, walls, and floor.

"Avery, it's not your fault. I went on an alcoholic binge. I, I, I'm getting back wit' my wife."

I feel a knot forming in my stomach.

I remain silent. I reflect back on him saying that they had been separated for six years. Now all of sudden, he wants to or rather *they* want to rekindle the flames. You gotta be kidding me.

I remain silent, with puddles forming in my eyes.

It hits me hard, especially in my time of need. He waits until after I find out that I have a sister who has died. After I find out that my parents were never married. After I find out that my mother had several nervous breakdowns. After I drive to and from North Carolina, Brick tells me unfeelingly over the payphone that he is getting back with his fuckin' wife who he has been separated from for six years. Is he for real?

Bricks tone becomes abrupt—obviously his mood swings have kicked in. My eyes widen, full of sorrow, because he can't even be a friend and console me in my time of need. The harsh words spew out of my mouth, "You are about to make the biggest mistake of your life!"

Brick starts yelling. "I LOVE MY WIFE! Wha' you wan' me to do!" and then I hear, *click.*

I stare at the receiver. Tears just fall from my eyes. I wonder why the sudden change. I can't believe my ears and my heart nearly drops to my feet. It hurts me deeply. I was misled into thinking that he truly cared for me. He expressed that he was falling in love with me over a quaint dinner. *All a bunch of lies.* The love he so-called felt for me somehow turned into "like" so very quickly. Then why would he go so far as to buy me a "friendship" ring that surely resembled an engagement ring? Why string me along by showing family the ring, especially his mom. A ring I only wore twice because his mind would change so often and words of what he really thought of me would slip. I had pulled the ring off and stuffed it in my dresser drawer. Brick was selfish and the treatment that he had experienced with his wife it all turned negatively on me. I became him and he became her. I was taking the punishment for something I had nothing to do with. At the most vulnerable time I am dismissed to heal on my own. The pain is excruciating. It is most difficult to function, to even breathe.

10

I receive an unexpected call from Jordan and it only resurfaces old hurts that make me lash out at him. I explain to him how I despised him for disregarding my feelings on our date. Jordan claims he didn't know. He later apologizes, anyway. We haven't really kept in touch since I called to let him know that I was out of town. An associate of mine slipped and told me that he was indulging in Spellman juice…Dolce. I was repulsed. A part of me wants to confirm from the source since he is on the phone but I don't care to know. I am already hurting and that will only push me over the edge to commit suicide. I wouldn't want him reading about me in the local paper, "LOCAL WOMAN DIVES OVER THE EDGE OF A HIGH-RISE BUILDING FOR OLD FLAME WHO NEVER GAVE A RAT'S ASS ABOUT HER. WASN'T SHE DUMB?!" I even chuckle off of that. I keep both ears open, and eyes, because I am hurting and can easily be manipulated into thinking that he is trying to comfort me. He did ask to come over and I said no. I don't want to be around a man. I just want to talk, to cry, to have someone, anyone who is willing to listen. Just lend me a pair of ears that won't go deaf. Jordan gives me his undivided attention. He respects me from afar and we just talk on the phone to help ease the anguish that I feel making me bleed out my pain.

Every day I insert in a DVD, *The Diary of a Mad Black Woman*, and just watch it and my wounds seem to open more and more. Even though I was not married to Brick the pain is still great because we had been through a lot together in almost a year's time. I thought we had each other's back but I was highly mistaken. I had his when two of his brothers passed on. I had his when he needed someone to listen to his drunken ass in the wee hours of the morning. I had his when he would confess of how much he missed his children, and what a rotten father he was back in the day. I had his when he would cry in front of me and would cry out for his mommy to help him. When he would cry out to God to help him and fall on his knees theatrically. I would just watch him, but I wasn't convinced. To his mom or God he would shout but to me it was just words that had no substance. No feeling. No sincerity. It was phony, as was he. He would even lie to himself. Trying to convince himself that he was pure as the driven snow, which we both knew he wasn't. So much bad had consumed his soul and it was wearing his spoiled ass down. I was there through most of the bad, good days were few and in between, but I was there. He wasn't there for me. And reality set in when he showed me his back.

When I feel the pain creeping up I slip in that Tyler Perry DVD and I cry at the same time because it hurts that much. I have a hole the size of a cantaloupe inside of me that will not close. It is agonizing. I feel myself getting sick. I have no appetite. I have lost weight, something I can't afford to do. I look as I feel—God-awful. It hurts so badly that I have to keep reminding myself to take my meds.

Jordan continues to call me and we laugh, but I am not looking for anything from anyone. I just want the pain to ease off. I begin to dig deeper into my writing allowing my character to feel what I feel at that time. I stop in-between to read what I have written to make sure it is exactly how I feel it cutting me to the bone. As I picture it in my mind. And how it twists and tangles my heart, and aches in my soul. I become hungry to finish this manuscript and I devote much time and patience to it.

One evening while watching *The Diary of a Mad Black Woman* DVD for the twentieth time I receive a call from Brick. My heart palpitates. I have a lump in my throat that feels the size of a twenty-five cent-gumball. And it is difficult for me to swallow. My fingertips tingle as well as my arms. I feel numb wondering why he is calling. I guess it all is coming to light when Brick returns back to his wife. The grass wasn't as green as he'd thought it would be.

"Avery, I, I, I, listened to you."

Dead silence.

"I, I, walked into the doors of a Narcotics Anonymous program to seek some help for my addiction. Avery, I didn't know. I didn't know that I was…am an addict."

I smirk slightly, but remain quiet. Then the rage erupts up out of me and I say, "Tell your wife! Why are you calling me?! Why are you calling me?! Isn't she there for you?! You were dying to be with her, now, you have *her* so tell her, not me!"

Numerous times in our past I had preached for Brick to seek some sort of help for his drinking and drug usage. He was completely out of control, hostile, nasty, and very, very lost. But he was living in denial and moaning and groaning for his love, his wife.

Unfortunately, *wifey* wasn't interested in him trying to rebuild himself so he ended up calling *me* stating that he realized he had the right woman all along. I cannot believe what I am hearing.

Okayyyyyyyyyyy. I am deeply distressed by his actions but then I realize for six years he was holding on to a woman who did not share his heart. Brick and I had something in common, we both loved hard. But we didn't have similar views on sticking things out and being supportive of the one who walked the walked with you. I had been there for him through storms and sunshine, but he wasn't for me. And it hurt like hell. He asks to come back and I swear that lump in my throat gets stuck. My mind, heart, and soul is flustered.

I speak with Jordan about my troubles. I can't think rationally. I don't want my heart to speak for me. I need help. I sigh so full of grief like I just witnessed my very own death. Yes. I have died of a broken spirit, and I am uncertain if I will fully recover. So much pressure is bestowed upon me and the weight overwhelms me tremendously. I have feelings for Brick. Love, I can't say. Truthfully and sincerely, the feelings have drifted slightly. It is still lukewarm. Jordan states that with the intimacy that Brick and I once shared there was a strong, spiritual connection that I had not shared with even him. I tell Jordan that just the intimacy with Brick and I taking baths together with scented candles surrounding the bathtub was a peaceful moment in quiet even though the city was full of noise. "Wow, Avery, it sounds like you guys had something special." Jordan says. I nod, but deep down I feel it was all a façade. Possibly he was just tired and I had nothing to do with that peaceful moment. I just happened to be there.

Brick continues to convince me that I am the one. That he truly knows what he wants. Still. I am not convinced because he is so easily influenced even a child could out smart him.

"I, I, know you the one. I, I, do love you. She doesn't love me. But, I know where your heart is. I know you care about me. You take good care of me. I know that when I grow old you won't desert me. I know that you won't put me in one of dem nursing homes to rot away. I know this. That's why I'm trying to get some help. I walked into the doors of the Narcotics Anonymous, and I thought of *you*. It was you who stuck in my rock head. You stuck by my side. Don't give up on me? You got me to come here. It was *you*, not her. She could careless. I, I, I'm gonna share somethin', huh, I'm tired. I know I got issues from when you told me to call that Alcoholics Anonymous hotline number at 1:30 in the morning and I asked the woman, 'How do you know if you a alcoholic?' And she said, 'Sir, 'cause it is 1:30 in the morning and you're calling me.'

I pause and then speak.

"Brick, I'm glad that you're getting help. You need it. Yeah, but look at what you are doing to *me*. You left me right after Jewell's funeral. I mean, c'mon, that shit hurt like hell. I needed your support! And you just disregarded my feelings, my heart."

"Look, I know. I'm, I'm, I'm sorry. I'm sorry. I know I got issues, the drinking, gambling, drugs, it's a lot, but I'ma do what I have to do to get myself together. Don't give up on me, I—"

Where the hell did the gambling come in? This nut is really trying to get killed. Lord, what do I do?

"What do you want from me? Why are you punishing me? I'm not her. I didn't hurt you. And yet, you keep hurting me for something *she* did to you. Why?" I ask.

"I want you, Avery. I love you. I've been afraid to share that wit' you. It's not easy for me, but yeah, I do. I, I, I, I do love you. I know you the one. I know it in my spirit."

He completely disregards my question.

"Uh-huh." Still, I'm not convinced.

Why is he doing this to me? Wait a minute. You longed for your wife for over six years. Suffering with booze, drugs, loose chicken heads, and God only knows what else. And now that you've been given the opportunity to be with the love of your life, all of sudden you don't want to be with her. Wait a minute. But this is the woman you loooooooooooove, the one I took all the punishments for, the one who you continuously threw in my face like acid. Now...that those things you envisioned aren't as you had hoped. Now...that you found out that her past is still her present of indulging in past bad habits. Now...you want to leave her and show her your back, as you've done me. But you loooooooooooove her, soooooooooooooo mucccccccccccccch that you won't stay to try to comfort, console, and possibly both of you need to get into some type of program. Now, you decide to leave with no thought in mind of making your marriage work only because she is doing something that was done in your past but yet you are still doing something that was from your past. You two belong together. And yet, neither one will help the other. Okayyyyyyyyyyyyyy. WHAT THE HELL AM I MISSING! Here I am devoted, committed, suffering with my own shit, you leave my ass to be with her, and then you leave her ass to be.... Isn't marriage about sacrifice...about togetherness, obviously you've both outgrown those vows, if they ever existed is unknown to me, but both actions of abandonment make me wonder if love ever existed.

After I vent in my mind, I take Brick back. *I must be high off of an over-the-counter drug called "Dumb Ass."*

After a couple of days of having a pity party I jump back on the saddle and return back to work. Anonymous won't survive on air.

Brick appears to be doing fine with going to his meetings, but somewhere along his journey of recovery he falls back and relapses. His motivation diminishes and the gambling fills the void as well as the occasional beer drinking. Brick calls and I immediately get annoyed because I'm growing tired of the same ole' shit. Then one evening, Brick calls me and I immediately let loose.

"Look, when you go to your meetings you need to open up to *share* your pain because it is not helping you to take in other peoples stories and not divulge your own issues. I am not a sponsor. I haven't lived that life of drugs, gambling, but I do know that if you don't open your damn mouth and set your soul free you are never going to recover. Next time raise your hand during 'burning desire' and get that shit out! If you don't you will use, whether it be drugs or booze—or both. Love yourself enough to help yourself."

"I know. You're right." Brick says, but his habitual habits remain the same.

He is lost. The alcohol, gambling, and the lies are thinning our relationship and friendship. We distance ourselves.

It really hurts me that he takes his anger out on me because I have done nothing wrong and yet, no matter what, I do to try to help him achieve his goal I keep getting shitted on. I get damned tired of hearing "it's the mood swings." I am not uplifted. I am being knocked for someone else's shit. *He's miserable.* He gets me to listen to him and then turns around and talks shit. But as I tell him repeatedly, "Karma will bite you in yo' ass when you least expect it." So I put all the insensitive things that he has done to me in the hands of karma. I dust my hands off and regroup back to the sane, free-spirited woman that I am.

11

Since Jewell's death I had to cancel Open Mike and reschedule. I get in contact with Travesty and we set up for her to come tonight. I'm looking forward to being around my extended family. I need the positive energy to surge within me. I take a nap until around 2:00, and then I plan out the evening. My phone is ringing off the hook from artists wanting to perform. It puts a long-awaited smile on my face.

Anonymous is almost full to capacity. The crowd is lively this evening. I am feeling on top of the world since I let my burdens down. There is no drama in my life at the moment. I walk on-stage dressed in a sexy basic black Michael Kors dress with high-heeled black and silver Jimmy Choo boots on.

"How's everyone doing?!"

Hands clap, making a roaring sound.

I am smiling from ear to ear.

"This evening we have a special treat. There is an artist here who will be reading an excerpt from her first novel titled, *Close-Knit.* Let's give it up for Travesty!"

This punk rocker-lookin' woman all dressed in black with eyeliner thicker than chalk and lips darker than black permanent marker comes waltzing on-stage in these high Frankenstein boots with black-painted fingernails. But when she opens her mouth you don't hear what you see. She has a soft-spoken voice that's childlike.

"Hello, everyone, I'll be reading a poem from my book, *Close-Knit.*" She takes a deep breath likes she's nervous. *How can she be nervous coming out looking like darkness*, I wonder. Travesty distracts my thoughts. "The title of my poem is "3 BIRDS OUTSIDE MY WINDOW.""

Tweet, tweet, tweet
I hear 'em singin'
That soulful tune
As I sit my lonesome self in my bedroom
Contemplating, what should I do?
Once, twice, three times
It's like a soul-sin, soul-sin, soul-sin song
As I plot to open the bottle of pills

And put one in my mouth
One after another,
Until my palm's empty
And my will cries helplessly
But I hear

Tweet, tweet, tweet
As if the birds are in the room with me
My mind grows sleepy
Eyes open and close
Close and open
As my life seems to be fading
Tears flow slowly down and leap off my chin
It's like a soul-sin, soul-sin, soul-sin song
That pierces my ears
Giving me the strength, the will,
To listen to the trio of life.
Tweet, tweet, tweet."

Then she begins reading the first chapter of *Close-Knit*:

"I loved him like no other. Like the moon was kissing the sun burning our souls. *I loved him more than life itself, but apparently he doesn't feel the same for me*, Mona thought. Is it my looks, she questioned. She wondered how she could make herself a beautiful vixen. She thought vixen because most considered her sweet and kind and maybe that was a turn-off for him. Why doesn't he love what she displays before him? Her pearly-white cashmere skin, red-colored lips, and brunette hair that coiled from the smell of him. Man hands that cringed to touch her bare skinned womanly shoulder. She glistened in the night, waiting in such agony for him to accept her, to love her, to yearn for her, but he yearned for another—a he. A tall, handsome, Mandingo man she could not compete with, unless she pretended in her head that she had a dick between her legs. But she knew it would not work because she smells of woman. His taste buds salivate for him. His warmth and passion spellbound his eyes. Who pleasured him into a bliss that she could not fathom. She was oblivious to that kind of love. That colorful love that stroked him lovingly, leaving him full as her heart wept of loneliness. That was when the thought of taking her life spun fast in her head as she lay across the floor balled in agony from a broken heart."

I can feel my skin wanting to wail. I was feeling so good up till now. I try to listen to Travesty, but my mind drifts to my own troubles. I try to fight the feeling, but anger displays as my veins pop from my temples. Each sentence Travesty reads, I grow intensely insane. I want to punch the lights out of her for coming in here disrupting my natural high with her woes of life. What's wrong with her! I find myself taking my anger out on her, but it is not her fault. She is or once was hurt and I have no right to disregard her anguish. I calm myself down and listen with an open mind. She ends her excerpt.

Travesty's eyes look weakened by her words. I can tell that she feels what she speaks and it is most troubling because I can relate. I feel empathy for her, as well as myself.

Travesty allows her tears to free from her eyes. She closes her book and stares into space before walking off-stage. I get a grip and walk back on-stage.

"Everyone, please give Travesty another round of applause."

The thunderous sound of support trembles the building.

"Our next performer is an erotic poet. Let's give it up for K-Luv."

This sexy creature sashays on-stage with a walk that oozes *Sex and the City*. She has a long bone-straight brown weave, C cup breasts that damn near stand up on their own through her skimpy blouse, and her jeans are glued to her skin outlining the crease of her crotch. All the men start lusting with their eyes poppin' out of their heads and their tongues dangling from their mouths.

"Hello. I am going to start my first piece off I call 'Inter-sex-tion'."

Eyes are glued and it is quiet as a mouse up in here. K-Luv uses a cell phone as a prop to recite her piece.

"Operator, send an ambulance quick,
There's been an accident,
At the inter-sex-tion, with my wet pussy and his smoky dick,
Yes, he is my secret lover,
Fine undercover brotha'
And we collided while he was licking my clit….

Oh Operator, you may have to make a U-turn,
And cum down Rt. 46 West,
Yes Operator, I think that may be best.

Ooooooooooh, What Operator? No…I wasn't moaning to you.
My mans doin' what he gotta do,

Ooooooooooh, Operator he is nowhere's near through,
(*she wets her lips seductively*)
Who? Oh, Operator, I won't kiss and tell
 (*she massages her crotch*)
But if you have a good nose you can probably smell—him.

Yes, I understand there may be a delay,
Traffic is quite congested,
Yeah…you think?
(*she smiles deviously*)
Just keep us abreast on it?
As I ride his dick
Can you do that for me?
(*she sticks her pinky in her mouth*)
I'm kinda busy at the moment,
Oh, I am steering him strong.
(*her face makes erotic expressions*)
No need to waste a "good nut"
Yeah…you know what I mean.

Operator, it was a pleasure talkin' to you,
But I really have to go,
(*she has an innocent look on her face*)
Dickey is starving for some pink tongue
Suck, slurp, lick, suck, slurp, lick,
Cum, pretty-boy, cum
Mmmmmmmmmmm, yum-yum-yum."
(*she licks her fingers like he tastes so good*)

ILK, ILK, ILK! I can't seem to get her words out of my head, especially…cum…yum, yum, yum. Damn, I guess her words do stimulate the mind and body. I'm all hot and bothered due to the fact that I don't have a penis breaking my back in and crumbling down my walls of frustration. I must say, the image is definitely thought provoking.

All the men clap with their heads bobbing and tongues dangling, dripping saliva. I fan myself because it is hot in here. All I can say is, "Wooooooow!" I feel a little envious of K-Luv. I mean she has this confident sex appeal that makes these men and some women fixate on her. I remember when I used to have that same effect on men. That seems so long ago.

12

Brick yearns for attention, something I try to give, but it is not me he yearns it from. He says he wants to change his life around, but the alcohol is burdensome. Even with attending his NA meetings it seems Chardonnay has a stronger hold on him. I want him to *love me like Chardonnay*, but deep within I don't feel that he can. *She* is his true lover, life-partner. *She* makes him forget temporarily, as he sips *her* passionately. *She* nurtures him in a way that leaves him shielded from his own reflection. He suffers inside and he doesn't know how to stop the noise that rings in his ears and shows images in his head. His past is drowning him. I cannot fathom how maim his internal is. But I feel great sorrow. Oh, I am wilting inside 'cause I can't help him surrender. All that I can do is support him in his endeavor to seek change. But I can't stop him from craving *her*—his wine.

I put up with the early morning and late night calls, trying to be supportive. But it isn't enough. He takes a spiral downward and I can no longer hold him up so I let go. I ache. I am left with no other alternative. He keeps relapsing and the anger leaps out on me. It's not my fault that he chooses to take a step backwards, and I refuse to carry the weight on my shoulders. I don't have the strength to hold us both up. I wanted him, and he wanted *her*. Chardonnay comes before any woman so I freed myself from the stress of trying to compete with his love of wine.

In letting go, I gradually begin to heal. It's not easy and each night I wrap my tender body in my afghan and weep so full of dismay. This is my only outlet that makes me feel a connection with myself—crying. The one thing Brick hates for me to do, but I do it anyway because it washes the old residue out of my system.

I choose to remain friends with Brick and move on in my life. By me making that choice it really makes Brick look himself in the mirror, but it is all words and no actions. My tolerance level becomes low.

I try to resume the friendship with Brick, but I pay a hefty price. He is still playing his little childish games. He is still drinking heavily, and he still is indecisive of wanting change. Many nights he calls me and gradually I feel myself reeling back towards him. But I don't. He is the only man that has actually provided for me, but as soon as the alcohol hits his gut the venom squirts out of his mouth.

And all that he had ever done for me comes ejecting out. I constantly hear it until I grow tired. I was there for him by listening, being an honest friend, sharing, feeding him some real shit, some truthful shit, words of encouragement, pushing him to seek more than the norm, and following through on my words. I may not have had money because everything is tied up in my business but I have a vision that is real. I can stand and touch my vision. It is more than he can say. I am devoted to my vision and it comes before any man.

Brick slowly makes progress, but somehow the mean and nasty seeps back as well as the man who could careless about others. It hurts me dearly because without the alcohol, without the verbal and emotional abuse, and without the compulsive lying, without the marriage, he could have very well been my future mate. Things seem to worsen instead of get better and my mind and spirit begin to feel greater pain. I have to make a choice and it is most difficult for me because I care for Brick, but he doesn't care for me in a way where he will stop punishing me, stop hurting me, stop making me suffer for someone else's doing. I support him by going with him to his NA meetings. I continue to encourage him. To forcefully give my hugs and kisses because I'm not the affectionate type. But I need a break from him, so I take it. It gives him ample time to realize what type of woman I am. How I want to be treated and respected and nurtured. It makes me question if he ever had love for me because he doesn't know how to show it to me without thinking that I will stomp all over his heart. It is a risk that he fights to take. I've become a non-believer when it comes to *love* from a man. His compulsive lying oozes from him like it is so easy and acceptable. And his favorite line, "You know how I am." *What does that mean?* That it's okay to treat people like shit? There is no excuse for his treatment. No excuse for misleading people. Neither having any regard for their feelings. It is definitely time to grow up and I do not foresee that happening in the near future. The forty-five-year-old man with the mentality of a five to eighteen year-old has a lot to learn about self-awareness, love, and peace.

Dear Brick,

I'm going to cut to the chase, I'm moving on. But I have some advice for you. Whether you take heed to it or not is totally up to you.

Grow the hell up! Stop pulling on your mom's skirt tail! And leave her nest. Continue to go to your AA/NA meetings and stop lying so damn much. Conning yourself to think that you got things under control, but in actuality you're just killing yourself slowly. Stop being selfish and greedy! Better yet, stop being a crook!

I wish nothing bad on you; if anything I wish only goodness to fill your heart, spirit, and life. I wish you peace and harmony. I wish you strength to find the courage within to fight your demons before they take you out of your misery. I wish that you find the confidence within to realize that "life" is valuable, not devalued. And that you remember all the bad things that you have witnessed in your own life and use it to enable you to seek better, and to be a better man, first and foremost to yourself, and then to others. I can only pray that you find your calling in life and devote to finding "joy" because when God or Satan calls you home it is non-negotiable, no second chances are given. When it is time to go, it is time to go.

I hope that when your time comes that, at least, one person can stand and say with sincerity, "He was a good man." No one wants to die knowing that they did nothing positive to contribute to society. And even though I know that you have a smidgen of good in you, I guess your only concern should be that God knows it too.

Goodbye,
Avery

I take a deep breath, crease the letter, seal it in the envelope, address it, and walk down to the corner to mail it out.

On my way back to my loft, I think about everything I said hoping that he really acknowledges the woman he used to have. I'm not perfect, but I'm worth so much more.

13

Ring…ring…ring.

"Hello," I say half asleep.

"Avery, I'm sorry I woke you."

I sit up against my headboard, "Who is this?" I ask, while massaging my face trying to wake up.

"Fever. Listen, I'm sorry to wake you so early but this is kinda an emergency and I didn't know who else to call."

"Is everything all right?" I ask, while wiping the crust from my eyes.

"That's the reason why I'm calling. Listen, I know you don't know me well enough, yet. Um, I feel a little stupid reaching out to you with all these folks here, but I don't feel like any of them will help."

"Help with what?"

"Well, a couple days ago Jo-Ruthie had a mild stroke. Well, Sisal has been running himself ragged that he ended having a scare of a heart attack. The doctor says he has to take it easy or he may have a massive one. It is difficult for us all that's the reason why he asked me to reach out to you to see if you could help out with Antwone and Tyree. I, I, know you don't have any children of your own. We just need someone we can trust. Someone already established. With your business and all we can't seem to find anyone else, reliable."

Silence.

I wipe my eyes and take everything Fever has said in.

"I, I, don't know what to say. Fever, I don't know if I would be the best candidate for this. I haven't even babysat a child before, let alone be a care provider for two. I'm flattered that you guys thought of me, but I, I, won't be able to do it. My business is strenuous enough. I'm sorry."

"No, don't be. I understand," Fever says, but deep down she doesn't. "Sorry to have woken you up. You have a blessed day."

"You too."

I can't go back to sleep. I look over at the clock and it is 6:20 a.m.—one day before Christmas. For some reason, I start thinking about how my Christmases used to be when I was a little girl. How Poppa and Ma'am would wake me up just to see me rip open the gift-wrapping and tear open the plastic cases to my Barbie dolls.

Then I think about that snake Verdi-Dee and Nana ruining my holiday. I frown. Then the frown dissipates as I think about Antwone and Tyree, the two little boys who just recently lost their mother. I must be the evilest person in the world.

I mope around the house. I cook a small breakfast. I call Dr. Fulmore to schedule my two-month appointment for Wednesday. I check my appointment book to see when my next visit to Dr. Cristal is. It's today. I smile because I'll have her to talk to. Well, I'll talk and she'll listen. I can't seem to get Antwone and Tyree, the little dark-skinned and light-skinned faces out of my head. Why?

By the middle of January of '09, I become a Good Samaritan. My plate is overflowing. My life has changed from single and free to care provider. What have I done? I am not a mother. I have no clue as to what being a mother means. But for right now I am considered a single-aunty to two little boys I haven't the foggiest idea how to care for. Me, a mother, I still beg to differ. I end up resigning from my position at Red Alert because there is no way I can handle a job, business, and two little boys. I'll be crazy before I reach my mid-forties.

Things are going rather well with having Antwone and Tyree as guests in my home. They are different from most children their age. Antwone's not loud or rowdy. He's polite as ever. He's tidy for a little boy. He likes to read books, lots of books, and watch cartoons. He cleans up after himself. Shoot, he's cleaner than me at times. He's actually a breath of fresh air. Tyree's more outgoing. He likes to mingle and get to know people. He craves attention. Or maybe he's just genuinely friendly. We recently celebrated Tyree's ninth birthday with cupcakes and ice cream. I smile because I feel I made the right choice even though it changes my life around. I mean, dating I haven't been doing much of that, lately. Jordan moved on with Dolce. Brick and I are over. No one from my past has ventured into my life so dating is extinct for the moment. And I'm okay with it. I nod my head.

I take the boys shopping at Old Navy for some up-to-date clothes. And at Foot Locker to get them two pairs of sneakers and some Timberland boots. I stop by a friend of mine's barbershop, "Diamond Cuts," for them to get fresh haircuts. And on our way back from New York we stop at Fuddruckers on Rt. 4 to get a bite to eat.

I enrolled them both into PS No. 117; I was lucky enough to know the superintendent so he did me a favor. Both are doing excellent—Antwone, in the second grade, Tyree, in the fourth grade.

But by the end of January Antwone starts complaining that his eye is bothering him.

"Single-aunty, my eye hurts." Antwone says, as he rubs it vigorously.

I stop washing dishes and kneel down and open his red eye wide and blow in it to make it water. Then I say, "Does that feel better? It is probably a piece of lint." He nods his head.

Later in the week I receive a call at Anonymous from the Child Study Team at PS No. 117 stating that they need to have a meeting with me about Antwone. I meet with them the next day. The Child Study Team sits on the second floor of the school waiting for my arrival. As I enter the room three women and one man are engaged in conversation. They all hush once I arrive and sit down.

"Good morning, Ms. Love," the gray haired man says.

"Good morning."

I cross my legs and listen to what is being said.

"Well, Ms. Love, we asked that you come because we are very concerned about Antwone. Oh, he's a bright kid. But we noticed a bit of a change in him. He seems hyperactive and we think Ritalin might work for him."

My lips press together. *Stay calm, Avery, stay calm.*

I take a deep breath. "I'm sorry, Mister...did you say Ritalin?" I confirm.

"Yes. Antwone's attention span is rather weak. He can't seem to stabilize himself enough to stay focused."

"Really." I pause. "Well, I disagree with your theory." I stand and walk out of the room as my long skirt sways in the breeze that follows me, into my car, blast the radio and cuss those assholes out.

I call Dr. Cristal and explain my situation with Antwone. She advises me to look into St Matthew's Hospital and Mental Health Services on Market Street, downtown Paterson. Since I'm already on the phone with her I ask can we have our session over the phone. She advises me to call her back at my scheduled appointment time. We hang up.

I call St. Matthew's Hospital and Mental Health Services and make an appointment for tomorrow. I also contact the Social Security Administration to see if Antwone can be evaluated and approved for supplemental income just in case his pediatrician finds that he is in need of the Ritalin. I don't know if they will be able to help with the prescription coverage, but I feel it's worth a try.

A friend of mine refers me to a clinic, Paterson Community Well-

Being Center, on Clinton Street to see if one of the pediatricians could discuss the matter of Antwone possibly needing medication. I speak with a Dr. Boyd and he adamantly states that if the Child Study Team wants Antwone on Ritalin then they have to do a complete evaluation on him to justify him needing the medication. And that he wants it in writing. I go back that same day and tell one of the members of the Child Study Team what Dr. Boyd said. I must say, things got pretty nasty because I wasn't willing to just give in and say, "Here, use my nephew as a guinea pig." I wanted proof just as the pediatrician had. Prove to me that this child absolutely needs to be on the medication before I just take their word for it. Antwone seems like the average child. I mean, he horseplays a little, laughs, and jokes around with his brother. All of that seems normal to me for a child. I don't see much hyperactivity. I figure he is bored. Antwone is very intelligent.

***

I call Dr. Cristal at 5:30 for my scheduled session and I let my breasts fall. "I'm under a lot of stress, Dr. Cristal." I wait for her to respond.

"What seems to be the problem, Avery?"

"I'm not quite sure. I mean, I'm not a mommy. I don't have the foggiest idea of what I am doing. And now the school is talking about this child needing medication. It is too much with my business and all. Then, I have to find someone to care for them while I'm at work. I feel like I'm gonna pop any minute."

"Welcome to motherhood," Dr. Cristal says excitedly.

I pause. Then break out into laughter.

"I guess I do sound like a mother, huh?" I sit back in the executive chair in my living room and absorb Dr. Cristal's comment. I smile as I stare at Antwone taking a nap and Tyree watching a DVD of *Fat Albert,* laughing his heart out.

"Avery, listen, you will be fine. You're learning. Just ask God to guide you. Is there anything else you want to discuss?"

"Well." I stand and walk into the bathroom for a little privacy. I shut the door and take a sit on the vanity chair. "I just found out that my parents were never married. And to make matters worse I found out that I have a sister, and the only reason I found out about her was because she was killed in a car accident in North Carolina. And to top that off I found out that Ma'am was in the loony bin." I suck back in some air.

"O-kay. It sounds like you have a lot on your plate. I suggest you take all of that in and just let it be. There is nothing that can be done about the past. You can't change it. So why stress over it?"

"Yes, I know, but now I have Jewell's sons to tend to and I don't have a man in this house to teach them how to be men. What am I supposed to do? Find a Big Brother's group?"

"Avery, that's not a bad idea. Big Brothers is a wonderful program. You should look into it. I say, do it!"

I massage my bottom lip.

"Well, I really don't have anything else going on. I guess this will be a short session. I'll send the check in the mail."

"Okay, talk to you soon."

"Good-bye."

***

Antwone's eye is becoming a thorn in my side. *Why does he keep complaining?* Now, he has headaches and his tummy is bothering him. I throw both of my arms up. I feel frustration brewing inside of me. And I hear Avona's voice. *Calm down, Avery, calm down, this is not this child's fault. Don't you even think of taking your anger out on that child, you hear me! You don't want the Division of Youth and Family Services running up in here handcuffing you, do you?*

I take Antwone back to the doctor and unfortunately Dr. Boyd isn't there so we see another pediatrician. Antwone is checked out and given a prescription. Things seem to be getting pretty hectic with me trying to split myself in two. I have meals to cook, homework to help with, clothes to iron, laundry to do, and I really don't need anything else added to my to-do list. I am overwhelmed. The phone calls and letters from the school continue to come. I am considering their behavior as harassment. I know they don't want me to call my lawyer, Mr. Byren Clausen. I'll sue their asses in a heartbeat. It is beginning to be a bit much.

In the middle of the night I have a premonition and I awake with watery eyes. I don't know what is happening to me. It occurs three times in three consecutive days and I immediately get paranoid. *God, am I about to die?* I can't understand for the life of me what is wrong. By the third premonition I am startled out of my sleep.

I see myself in a funeral home with people that are familiar to me. But most are dead. There is a guest book on the right-side corner of the room. There is fog in the room, lots of it, so I can't see clearly. There is a small casket but I can't see who is in it.

That scares the shit out of me. I think my mind is playing tricks on me. In-between all of this, I still get more calls from the school this time stating that Antwone is sleeping in class and I'm the one keeping him up late. Absurd! It is simply untrue. I take Antwone back to Dr. Boyd, and again he isn't there so we see another pediatrician and another prescription is given for what might be a stomach virus.

The next day, Antwone still doesn't feel well so I change my schedule around, drop Tyree off to school, and keep Antwone home with me.

I scrub the oven cleaner out of the oven, scrub the top of the stove off, wipe down the kitchen sink counter, sweep the floor, and empty its debris in the garbage can, and by the time I turn the nozzle to the bathtub to fill the bucket with water, and drag the bucket into the kitchen to mop the floor, and pick all four chairs up and sit them on top of the table, mop the floor, and tip-toe out of the kitchen, and by the time I sit down and start to read an *O* magazine, something tells me to go and check in on Antwone in the bedroom.

I hear Antwone whimpering with his knees buried in the bed. His head is lent over in a pillow like he is in so much pain. He looks me dead in my face and says, "*Mommy*, I don't feel well." I pick him up dressed in his blue denim jeans and orange long sleeve Polo shirt and take him back to the clinic for the third time.

As we enter the clinic I greet the receptionist with a curly kit do and politely tell her that we need to see Dr. Boyd. I tell her that it is an emergency. She looks me in my face with her Big Bird eyes and says, "He looks fine to me." I want to snatch her up and knock every last freckle off her face and read her from top to bottom, but I don't. I look over at Antwone and keep it civil. We sit in the waiting area until his name is called. And as soon as we get into the room, my seven year-old sits on the examination table and within a second's time he lays back and falls asleep. I explain everything that has been going on to Dr. Boyd. He then takes a instrument hooked on the wall and uses it to examine Antwone's eyes. A couple of seconds later he picks up his wall-mounted phone and calls someone. I don't know what is going on at the time so I patiently wait for him to explain. Inside I feel nauseous. Antwone continues to sleep. When Dr. Boyd gets off the phone he looks at me strangely.

"Ms. Love, do you have a car?"

"Yes."

"I need you and your son to go straight to Hopkins Hospital."

I don't bother to correct him about Antwone not being my son.

"Okay."

A few seconds later I ask the question that anyone would ask.

"What's wrong with my son?"

The doctor looks at me with his spiked hair around his Caucasian ears, sharp-fanged teeth, and small bubbles of saliva in the corner of his mouth and explains to me that one of Antwone's eyes looks to be protruding outward. Concerned, I immediately take him to the emergency room because the doctor says that they are waiting for our arrival.

My drive to the hospital is like I am on pins and needles. I am shaking and cutting my eyes at Antwone and the road, the road and Antwone, until we arrive at the hospital. I have to remain calm because I don't know the severity of what is going on as of yet. And panicking will only frighten him. I am terrified. What parent wouldn't be? I don't understand what is happening. Everything is moving so fast. I am weighed down with internal emotion that I can't display on the outside. *Something's wrong with my baby*. Two weeks of thinking that he has this or that leads us rushing to the emergency room.

When we enter the hospital I speak with the pallid-faced triage nurse and she escorts us into the emergency room. My stomach has butterflies. Not even twenty minutes later we are escorted upstairs to a room assigned to Antwone. Minutes later a transporter comes and carefully steers him onto the elevator. My stomach is churning and I feel so sick. *What, what's wrong with him?* I have to lie to myself and say that everything is okay, but consciously I know that it isn't. The signs are obvious that it isn't. All I can do is pray and wait.

When we enter the hospital room, there is a Hispanic woman already occupying the bed by the door. Antwone's bed is near the window. He is given a gown and I help him get undressed. He lies in the bed and we just stare at each other. I connect eyes with the Hispanic woman, but we never say anything to each other. I just crack a smile, trying to convince myself that everything is fine—that my son is fine.

It is getting close to two-thirty and I have to leave to pick Tyree up from school. I explain to Antwone that I have to go and get his brother and that I will be right back. I promise that I will be back so that he knows I mean it. I turn to look at him before I walk out and I notice that the bed is swallowing up his frail body in his gown. His skin tone is flawless and dark, smile bright, and eyes wide. He looks due for another haircut. I smile and then walk out to rush to the school.

On my way to my car I am anxious. I need to know what is wrong, but I also need to be cautious when I drive to pick Tyree up from school. I keep trying to figure out what the problem can be, knowing full well that that is impossible. When I arrive at the school I have a few minutes to get myself together. Five minutes later the bell rings and out come all the children. I open the driver's seat door and stand waiting to see Tyree's face. Then I walk across the street to greet him. Tyree looks in the backseat and asks, "Where's my brother?"

I ignore him trying to think of a way to break the news. Then as we get into the car and buckle up he asks again, "Where's my brother?" I palm the steering wheel, take a deep breath and look over at him.

"Your little brother is in the hospital. I don't know exactly what's wrong with him, um, but I did tell, actually I promised him that I would be back after I picked you up."

We drive home and as soon as I get in the house I have a message on my answering machine.

"Ms. Love, I'm a surgeon at Hopkins Hospital. I need you to return to the hospital and to bring immediate family."

Immediate family! Immediate family!

I panic and grab Tyree's hand and we dash down the stairs to the parking lot as I tumble over my feet. I fumble with the keys to unlock the car door; we enter the car and I fumble to put the key into the ignition. Tyree buckles up. I take a deep breath and drive off like a bat out of hell. Tears scroll down my face. My hands shake like I had too much caffeine as I drive up Main Street. I can only think the worse. I pray and think the worse. I park the car and Tyree hops out and we quickly run across the street into the hospital and I push the elevator button. The elevator opens and we get on. It stops on the sixth floor and as the door opens for us to exit my feet will not move. *Move feet, move!* The closer we get to the room, the more I feel sick. The more I feel sick, the more I want to run and hide, but I can't because I need to be with my baby. I need to know the cause of his illness. I need to comfort him no matter what the outcome.

I suck my gut in as we get closer to the room and sitting in a hard plastic gray chair is this Caucasian man in green scrubs. Antwone is lying in bed and they are having small talk. We immediately enter.

"Hi, Ant!" Tyree says excitedly, with eyes as big as headlights.

I question what is going on. But the man says, "Please, give me a minute." I grow impatient. But Antwone appears to be calm. I can't wait so I interrupt, again. And again the man says, "Please, please, be patient?" I nod in acknowledgement as my legs feel like they are about to give way. My eyes cut over to the Hispanic woman and she puts her head down. She looks to the side, almost like she is avoiding me. *Something's wrong. She knows more than I do.* I can tell by the fact that she can't look me in the eye as she had done prior. *What is it?*

Minutes later, the Caucasian man addresses me as he stands and smiles at Antwone. We proceed to walk out of the room, while Tyree and Antwone bond. I follow him out to the hallway. His blue eyes are assertively piercing mine through his glasses. He isn't smiling or smirking. He wears a tight face and that scares the hell out of me. He removes some paperwork from under his armpit and places it smack dab in front of my face.

"Ms. Love, you need to sign these papers."

"What for?! What's wrong?" I ask as my forehead crumples.

"We don't have much time."

"Time... for what? What do you mean?" My eyes tear.

"While you were gone we took your son down to have a CAT scan and we found a tumor on his brain. I have scheduled his surgery for tomorrow morning around 7:00 a.m."

I sigh. My heart beats erratically. *Tumor.* I can't function. It brings back memories of Poppa. Oh, God! Oh, God! And then I pause for a brief moment and ask the question that is tapping my brain. "Will he be okay?! What...what... are his chances with the surgery?! Brain tumor!" My hands massage my forehead.

The surgeon sighs. "I can't say. It's about...*fifty-fifty* chance." His eyes pierce mine. "Just pray."

My eyes widen and then shut tight. I start to hyperventilate in segments to myself, not trying to make a scene of any sort. The doctor escorts me to the nurse's station and staff that have been obviously waiting for my arrival surround me. They are waiting for some kind of reaction, faint, cry, or scream at the top of my lungs. I want to so badly, but I don't. I pull out my cell phone and speed dial Sisal's home. I relay the message to Sisal and I can hear Jo-Ruthie in the background crying hysterically.

"What's wrong with my grandson?!" she screams.

I don't know how she knows I am on the other end of the phone. Sisal didn't say anything about me being on the phone, but she knew. Tears flow slowly down my weary face. Everyone around me has close eyes on me. I tell Sisal that he should come up because the surgery is scheduled for tomorrow and nothing is guaranteed. He says, "Okay, sugar. We will jump on the road tonight."

We hang up.

I look through my contacts on my cell phone and I dial Xavier's number. Three rings and he picks up.

"Hello."

"Hello, Xavier, I didn't know who else to call."

"Avery...Avery, are you okay?"

"Um, no, um. Would you be able to come to Hopkins Hospital?"

"Are you ill?"

"No." I clear my throat. "Um, my son, I mean, nephew is ill. I just needed a friend, you know what I mean?"

"Yes...yes, I do. I'll be there."

"I'm on the sixth floor under Antwone Robinson. Room 619. Thanks, Xavier."

Tyree and Antwone grow curious about my whereabouts. I return to the room. A part of me wants to go down to the chapel to pour my soul out to God. Asking Him why this is happening to Antwone, but I don't. I always believed that God is everywhere you are, so therefore, I can sob uncontrollably in my car, if need be. The severity of the surgery, I share with no one. The chances of Antwone survival repeat in my head. Over and over I hear the surgeon's voice. Each time I look at Antwone, over and over I keep hearing *fifty-fifty*. My eyes blur as I try to keep a warm, pleasantness to my face, which is the hardest thing for me to do.

Finally, Xavier arrives. He sits down in his camel-colored Brooks Brothers trousers, cashmere fudge-colored French Connection sweater with suede chocolate-brown Steve Madden boots.

"Hello," he says to the boys.

They both say hello.

I am so relieved that I have a least one person I can count on. Antwone is full of smiles. At his worst he still continues to show all of his brightness and things are pretty bleak. I am almost positive he knows what lies ahead come tomorrow because the surgeon explained everything to him. His mind is sharp-witted for a seven year-old. He understands just like us grown folks.

I glance over to Xavier and there is this strange glare in his eyes. A look I've seen only one time before. I remember the distant look in his eyes when he talked about his sister, his friend, and his aunt. How it drove him to start his non-profit organization, Red Alert. He comes to and catches me staring at him. I lower my head, giving him a moment of privacy.

My eyes are red with exhaustion. It's getting late and I know I have to prepare for the next day. Xavier stays for an hour and we talk a little. We mingle with the boys and have moments to ourselves. It's near 9:00 so I let Antwone know that we have to be going so that I can get Tyree ready for school tomorrow. He sulks and pokes out his bottom lip.

Tyree walks over to him, "Ant, you gonna be fine. Don't be scared. Here." He pulls off his shirt. "Remember when momma used to give us something of hers when she would have to go to work and we didn't want her to leave us."

Antwone nods his head.

"Well, take my shirt and sleep with it, okay."

"Yessss." A rather weak smile appears but then his pearly whites beam.

We give our hugs and kisses and say our goodnights.

I glance over to the Hispanic woman and she connects eyes with me. I'm more than positive that she knows what is going on. I feel empathy from her eyes.

"Antwone, I'll be here bright and early. I promise." I nod my head.

"Okkkkayy," he dryly eases out with a sulky look on his face.

We leave out of the room and head towards the elevator. I pause at the elevator so full of grief.

"Xavier thanks again for coming. I really appreciate it."

"Avery, say no more." His manly hands caress my shoulder.

I feel helpless trying to pull myself in two. But I have no choice because no one else is here. I guess this is motherhood. I am restless. I try to ease my mind by listening to some gospel music. Ma'am used to do that when she was stressing over something or another. Poppa used to pace back and forth and Ma'am would say, "Poppa sits down before you wear the floor out." I smile. But my smile turns upside down as I lay Tyree to bed and listen to him say his prayers.

"Dear Lord,

I know I haven't prayed in a day or two or maybe three, but I need a favor. Lord, momma died, and my single-aunty, Avery, took my lil' brother and me into her home. It's a nice home. Well, my brother is sick. Very sick. I don't know the name of his sickness. Well, I don't want my brother to leave me, Lord. I don't have too many more people left. I don't ever see my dad and truthfully it's probably for the best. Please, Lord, don't take my brother from me. He's all I got. Amen."

I wipe the tears with the back of my hand. I know how Tyree feels all too well. I'm lonely, have been for quite some time. Even with people in my view, in my space, in my life. Oh, his words pierce my heart as I walk into my bedroom and cry into my pillow sham. I keep seeing Antwone's face wondering if he is okay alone in the hospital. A part of me wants to call him, and then go up there, but I don't. I get my clothes out, take a shower, and try to relax, but it is so hard. I reach into my purse, pull out my checkbook to check the date and circle February 2, 2009—the day that I found out that my nephew has a brain tumor. I cry, stop, cry, and stop until I finally fall asleep.

14

February 3rd...

I awake a nervous wreck. This is going to be a day of the unknown and it frightens me so. I get Tyree up to get ready for school. The surgery is scheduled for 7:00 or 7:30 a.m., and I don't want to be late. I want to greet *my* baby, to see his chocolate face, and bright smile. I take Tyree with me so that he can see that Antwone is okay before I take him to school. I remain calm when we arrive at the hospital. Antwone seems pleasant as always. I give him a hug and kiss and so does Tyree. Soon the transporter comes to take him down for surgery. I feel my knees buckle, a lump in my throat, eyes twitch, but I manage to crack a smile when Antwone looks over at me.

When we land on the floor, the elevator door opens; I can feel the soreness in my throat inflaming. I pant and slowly step off the elevator as if I have just learned how to walk. The transporter takes Antwone into the operating room. Tyree and I sit in the waiting area up until it is time for him to get to school. We leave. There are these fine hairs that stand on my arms and I gently brush them down. I drive him to school. I shiver because it is chilly and I try to occupy my mind with other thoughts, but I can't. Tyree sits quietly.

I drop him off and head back to the hospital. A few minutes later I receive a call from Sisal saying that they just arrived in Paterson. I give them directions to the hospital and wait for them to arrive.

Unexpectedly, Sisal and Jo-Ruthie bring a tag-a-long, Sin Grayson. My eyes do not deceive me. *Oh, my goodness, I can't believe this shit!* My old flame. The man *I* lost my virginity to. The man I loved with mind, body, and soul had dated and conceived children by my baby sister, Jewell. Antwone and Tyree's long lost daddy. I can't believe it!

This ink-black skin-toned, six-feet, bow-legged, scruffy-looking man with dark eyes, and big, thick lips extends out his hand for me to shake it. I scrunch my nose up at him because he reeks of something awful. I cut my eyes at Sisal and pace the floor. I talk in my head. *Why would he bring this...this man here? After all these years, his black ass wasn't even at the wake or funeral. I don't care if he is their daddy; he has no say in nothing. No say. I'm their guardian. They asked me to be his single-aunty. Negro, take your ass back where the hell you came from. The fuckin' sewer.*

I pace and finally stop. I sit to myself waiting for the surgeon to come out and tell me that *my baby* is doing well. My baby!

My blood is boiling because Sisal never forewarned me about this man—Sin. He didn't say a word. He is just springing this on me now like I'm supposed to be okay with it. Well, I'm not! How am I supposed to explain him to Tyree and Antwone? What am I supposed to say, "Oh, all these years your daddy was lost in the forest somewhere." Bull. It's a bunch of bull-crap!

I sit down and tap my feet against the granite floor. I fold my arms across my chest. And I just stare blankly into space. Finally I ask Sisal if I can have a moment of his time.

"Sho'." He stands and follows me near the elevator.

I cut to the chase, "Why is he here?"

Sisal heaves heavily and his eyes pierce mine, "Avery, he's dey father."

I become defiant, "Where the hell was he when Jewell died?" I get right in Sisal's face damn near spitting in it. "He didn't even have the courtesy or dignity to show up at *her* wake or funeral. What kinda father or daddy is he? Obviously, Jewell knew how to pick 'em."

"You have no right to judge him!" Sisal's eyes enlarge and then squint.

"Excuse you!" My forefinger sways from side to side. "I have every right to judge him! All of a sudden he wants to play 'Daddy Dearest.' Coming in here smelling like a brewery or something! You must be kidding me!" I roll my eyes.

Sisal walks away from me huffing and puffing. I walk away in the opposite direction, full of disgust.

I am pleading within that when the surgeon comes out of the operating room that he will say that everything went well. That Antwone survived. I ball my fist and raise it up to my mouth, patting my lips. I return back to my sit and patiently wait. It is possibly a half hour later and the surgeon comes out with his green scrub cap dangling from around his neck.

"Hello everyone, everything looks to be a success."

I hear Sin gasp for air. Then he starts coughing and rattling some phlegm sound in his throat. I turn around and give him a dirty look. *Shut the hell up!*

The surgeon continues, "We still have to keep an open-mind that any problems can arise. I am hopeful that all will be well. Your little boy is strong."

Sin cuts his eyes at me as if to say he is not your son, he's mine. I ignore his little rendition of "Daddy Dearest."

"Can we see him?" I ask.

"Sure. Just two at a time, okay. You all can follow me."

I go first and Sin invites himself into the intensive care unit. Sisal and Jo-Ruthie wait in the waiting area for us to come out. I plead with God to help me get through this trying time.

Sin and I walk into Antwone's room and there is a chill that runs down my spine and sweeps across my body. There are so many wires and machines all intertwining. There is a balloon attached to his head and fluid is draining from his brain into the balloon. All I see is the color red. *Oh, my God.* His eyes are moving underneath their eyelids. His body is stiff. A long tube is in his mouth as he breathes in and out with the help of a machine. Tears saturate my face, shirt, onto the floor. I am petrified after witnessing Antwone's state. I put my head down and run my fingers across my scalp as my eyes weep with heartache. I don't know the reaction of Sin. As a single-aunty it is about my son and me. At this moment, I am being selfish because I took him into my life. Even though Jewell carried him in her womb I feel a strong motherly hold. I have a connection that no long lost father/daddy can ever conceive of having. It is personal. This is just the beginning because we have to wait two weeks for a biopsy to be done to alert us if his tumor is benign or malignant.

Two weeks of numbness, teeth chattering and loss of weight for me.

15

On one of my visits to the hospital I stop in the chapel to have a talk with God. Immediately, my chin starts to vibrate. Tears stream down my wary face. I practically beg for forgiveness because I personally take Antwone's circumstance as my cause. Possibly I didn't do something right in my life. I made mistakes. He knew that. I committed sins. He knew that. I suffered as a young adult. He knew that. I lower my head, feeling so low and lonely.

I say a little prayer and then I head toward the elevator to go back upstairs to Antwone. My mind was flustered and I happen to get off the elevator on the wrong floor. I roam the halls. On both sides of the floor I see rolling carts with cartons of masks, latex gloves, and disposable gowns. As I slow pace the floor my eyes cut from room to room seeing bold green signs that read "Acquired Immunodeficiency Syndrome" plastered on some of the closed doors. The doors that are open are people in their mid-twenties, early thirties, latter forties and fifties, if not older than that.

My body is shaky; eyes are sharp along with my mind. I am very observant of my surroundings. I take deep breaths 'cause deep down I am afraid. I am afraid of the reality of what runs through my veins. AIDS is my biggest fear.

As I continue to walk the corridor I see a man lying in bed nearest the window. The room is desolate, but an aura sweeps across me as I stand in place in front of Room 566 and stare at him.

Since I don't know the man's name I name him Epidemic. I stand close to the doorway of his room and a shiver crawls up my spine. The sun is beaming through the window ever so bright. There is no one in the room with him. I can hear Epidemic breathing. He is not breathing smoothly. I can hear it keenly. I can hear him as if he is standing right behind me. I stand quiet not to disturb his peace. His breathing is loud in my ears, nerve-wracking to my solitude. I see his dark skin that brings out the white sheet that covers him up to his neck. He face looks small and thin along with his body, but yet his eyes bulge so big like their stretching his skin to be seen. I see them plain as day. I hear him so loudly.

This white nurse with pale skin, crimson cheeks, and curvaceous bottom comes waltzing in while I am standing in the doorway. She says hello and walks into the room assuming that I am a visitor of

Epidemic's. Epidemic's breathing is erratic, short-winded, and alarming to my ears. I see him lying there as if he is lying in a casket, stretched still like a cadaver. I turn to look the other way. The nurse says, "Hello, Ely," while she observes him. I don't say anything. I just stare. I hear that scratchy, scatting sound so loudly. Epidemic is barely able to catch his breath. I hear him fighting for air. He tries to prolong each breath. He tries to savor his inhales and exhales. He tries with all of his might. I hear the fight in him. Suddenly, I feel weak. Helpless. Afraid. Alone. Emotional. But I don't shed a tear, even though my eyes are watery. No tears break free. Shortly after, I hear a long gasp and then the sun tucks and dims the room. I bow my head as I listen to Epidemic take his last breath. This kind of death is new to me. I have never experienced it before. Not even with Johnnie because I missed the opportunity as he leaned toward Javis Cline to watch him take his last breath. This is the first I've come so close to it. Never have I gazed at it in its realest form. And it is real. It is evident. I hear no more erratic breathing. I hear nothing. Epidemic lies stiff as a rock. His eyes wide open. Death changed his look. He looks like an old black man. It is evident. AIDS does kill the young, old, and adolescent. I listened to death squeeze Epidemic dry. I listen to the sound of silence as he lay in his bed. The nurse covers his face with the white sheet and stares for a brief moment as I glance at a man hidden underneath the white sheet. I sigh and walk the halls.

Epidemic didn't die alone in that room. I was there, as well as the nurse. At that moment I felt like I had given or done something good for a woman who was years oblivious to this deadly disease. Epidemic touched a part of me and I will keep his memory as my message to what could be so easily me. Just as I keep Storyteller with me. Epidemic is another statistic, another number to add to the list of lists. I hate to put it this way, but I am no different and if I become full-blown, I will become another number added, as well. I am learning whether this disease is self-inflicted or not it is most devastating. I am learning to acknowledge it instead of deny of its existence, even though it runs through my veins. I am a young black woman. This disease does not discriminate. This is a known fact to me.

16

I sit in Antwone's room watching him color in his Spiderman coloring book. Dr. Boyd stops at Hopkins Hospital to talk to me. We walk into a little room on the floor. He doesn't beat around the bush. That's what I like about him. The word "malignant" slips through his lips and into my ears. It is my worst nightmare ever. It is a very moving conversation for him and me. He literally takes Antwone's illness to heart. Like, guilt is compressing him because it wasn't caught in time. But no one knew. The Caucasian doctor tells of a story of his internship and how it felt to him when one of his patients died. How it influenced him into thinking that he should possibly reconsider becoming a doctor. God doesn't make mistakes. He was meant to be as such for the simple fact he showed enormous compassion. His story is a reference for me to prepare for the best/worst road ahead. The word "glioblastoma" is a scary son-of-a-bitch because Antwone is diagnosed with it. Tears burst from my eyes. I don't want to believe it. No, no, no! Please let this be a mistake. But Dr. Boyd's face confirms that it is not. We have a fight on our hands.

"Ms. Love, glioblastoma is a monster. It is a very, extremely aggressive beast. So, yes, you have a fight on your hands."

His words eat me up. I sit pondering how all of this is going to change this seven year-old little boy.

"There are things to consider: abnormal pulse and breathing rates, deep, dull headaches that recur often and persist without relief for long, periods of time, difficulty walking or speaking, dizziness, eyesight problems, including double vision, seizures, and vomit." Dr. Boyd pulls out a handkerchief and wipes his forehead and around the back of his ears.

I recall Antwone's symptoms were headaches, constantly feeling as though a piece of lint or eyelash were in his eye, vomiting, appetite decreased, loss of weight, and the constant sleepiness. It never affected him mentally as far as his intellect. There were two other things that come to mind that he did which were pretty peculiar.

First, he came upstairs one day and turned the stove on, lit a piece of paper, and threw the burning paper into the garbage, and then had gone back outside to play basketball in the playground. Secondly, one morning before getting ready for school my boys were looking out of the back window as they saw Mr. Reynolds my next-door neighbor getting ready to leave for work. Apparently Tyree yelled out the window to Mr. Reynolds that Antwone had told him to tell him "to kiss his ass." Wow! I didn't believe it either, but it surely was true. Antwone said, "Tell that man I said to kiss my ass."

Mr. Reynolds had gone to work, but as soon as he got off work and had gotten home, he parked his truck in the parking lot, had come ringing my door looking for Antwone and asked that he speak with him. He asked him if he had indeed said it, and my youngest nephew never backed down to deny it. He took his punishment like a man. No video games, TV, park for two weeks. Those last two things were like "red flags" because it was truly out of his character.

Dr. Boyd mentions another hospital that specializes in children with cancer, Jaysen University and Medical Center-Children of Tomorrow Institute in Hackensack, New Jersey. Sin and I are both told in the most sympathetic way that *our* child had a malignant brain tumor. It is a hell of a blow for me to take. In that instance, my life changed. Our lives changed.

Sin and I are scheduled to meet with a team of specialist to discuss Antwone's treatment. We meet with a female doctor, Beatrice L. Rice Pediatric Hematology/Oncology/CTI, two social workers and a psychologist. We are informed that Antwone will have eight specialists on-call. *This is surreal,* I think.

It is very difficult to hear all that they want to treat Antwone with: radiation, chemo, and harvesting of the bone marrow. All I can think is, *Wow! How is he going to withstand all of that?* It seems the expression on my face gives me away and one of the specialists in an assertive, manly tone expresses the fact that Antwone has to undergo so much is non-negotiable. The reality is that whatever will keep him alive, will be performed. I have to take myself out of the equation because it isn't my body—my life. It's Antwone's. But as a single-aunty I don't want him to hurt, feel pain of any sort. I am just being who I've become within the last month or so of Antwone's life—his protector.

When I have to explain what is going on to Tyree it is so hard. At the age of nine he really can't fully understand the magnitude of the situation. His brother isn't going to be able to do as he'd done before. He has to be cautious. His doctor informed Antwone of his condition and I can't recall if he ever cried. It was like "Okay. You told me, so what's next?" That's the only way I can explain it because his mindset of life is so profound. Seven years old and articulating like an adult, truly amazes me. He makes his stay in Hopkins Hospital a pleasant one.

Antwone gets his strength up, and he is up and about. Keeping busy in the little group sessions of coloring, crafts, and reading. He helps out the volunteers in the hospital pass out goodies to the other patients on the floor. Majority of the time when I go to visit, he is never in his room. Either he is at the nurse's station with his Batman slippers on, green sweatpants with white T-shirt, and royal blue bathrobe with red trim around the collar, engaging in conversation or somewhere on the floor helping someone with something. Yes. It is in his spirit to be generous with his time. It doesn't cost him anything. His stay in the hospital is lengthy but when he is released he is the happiest kid in the world. Him and his brother bond even more, but it isn't the same because he knows that he can't roughhouse, jump off the monkey bars, standup on the swings at the park, and most of the time he has to be supervised by me. If you look at him it isn't evident that something is different. He is always friendly, but his heart has grown bigger for people.

Our playtime consists of Antwone and Tyree watching *Batman,* which is both their favorite movie. They watch this movie so much that they know the lines verbatim. They watch cartoons when Tyree gets home from the after-school program at the YMCA. I enrolled him about a month ago so that he could have some free time away from home. It is a lot to take in and the time away would do him some good. Antwone has to stay home with me and the bond between us has grown even stronger. It is a tiresome task of raising two boys and one having cancer grows even more straining, but I keep my ground and do what I have to do. I have no choice; no one else is going to join in.

With Sisal and Jo-Ruthie and Sin I feel like I am in a battlefield alone. I mean they come over to show their faces, have tea, and stroke Antwone's hand but when it comes down to giving him a bath, making meals, reading to him, or just having general conversations, they are off doing other things. I don't say a word to them about not lending a helping hand. I just note it in my memory bank. *You guys asked me to help the very least you could do is do the same.* Nope. I don't say a word.

After a few weeks of Antwone being home he is bored out of his mind.

"Single-aunty, why can't I be with other kids? I want to go back to school and go to the after-school program like Tyree, to the park, and run around like the other kids."

"I know, I know, you must be patient."

"Ah man, I hate being patient." He balls a fist and leans his face on his knuckles. "Why did I have to get sick? Why me?" he walks into the living room and sits down on the loveseat staring into space.

It breaks my heart seeing him so blue. I know Antwone feels smothered, like a ball and chain is at his ankles. The doctors keep reinforcing in me to be "cautious and careful," which I am, but I fully understand how he feels. He isn't living life. Life is drifting as the days, weeks, and months pass. Antwone is in the process of receiving his radiation treatment, which is to last for six weeks. And the talk of chemo will follow. I have to take a step back and reflect on the life Antwone had prior. His argument of wanting to be a "normal" kid makes sense to me. He is looking at his life from a different perspective. He doesn't feel like he is living because everywhere he turns the word "cautious" stares him in the face. And it doesn't help with me constantly breathing down his neck, either. "Baby, watch it," "No, no, baby, you can't do that," "Baby, the doctors said," that seems annoying. Don't get me wrong it was important that I stand with a stern voice of reason for his actions because one fall can possibly be fatal. But I have to trade places for a brief second. Logically, I can't fully understand what it feels like inside his body—his brain. But I know what he was like *before* the surgery, a vibrant little boy.

17

I can only imagine Antwone feeling like he is walking on shattered glass hoping that he doesn't fall and get cut and bleed. Then everyone will be looking at me saying, "Why did you let him…." And I will simply reply, "Because he asked me to let him live with normalcy." I must say, he won his argument with me and I allow him to be a kid—that is who he is. He spirits rise to higher grounds, smile expands, and his strength increases, and life blooms. Antwone is his best counselor because he knew what it would take to keep him going, not the doctors, not me—him.

It is a demanding time keeping up with his meds, making sure I give him the right amount, at the right time. Keeping up with Tyree as far as school and homework is a task. It is pressure. Sin isn't around much. He comes around when he wants to. Around the weekend is when the boys see their father and most of the time he is not in his right mind. At times I have to find him to drop them off for an hour or two since he is now living in Paterson with some relatives. Sin asks me to drop them off by his girl's house. And I notice his ass is high and I kindly keep driving.

"Single-aunty, where you going?" the boys ask in unison.

"We're going to the movies!"

"Yehhhhhh!" They hoot and howl so full of excitement that they forget all about their daddy. Even though, they've seen him struggling down four steps. I had to think on my feet because they might have asked me to take them back to their father.

I cut my eyes through the rearview mirror seeing Sin walking down four steps that seems like eternity to come down. His eyes are droopy, movement is of a snail, and mobility is like the Matrix. His bottom lip droops. Brotha' is stone to the bone. Sweat is drenched on his face and his shirt indicates that he is sweating profusely. He looks like he stinks. His hands are scratching all over his body. My body shivers by the look of him. Days later I hear that Sin is indulging in some heavy stuff that could knock him on his ass. I needed confirmation so I called Sisal. Sisal denied ever knowing anything about Sin's habitual cravings. But the scene is clear as I receive confirmation through the eyes of the addict.

After some weeks of Sin not visiting his sons it is brought to my attention that Sin has upgraded from crack to heroin.

I ride through the block of Governor Street and I see Sin barely able to stand, holding the porch banister for dear life. Brotha' is strung.

Several weeks later, Sin comes to visit the boys, saying that he wants to take them out for a bite to eat, dressed in a fleece sweat suit with sweat glossing his face.

"Sorry, they ate already." I say right in front of the boys.

"Well, let me take them to get some ice cream. Let me take my boys! Dey my sons, not yours! Let me take my boys out! Why do I need your approval anyhow? You not dey momma. Dey momma *dead*!"

Antwone and Tyree burst into tears and run into the bedroom and slam the door. My eyes spread wide full of burnt orange flames.

I take two steps forward and pierce Sin's face. "You listen reallll good, Mr. Grayson! Don't you bring your smelly ass around here anymore you got that! That's it! I didn't take to you when I first laid eyes on you. I don't know what Jewell saw in you. But she must've had her reasons for dealing with a low-life like you." I walk closer our lips almost touching as my breath greets his smelly ass, "You disgust me! Now get the fuck out of my house before I personally escort you out through the window! Take your pick!" I don't budge.

Sin turns around and leaves without a word being said. Tears engulf my eyes as I walk into the bathroom to regain myself. I stare in the mirror and speak aloud, "He hurt my boys. My boys." My head falls, as my heart is full of gloom.

***

I take Antwone and Tyree with me to my doctor's appointment. As we walk into the office I greet Violet.

"Why are we here? I have to see another doctor?" Antwone asks.

"No, I am here to see the doctor," I say.

"You sick single-aunty? What's wrong? You have a cold?" Tyree asks.

I smile. "No, I just have to see the doctor, nothing serious." I pat him on his head.

Violet slides the glass partition aside and says, "Hello. Who are the cutie pies with you?"

The boys giggle.

"This is Antwone and Tyree."

"Nice to meet you guys."

"You too," Tyree says with his finger in his mouth.

I have never seen him act bashful until he laid eyes on Violet. Violet has a slender frame, long, curly, red hair, sea-blue eyes, and a pointy, freckled nose. Tyree seems attracted to her. I smile because it is his first crush. And I get to witness it.

Violet kindly oversees the boys while I go in for my fifteen-minute visit with Dr. Fulmore. I sit on the examination table patiently waiting for him to come bursting in full of smiles.

"Hello Avery, it is always good to see you."

I smile.

"You're actually glowing Avery. What's new in your life these days?"

"Oh, I'ma single-aunty." I chuckle.

Dr. Fulmore looks at me in awe.

"Allow me to briefly explain." I make a long story short and he takes everything I said in.

"Well, I must say it is doing wonders for you. You look great! Now, let me check to make sure you feel the same."

"Okay."

***

April is the month of great concern. It is the month of spring, but springing back into normalcy is questionable. I have to rush Antwone back to Hopkins Hospital because he isn't feeling well. "It can't be," whispers under my breath. Two months have past since his diagnosis in February. Radiation treatment is complete as of six weeks and the tumor resurfacing is a total nightmare. Unfortunately, glioblastoma is definitely back. The bastard is winning and I am furious.

Antwone's health is depleting and my confidence is lessening. I am in a state of defeat. The probability of his tumor growing back so soon was not known. I am in awe and a part of me wants to throw my hands up and cuss God out. It is the absolute truth. I am angry and vindictive, struggling to understand why He is allowing Antwone to suffer. What is He trying to prove to me? Why can't He realize that I have had enough suffering for one woman? I am not trying to compromise anymore. I am not trying to reason with Him anymore, basically kissing His butt. No! I am trying desperately to move on and get my life in order, cleaning out my damn closet to start anew. What more can I do? I have admitted my faults. But He isn't making things easier for any of us by having me have to deal with the agony that I am enduring. That we are enduring. I say this with all honesty. If I have a way of reaching heaven I would punch His walls, knock down His gate, and boldly address Him by asking one simple question, "Why?" and then repeat myself, "Why?"

I know I have no choice but to keep doing what I am doing no matter how tired, frustrated, or aggravated I get because my boys will be damned if I have to rely on Sin, Sisal, or Jo-Ruthie. Instead of Sin trying to work with me—he is making it more difficult for me. Brotha' is hooked on drugs. And I feel bad for the boys because he is wasting his life on drugs that can undoubtedly kill him while his son is taking drugs to help him stay alive. Ain't that a blip?

Jo-Ruthie will be the first to retort, "That chile is going to hell speaking to the Lord in that tone." And I would have to respond by saying, "I've already been to fiery hell with Satan's wife, Aunt Bitch." If God decides that He doesn't want me in heaven, what can I possibly do? Nothing! I don't feel that I should hold back my true feelings even towards Him. He made me this way to speak up and voice my opinion. And I am only doing what I know how to do and that's to be candid. Why should I be deceptive in having people think that I am embracing what is happening in my life. No, I am mad as hell. And He can kiss my ass! I feel that I should be able to express myself. He's the Higher Power—the Almighty. I can't conceive of His reasons for my family constantly going through turmoil. And in order for me to move forward I have to be honest within myself. If I feel angry, I express anger. If I am content, I express content, so forth and so on. Of course, I expect uninvited advice, which is for me to get into a church to find God. He is already by my side. It is just that my distress sometimes will overpower even Him.

I finally take a moment to skim through my pile of mail, mostly bills. But something catches my eyes. A letter addressed to me from Brick. My hands shake and I pull the sheets of paper out of the envelope. I squat on the living room floor and begin to read:

To Avery,

I am very sorry how I treat you, Avery. But I am not *pervect* (perfect) Avery. I have problem being nice at time, Avery so don't be mad at me, I *trys* (tries) to *till* (tell) you that, *wear* (where) I come from *thear* (there) *or* (are) not nice people *thear* (there) I been *lier* (liar) and *theve* (thief) for a long time, so this is new Grounds for me to learn about me about being real, my life was bad so I am trying to get on track, Avery. It is not easy to be nice to people, *becaus* (because) I am not use to that *cind* (kind) of life, I am trying to learn to be real, it is not easy, Avery, *none* (now) you *no* (know) a little more about me, but I can be *sweat* (sweet) at time, and *lovein* (lovin') but, I am sad a lot you don't *no* (know) that *wry* (why) I am *whiting* (writing) this letter so will *realy* (really) *no* (know) me, I was hurt *win* (when) I was a child so don't be mad me *none* (now) *becaus* (because) I don't *no* (know) at time *whin* (when) I am *beon* (being) mean, I don't *no* (know) sometime I *realy* (really) don't sometime. Avery, bear with me, please Avery, I am very sorry, Avery, how I treat you. God, please forgive me how I treat her and myself,

Love Brick

Tears drip upon the letter. I wipe them with the back of my hand and stare at each misspelled word. But what really makes me weep is the word "*sorry.*" No one who has really hurt me has ever let that word escape from his or her mouth. In this moment, I have the utmost respect for Brick. For taking the time to write this letter and for being brave enough to mail it out. I never knew how *illiterate* his lifestyle has made him. But now I know firsthand how influential and detrimental "street life" can be. Hustling is all Brick knows. It must be a struggle within himself, I think. How can it not be? Just having limitations is enough, but to go through life just getting by, just flipping the buck and using others to camouflage your shortcomings must be a hells of a ways to live or rather exist.

18

Many thoughts run through my head about different options for Antwone. Everything that comes to mind has a question mark after it. I can't function. My heart is heavy with emotion. My shoulders carry enormous weight that is weighing me down. I immediately stop torturing myself realizing it is not a question that I can answer in a split second. I am beating myself up trying to fix something that I can't fix. I go to the hospital to visit Antwone and the surgeon who performed the first surgery is standing in his room having a conversation with him. I can't tell if Antwone is coherent. I walk in and greet him, as he ponders in thought staring at Antwone. Antwone's eyes are shut and he looks asleep or in a state of relaxing. I can't tell. My eyes wander around the room. Then I ask the one question that I dread to ask.

"How long?"

The surgeon looks at me with his bluer than blue eyes.

"Don't give up. If I perform another surgery that would prolong his life—how long is unknown. Or you can decide not to do the surgery and the hospital staff will keep him comfortable. He will be sedated with morphine so that he won't feel any pain."

I sigh. Then I start biting my nails.

"What would you do if he was your son?" I ask.

He immediately answers.

"Your son is a fighter." He smiles. "I would continue to fight with him until he couldn't anymore."

Then he walks out of the room and leaves me with Antwone. I walk over to the left side of the bed and I ask if he is asleep. He opens his eyes.

"No."

I get to the point and explain his options as honestly as I can.

"Ant, the choice is yours. Only you know how much you can take. Only you can fight this fight."

He quickly answers as if he has been thinking about it for a while.

"I wanna go back to school."

I take that for what it is worth. I have one of the nurse's contact the surgeon and the second surgery is scheduled for the next day.

I stop at a local Dunkin Donuts and buy a glazed donut and a small French vanilla coffee—light and sweet. I arrive early at the hospital just pacing the floor trying to waste time. Finally, I walk into Antwone's room and greet him and the stout male social worker with a hello as they are already engaged in small talk. I sit down nibbling on my donut until the social worker looks at me and says, "That's not a healthy breakfast." I shrug my shoulders with a dumbfounded look upon my face. The social worker leaves the room and I quietly walk over to Antwone and kiss him on his forehead. I am so nervous.

A couple of minutes later the transporter comes to take Antwone down to the operating room. I shiver, but remain calm. The down button for staff-only is pushed for the elevator. We step on the elevator and I discreetly keep looking at Antwone with his marble looking eyes. I smirk. The elevator stops. My feet feel stiff and heavy like lead. I pause for a moment as the transporter carefully steers him off and into the operating room.

I don't want to leave him, I think. One surgeon must've read my eyes and he allows me to stay while they are preparing. My mouth is watery like I have to vomit. Antwone lays back and his big eyes wander, fascinated by all the equipment. It is chilly in here. A few minutes later a Caucasian male surgeon comes over to us and greets us with a smile. He has a friendly disposition as he plays with Antwone. Then he reaches over and pulls out a mask and asks Antwone to smell it. Antwone blurts out, "It smells like cherry!" We laugh. Water floods my eyes but a tear does not fall. I am trying with all of my might not to cry in front of him, but a mother's love is so strong.

The surgeon nods signaling for me that it is time for me to leave as they try their best to remove the tumor from Antwone's brain. I walk out of the operating room uncertain of what I am facing. It has already been an ordeal of emotions scattered, but I am hoping that the second go-around will be most promising. I wait in the waiting area with great patience. Not thinking of rushing them. Not thinking of panicking, but soon the anticipation gets the best of me and I end up leaving to get some fresh, cool air.

I drive to downtown Paterson, to the barbershop on West Broadway, Cut-it-Off that Poppa used to frequent just to be around familiar folks. My mind is flustered and it doesn't dawn on me that I have locked my keys in my car, until I am getting ready to walk out of the barbershop and I can't find them. I walk out of the barbershop and sure 'nough my keys are dangling from the ignition. I panic. Then I start asking folks if anyone can get my car door open to get my keys out. I have to get back to the hospital! I have to be there when my son's surgery is over! I have to get help! There is this gentleman, DC, who leases a clothing store called Slouch Wear on the block and I go to ask if he can help me. His light complexion, string-bean frame, tries with a wire hanger, but is unsuccessful. I didn't want to call the police because they will have me call AAA. I grow desperate.

There is another man, tall in height, medium build with a mustache and low cut walking up the street and he notices that I am distraught. It is so evident that he stops on his way to work to help me in getting my car door open. He is successful and I thank him for his help.

By the time I arrive back to the hospital and sit down in the waiting area, a few minutes later the surgeon who performed the first surgery comes out of the operating room. He pulls off his scrub cap and stands before me with his eyes glued to mine.

"I went too deep," the surgeon says.

I didn't know exactly what he is talking about. I mean, nothing is registering.

"He can't...." He lowers his head as if he is reprimanding himself for whatever reason. I look at him.

"What are you saying?" I ask.

"He can't move. He felt cutting. The anesthesia hadn't.... We didn't know he was still awake until.... He didn't feel much."

I stare at him for a brief moment. Then I take a deep, deep breath.

"He can't feel his legs," he says still with his head dangling downward.

"Can I see him?"

The surgeon escorts me into the recovery room.

The expression on Antwone's face is of utter fear when I first lay eyes on him. The balloon is attached to his head full of red liquid. There are so many wires and equipment. Antwone opens his eyes wide and says, "I can't move, Mommee." Tears release down my face to watch his chap lips shake, releasing that he can't move. His left side is paralyzed. It is not certain if his paralysis will be permanent or temporary. Time will only tell. Physical therapy will be needed to help him recover. I am hopeful that he will learn to walk again. My faith begins to peak like a flower in bloom because I have a child that is not afraid to fight, the most challenging fight. I believe in his capabilities. That he will conquer all that is placed in front of him. I believe that he is undoubtedly a blessing, a messenger—an angel sent from God.

19

Sin staggers his worthless ass in Hopkins Hospital to see Antwone and as soon as he sits down he nods out with his bottom lip hanging. Ooh! I am furious. I try to get the hospital to stop him from coming to visit but I can't since he's the biological father. So I sit sulking the whole time I am there. I stare at him as if he is translucent, wishing he were dead.

During another visit from Sin, Antwone is sedated with medication. I had just arrived as the social worker comes into the room and slips Antwone's wallet (his uncle Tyrell had given...him), which has five dollars in it, in the table drawer. At my departure I forgot to take the wallet home with me. By the next day, I get up early to get to the hospital and the first thing I do is check the drawer for the wallet. The wallet is there but the five dollars isn't. That bastard! Sin stole the money. I know it in my gut. When I did speak with Sin he gives me some lame excuse that he asked Antwone if he could borrow it. And Antwone supposedly said yes. Bullshit! Asshole!

Antwone's stay in the hospital is one of many, many weeks. He is monitored regularly. The doctor's notice that his head is swelling and the fluid has to be released with a spinal tap. Antwone is taken in this room and I stay outside the door. I hear him screaming. Oh, a mother's worst fear is not being able to hold her child's hand during such a traumatic experience to prolong his life. My body slides down the door, onto the floor and I hug my body—each scream—I hug tighter and tighter—desperately wanting to knock down that door, grab him in my arms and console him. My flesh shakes. Scream after scream. Cry after cry, literally tears me to pieces. Stain tears roll down my cinnamon skin, eyes redder than beets. Then a few seconds later, the door squeaks open, and out comes my nerve-wracked, frazzled, shaking like a leaf, boy. I grab him as he holds onto the wall and my body shakes with his as we wobble back to his room.

During Antwone's stay at Hopkins Hospital, he slowly regains feeling in his leg. One of his arms appears to be smaller than the other, but his smile is ever bright. He goes to physical therapy and it is paying off. He's doing very well.

The mornings that I don't make it to the hospital, Antwone calls me from his phone in his room to have brief talks. He mostly squeals on the nurse's aides. When he calls me he says, "Mommee, I haven't been washed, yet. It is almost lunchtime. And no water has touched my body." Or, "Mommee, I got the same underwear on from the day before and my breath stinks. Now they know that I can't get up to brush my own teeth and I keep pushing the red button and no one is coming. No one has come, Mommee," in his husky voice. Folks can't get over on his precociousness. I start cackling in the phone because it is hilarious. Sometimes he calls to say, "Mommee, please bring me some clean underwear, T-shirt, and socks, hurry?!" *Goodness, the boy is a piece of work for a seven year-old*, I think to myself.

The male social worker from Hopkins Hospital has a big surprise for Antwone. He put a request in to the Make-a-Wish Foundation and they contacted me to inform us that we are going to Disney World in Kissimmee, Florida. The boys are thrilled. The boys blurted the news to Sin and he is thrilled as well. I wait to tell him the bad news. I pull him to the side while the boys are chitchatting.

"You really don't believe that you are going with us, do you?"

Sin eyes darken.

"I mean, let's keep it real. Sin, you rarely come to visit your children and you think that I am going to reward you with a trip. No!" I say with a smug look upon my face.

There is a look of misery on his glossy face. "I have a right to be there. He is my son! Dey are my boys!" His index finger pokes into his frail chest.

I am not impressed with his audition. I nix him off.

"You are wrong, Ms. Avery, dead wrong!"

"And you're a junky! Stop drugging and gain some respect back. Then you can rebuild a relationship with *your* kids, but until then I am not going to let you devastate them anymore. "

He storms down the hall as an eerie aura surrounds me. Before exiting, he turns and sneers at me.

A week later I receive the tickets in the mail for a stay for a week in the middle of June. There is a scheduled limo to pick us up at 6:00 a.m. to take us to Newark Airport. The boys can't stop talking about it. I make arrangements with the school for Tyree to be out for a week. It doesn't surprise me that they are cooperative. We are to stay from the 10th to the 15th. Before our departure date, the faculty at the school gives us some parting gifts to take to Florida. The boys receive Disney hats, cards, and the principal hands me an RCA camcorder. They faculty yells out, "Take lots of pictures!"

The anticipation is getting the best of us. We pack the night before. We go to bed early and around 5:00 o'clock in the morning I wake the boys up to get dressed. The limo arrives on time. When we arrive at the airport I feel queasy. I have never flown before and I am quite uneasy about it. Tyree and Antwone are laughing and joking at me.

It is time to get on the plane. My legs are wobbly, my stomach aches and I feel faint. The boys hop on the plane and sit in their assigned seats, still talking and having a blast. My ears are popping and I am chewing the hell out of some Double Mint gum. The boys turn and poke fun because I am afraid. I smirk.

We arrive in Florida and go to pick up our rental car, which is silver Ford Taurus, and we head for Kissimmee. It is a beautiful place for children to be. We stay at a lovely yellow cottage that is nicely decorated on the outside. As we pull up in the driveway I can hear the boys saying, "Wow!" They are really excited.

It is hotter than fire as we exit out of the car. We enter our cottage and it looks like a condo inside. It has a living room, kitchen, two bedrooms, (the boys have a bathroom in their bedroom) and the other bathroom is across from their bedroom. We have an itinerary to follow. After we get settled we enjoy the scenery, but mostly at night because the heat is brutal.

The next day, we go shopping at the Nike Outlet to get the boys some new sneakers and short sets with the American Express Traveler's Checks given to us by Make-a-Wish Foundation. We go to dinner and the nice people give us Indian hats, as they are dressed like cowboys. They sing and dance. It is a hoot!

During our stay at the cottage I mingle with other mothers whose children have illnesses as well. The whole premise is full of ailing children from all different walks of life. The children play like nothing is wrong with them. At the Kissimmee cottage there is a merry-go-round, and different things for the children to do. We go swimming and later head back to our cottage to relax. Antwone isn't feeling well so I have him lay down for a bit. The boys keep me pumped. We enjoy ourselves.

It is a scorcher during the daytime and Antwone can't take the heat. It literally drains him so we stay indoors during the day, and go out during the evening. Our last couple of days, we drive to Disney World to see the fireworks. The boys love the bright-colored fireworks. Just hearing the loud BOOM!! It really makes their day.

When we return back to Paterson, Tyree returns back to school. They seem fulfilled. A feeling of happiness engulfs me and I feel full

145

for the very first time in my life. These children complete me.

Blood is thicker than anything in their eyes. I idolize them. I haven't birthed them, but I feel like Jewell did a hell of a job of raising them as a single mother. I am truly proud of my sister.

It is back to the daily routine of taking Antwone for his first visit of physical therapy as an outpatient. I must tell you, our first visit is a very quick one.

The next day, Antwone and I get up early to go Hopkins Hospital for him to start his treatment. We walk into the physical therapy office and meet with a Caucasian woman named Jean, who seems very pleasant. There are four steps that she wants Antwone to walk up and down. Antwone sucks his teeth and turns to Jean and say, "You had me and my mommee get up early for this?! I have more steps at home to walk up and down. Mommee, let's go." I put my hand up to my mouth trying not to smirk, but it is certainly funny. We walk out of the door and head home. Antwone crawls his way up the stairs at home. Everyday it is part of his regimen. He becomes stronger by the day. His arms and legs regain extraordinary mobility. I am truly amazed at his tenacity. This boy is no joke.

I go pick up Tyree and get the boys settled. Cook, wash the dishes, and have everything tidy so that I can sit for a bit. Sin hasn't popped around and I can see that the boys miss him. I feel kinda guilty. *Maybe I should have let him go to Disney World.* But my instincts tell me that I did the right thing. I have to protect the boys.

Every Saturday is movie night, and Tyree, Antwone, and I will sit and crunch on popcorn while watching *Ninja Turtles*. I am learning from them how to be thankful for family.

20

Things are unpredictable with Antwone. One minute he is flying high on life, and the next he is at his lowest. I rush him to Jaysen University and Medical Center because he keeps falling down. And when we arrive at the hospital I quickly park my car by the security guard, and fetch him my keys, and lift my son's head up, and slowly guide him out of the car into the emergency room. The woman in the triage office tells me to sign in and have a seat.

"Look, lady, this is an emergency. I don't have time to sit here. My child is ill. Can't you see?!"

"Ma'am, you're gonna have to take a sit. Others are waiting just like you."

Ooh, I want to reach through that glass and whoop her black ass.

"His doctors are waiting for our arrival."

Again, she says, "Please, have a seat."

And again, in a voice of panic, "My son is sick! He needs immediate attention." She blows me off.

As I turn around Antwone is lying on the cold, marble floor. He has fallen asleep. I turn in her direction, "Didn't I tell you that he is sick!" She immediately calls for a doctor. I raise Antwone's head, and the people in the waiting area watch me as they whisper among themselves about me persistently telling her that we needed help. As I lift Antwone midway he vomits all over his clothing, and it splatters onto my blouse, as well as the floor. A stretcher is brought out and we are finally able to be seen. After the doctors observe him they discover that his medication dosage is too strong and lowers it. Antwone stays overnight for observation. The next day he is discharged.

Weeks later, Antwone is back in the hospital at Children of Tomorrow and this particular day he is scheduled to go to the imaging center for an MRI. The transporters have an issue of wanting payment of one hundred dollars in cash before they take him. At the time I don't have any extra cash on me. We wait trying to get the issue resolved. The clock ticks and then something happens. Antwone's body tightens stiff as a board, and his mouth is that of a water fountain just spewing out everything in his belly, as his eyes spread big like he has been spooked. It happens right in the hallway of that floor. And I raise my body off the seat and I panic in the square tile where I stand as I watch him harden like a rock. I can't move. My arms reach out for him, but I can't move to wrap my arms around him. To comfort him. Oh God, I am as stiff as he. Big gulps of saliva slither down my throat. Face full of blots of beaded moisture. Eyes flooded with desperate emotion as I echo shrieking sounds from my mouth of sorrow and pain. I witness it with my own eyes. Antwone suffered a stroke. My seven year-old suffered a stroke! Lord, why?

I keep my head up and finally come to grips with, *what if*. Yes, what if things take a major turn for the worst. Many thoughts run through my mind. *What if I awoke one morning and receive a call that my son remains asleep. What if he suffers tremendously and I have to helplessly watch.* "What if" sticks in the back of my head as if I have folded it and carefully laid it down, and zipped it in my luggage—waiting—waiting for the inevitable to occur. *Honey, erase that from your mind*, I hear Avona say. She is my biggest motivator. Antwone's cancer is wearing me down, but I keep fighting to get up. I have no choice because *my children* are now my survival. Yes. They keep me going even though I shut the door to my bedroom and weep in silence. Hugging my pillow and inside of me the little girl throws a hell fit. I want Antwone to be a child, not growing faster than his years, but I have no control over his mind's maturity. I have to face reality, which is to allow him to live as he chooses, young or old. He is different in his mannerisms, not as a child, but more as an adolescent. No, he has changed and I adjust. Laughter fills our rooms, smiles and kisses are ointment for my wounds, and I begin to feel the acceptance of what I have. I deal with the emotional roller coaster. I have to take the ride and be happy with the fact that I am not riding it alone.

I go early to Children of Tomorrow to see Antwone after dropping Tyree off at school. There is constant movement throughout the halls. My whole visit, Antwone is in a coma. The nurse's aide comes into the room to check his diaper and pulse. And he still hasn't awakened from his dead sleep. I try to distract my thoughts. In my mind I pretend that he is just sooooo tired. Like, he was up late last night. I sit up there from 9:00 to close to 2:00, and then I prepare myself to leave to pick Tyree up. As I step one foot out the room it is like an army waiting for me. No one ever came into the room, except the nurse's aide. There is the nurse, social worker, a doctor, and other folks that I can't recall who they are. And one of the social workers asks me where I am going.

"I'm going to pick my son up from school. I'll be back."

"No, Ms. Love, you shouldn't leave," the social worker says.
"Why?"
"You may not get back in time."
"In time for what?" By now, I have a look of utter frustration on my face. All this time I've been here you haven't said a word, and now that I have to leave you're telling me I shouldn't. She can tell that I am bothered.

The social worker lowers her head as her blonde hair hides her face. Then she raises it and looks me piercingly in my eyes.

"Can you call someone to pick your son up?"
"There's no one to call."
"We can call a cab for him and have the driver bring him to the hospital."
"I've taught my son not to get into cars with strangers and I know that he will not get into a cab alone."

Then a few minutes later Never comes sashaying off the elevator. She is a pleasant but unexpected surprise. After she arrives, Dr. Rice takes us into a room off the corridor. We sit down to talk privately.

"Ms. Love, There is no easy way for me to say this but Antwone's health is depleting and the staff feels that if you leave, you may not return in time."

It still has not registered in my brain. And I guess Dr. Rice can tell by the expression on my face. Never seems to catch on before me.

"Ms. Love, Antwone may die, today."

My eyes water just by her words. I tighten my lips to fight the tears away, but I can't. I just can't. So I let them pour from my soul.

Never immediately gets on the phone making phone calls. I call the only friend I can depend on Xavier and ask for another favor.

"Hello, Red Alert, Marilyn speaking, how I may direct your call."
"Yes, may I speak with Mr. Combs, please?"
"May I ask who is calling?"
"Avery...Avery Love."
"Ma'am, please hold while I connect you."
"Thanks." My body is fidgety and my eyes are swollen and red.

I sniffle in between the 101.9 AM music playing until Xavier picks up.

"Hello, Mr. Combs, speaking."
"Hi Xavier. I need a favor, a quick favor. Um, is it possible for you to go to the YMCA on Ward Street to pick Tyree up for me and bring him to Children of Tomorrow in Hackensack?"
"Avery, are you crying. Is it your nephew?"

"Yes. They don't think that he is going to make it and I was going to leave but they don't want me to because they think I may not get back in time."

"They're right. I'm leaving now. Do not worry yourself."

He hangs up before I can even say thanks.

Never is calling around to inform relatives. She calls her father Chaelbert's house and Sisal and Jo-Ruthie and others rush to the hospital. I try to reach Sin on my cell phone but no one has seen him. I contact Sin's youngest brother Kye and wife Lee and inform them of the news. And then I just sit and wait in Antwone's room praying for a miracle. Hoping that he makes it through because I don't know what I am going to do should he leave us.

In about a half hour to forty-five minutes Antwone's room is full of folks. Somewhere along the way Kye picked up Sin hibernating on Godwin Ave. I remain silent in a world of my own. Praying underneath my breath as everyone voices muffle together.

I can hear the elevator door open and off walks Xavier and Tyree. I smile and embrace Tyree with a hug as well as Xavier.

"Thank you so much." I wipe my red eyes.

"Avery, you don't have to thank me. I would do just about anything for you." He stares into my weak eyes.

It catches me off guard but I don't embellish his words. Xavier is just being himself, a very giving man. But when he reaches in to kiss me on the cheek I know that it means more than I expected. I smile softly and stare back into his eyes. We walk into Antwone's room as we shut the door behind us.

The room is full of voices chattering as Antwone lies still. I am at this point stressed out not knowing if he is going to live or die. In that moment Tyree walks over to the right side of the bed and stares into Antwone's face.

"Hey, Ant," Tyree says, looking around at everyone.

Tyree doesn't know the severity of Antwone's condition and I don't have the nerve to tell him. I just can't do it.

Tyree is chewing gum and out of nowhere, with everyone in the room, Antwone opens his eyes.

"Whachu eating?" Antwone asks.

Everyone's eyes widen with astonishment, including the social worker, nurse, and doctor.

"Gum."

"Can I have some?"

I nearly fall to my feet. The look of surprise and relief on their faces says it all. I have been up here since 9:00 in the morning and the child gave me no response whatsoever, and as soon as his brother comes he wakes out of his coma. That makes everyone and I mean, everyone, open their mouths in awe. I will never forget this day. I will never underestimate the power in God as I have in that moment thinking that He was truly going to take my child away from me. I will never underestimate the power of true brotherly love. Never again will I underestimate the power of love! Thank you, Jesus!

21

The request to go back to school from Antwone has come. He is ready, but PS No. 117 isn't. The Child Study Team has cut me some slack after finding out the news of Antwone's condition. In the beginning they didn't embrace me with open arms because I was difficult. But being difficult worked in my favor because if I had not been, Antwone possibly would have died back in February. I listened to my gut instincts and his doctor. I remained cemented to my words and it paid off. But I see I have another fight on my hands with trying to re-enroll him.

Numerous times I call the school to see if I can get him back in, but it is so damn frustrating. Time after time, the Child Study Team will come up with some bogus bull that makes my blood boil even more. I make an appointment to meet with them at the school to discuss re-enrolling Antwone, but they are defiant. Bringing up the fact that Antwone walks with a limp due to the fact that his foot is not straight, his mouth is slightly crooked from suffering the stroke, and one arm is smaller than the other. They fret that he may not be able to walk up and down the stairs. But he still functions properly. And I'd be damned if I am going to allow them to stunt my son's growth because of their small minds. I'd be damned!

I have put a request in for a home tutor named Simone Vincent, a young mocha-skinned woman, with a great big Kool-Aid smile, and friendly disposition. Simone willingly comes to our home to help Antwone. At first he didn't seem too fond of her. I think he was testing her to see if she could cut it. And she passed with flying colors. They have built a good rapport. Though, there are times when Antwone doesn't want her to leave and he hides underneath the kitchen table to prolong her stay. Simone has a lot of patience and I can see her being a great teacher. If she can deal with Antwone and his many mood-swings and still keep a smile on her face there is nothing that will get her down. I still continue to pursue getting him back into school, though.

The next meeting that is scheduled with the Child Study Team I have to get down right dirty. I have a surprise for their asses. Yes, Antwone. It has gotten to the point where I am tired of speaking up for him and have come to the conclusion that you must fight with wisdom. And the young wisdom I have is Antwone. I feel that if they hear him speak on his own behalf that maybe it will make a huge impact on their decision. All I can do is try and hope for the best.

Three white women and one gentleman sit at a conference table on the second floor waiting for my arrival at PS 117, which turns out to be *our* arrival—Antwone and me. We both sit down. The Child Study Team has peculiar looks on their faces. I guess wondering why Antwone is here. The dialogue begins and in response to any comments or questions that come about I remain silent. I nod on what I agree with and shake my head on what I disagree with. Antwone remains silent. His eyes bright, face full and round from the weight gain, skin of dark chocolate glistening, he sits in his multi-colored pinstripe jean shirt, jeans, and black Nike sneakers with his head held high, neck tall, as he listens attentively.

After listening Antwone speaks in his husky voice, "Why can't I come back to school?" Eyes wander, fingers tap, and toes probably curl to the sound of child's voice. He repeats. "Why don't you want me to come back? I can walk, talk, the stairs won't be a problem for me because I will hold onto the banister. I promise. I won't misbehave. I just wanna come back to school. I miss it. Give me one reason?"

There is deadness in the room. Inaudible silence. The unanimous decisions of not wanting him back changes as the brunette haired woman caves in. In a soft-spoken voice she says, "Let him back. If he wants to come back to school, let him."

After her words are spoken, all join in to allow Antwone back and I am a teary-eyed mom as Antwone sits enthralled by his great accomplishment. He fought for what is right for him and I am as proud as a mother can possibly be.

I awake that next morning feeling alive and refreshed. I raise the heads of my boys and help Antwone get dressed and ready for his day back to school. He is so happy—laughing and joking. Tyree teases him in a good way. I get myself ready in no time because I don't want them to be late. This is a new day of beginnings.

We head out and into my car. As we exit out of the car and enter the school we greet the principal, a middle-aged, brunette hair, slender-framed Caucasian woman named Mrs. Barberry. She in turn calls Antwone's teacher, Mrs. Guess, to meet us out in the hallway. Tyree heads for his class. Mrs. Guess kindly escorts Antwone into class with the biggest, brightest smile I'd ever seen on his face. I smile as I leave out of the school and head back home. After about an hour of being home alone I am going crazy. I get paranoid. I start thinking that something is wrong. I keep checking the phone wondering why no one from the school is calling me to come get Antwone. I turn the TV on to distract me. I peek toward the clock. Turn the channel. Watch the clock. Turn the channel. My mind is tormenting me to think that the worst has happen. That Antwone will come home in a bad mood because the students were mean to him and the teacher yelled at him. All of this I make up in my head.

When it is time to pick the boys up, I grow anxious. I need to know that Antwone's fight to go back was not in vain. That everything worked in his favor. I need to know that he is all right because we spend so much time together that I worry even more with him not in my presence. I leave the house a few minutes early, park my car directly across from the school's door and sit waiting while listening to the radio. I stretch my legs, wiggle my toes, and extend out my arms to relax but I simply can't. I am too wired.

The school bell rings and all the children race out. I get out of my car and greet Tyree and we walk into the school to greet Antwone. I meet with Mrs. Barberry, the slender brunette principal, and she escorts us to Mrs. Guess. Mrs. Guess has a huge smile upon her ivory-colored face. Her blonde hair is pulled back in a bun and it accentuates her blue eyes. She hands Antwone a piece of paper with a heart drawn on it with an arrow and inserted in the middle is an, "I love you." The little note reads:

Dear Antwone,

I am so proud of you. You are the best student for the day.

Love,

Mrs. G.

Then he shows me his other note that reads:

"Antwone did very well in reading and math today. He got a star!" It has a smiley face on it.

On our way home the boys talk about their day. It is great!

22

The next day there is an unfamiliar scent that invites itself through the cracks about the window. There is an echo in the house of the refrigerator humming. There is a whisper in my ears. There is throbbing in my heart. There is a fiery sensation in my gut. There is quietness, stillness, and it frightens the hell out of me.

Morning is upon me and my feet drag as I plant them on the black tweed multi-colored rug, scraping the soles across trying to buy time. The laughter from the day before is heard only in my head. Memories—flashbacks reflect. *Something's different.* I can feel it in my bones. And confirmation surfaces when I walk over to Antwone. He has a fever. He looks different in his face. His body is frozen, but I think it will pass and he will be able to get out of bed within a few minutes, but I am wrong. *Oh God, please help me?*

School is near its end and summer break is just around the corner. I wake Tyree and tell him to get ready for school. I ask him if he thinks he can walk to school on his own this morning and he says yes. He is so helpful and understanding when I need him to be the bigger brother. Jewell taught him well. I call the school and inform them that Antwone won't be attending because he is under the weather. The school staff seems disappointed and sends their blessings for him to get better. I am proud of Antwone because he accomplished his goal of returning to school, even if it was for only one day. He did it.

Tyree heads out the door as I watch from the living room window. He's wearing his Air Force One's, South Pole jeans, and T-shirt to match, with his backpack string dangling in the faint breeze. A smile spreads across my face. I give Antwone a sponge bath. I feed him breakfast, but he eats minimally. I give him his medicine and we talk minimally. When he sleeps, I sleep. When he wakes, I wake. And this continues up until he regains his strength to get out of bed. I keep in contact with his specialist to let her know of his progress. They send a nurse to check on him as well. I have to keep Anonymous closed for the week because I just couldn't leave Antwone at a time like this. He needs me and I need him.

During Antwone's downtime I have had many disturbing thoughts travel through my mind. I sigh. I thought his time was near. I close my eyes and cover my mouth with my palm. Yep. That time to express my "see you later" time. I am not prepared. Even though I feel the need to go to Booker Prayer Funeral Home in Montclair and start the preparations just in case. My ears keep hearing Avona say, "Avery, go ahead and start the prearrangements because you don't know how your state of mind is going to be when that time comes." I interrupt her, "If that time comes!" Sometimes I wish she would shut the hell up! I decide once Antwone is on his feet I will look into it. I am not looking for it to happen, but I have to be realistic; things aren't good. Every day is unpredictable. And I think my mindset will not be up and running so I better take heed to that little voice.

I think I jinx things because within the same week or so Antwone and I have a conversation about death. He is very serious about what he wants.

"Single-aunty, I don't wanna die."

This catches me totally off guard and I try with all of my might to compose myself.

"Single-aunty, how come God wants me to go to heaven?"

I try to tune his husky voice out. I don't want to talk about this. *Please, Lord, stop making me suffer?*

"Single-aunty, why aren't you talking to me? Are you mad at me?"

I wipe my eyes and say, "No, baby, no I have no reason to be mad at you."

This is too damn difficult. I can't answer his questions because I don't know, why. I feel like I am failing him in his time of need. Guilt lays heavy on my heart.

During our talk Antwone turns and looks me dead in my face and says, "*Mommee*, I don't wanna leave you and Tyree." I remain silent, but inside I am crumbling. Antwone mind changes from not wanting to die to accepting his fate. "Okay...*Mommee*, you can go. Go and pick out my outfit to wear, but you cannot buy it until after I'm gone." I look at him with surprise in my eyes. "Promise me, mommee. Promise me that you won't buy it until after, but you can go look and pick it out." I am floored, ready to drop to the floor and bawl like a baby. *Sweet Jesus.*

"I promise," I say, with swollen glands.

Sometime after our conversation I call Chaelbert's home to ask Sisal to babysit while I run some errands. I go to Booker Prayer Funeral Home to make the prearrangements. Then I start looking around for the proper attire. I find Barry's store in Passaic, New Jersey, and I walk inside to inquire about a specific outfit. This short Hispanic woman greets me and asks if I needed any assistance. I say, yes. But I can't seem to tell her what I want. It is too difficult. She tries to help me by asking questions.

"Ma'am, what occasion is it for: communion, bar mitzvah, wedding, or baptism?"

It is hard to get my words out, but I struggle and say, "No." I clear my throat.

"It's….um… um…ah, it's for a funeral." I lower my head and take deep breath. The sales associate remains quiet for what seems like a minute.

I take a moment and then explain what I am looking for. "Um, do you have a white tuxedo with Mickey Mouse cummerbund and bow tie for a seven year-old? And a white dress shirt with black ball buttons on it?"

"More than likely I will have to order the Mickey Mouse cummerbund and bow tie. Once it comes in I will put everything aside for your return." She smiles.

I exhale as she writes out a receipt for me. This is just the beginning but I feel with her help I passed the first test. Antwone really put me in an uncomfortable position, but who else is going to finalize his requests. Sin hasn't been seen in weeks. And he's too high to even conceive of preparing for his son's death. This is the first and I hope the last time anyone asks me to do anything like this. I fully understand why Antwone asked such a thing because he is trying to make it easier for me when that time does come. I won't have to frantically look for an outfit because it is already prepared. It makes me wonder about what else he will ask of me that I probably won't feel comfortable in handling. I feel another request coming on.

I think about Poppa on my way back home when he used to say, "suffer the child no mo." He used to say it quite often when hearing that a child had died on the news. He also said, "What man in his right mind would possibly want a woman with so many troubles in her life—back to back?" It makes me think about how much I have endured and how far I have come. I have to remain calm for my boys. As much as my heart bleeds I have to put my children first and I keep my head mid-level and do what any loving mother would do—stick it out, straighten up, and fly right. I literally have to convince myself that I can do anything that God puts in my lap. That I can conquer it all and keep moving forward, but truthfully I am not totally convinced when it comes to Antwone being ill. It isn't that cut and dry for me. It isn't.

Many a nights I have panic attacks because I keep seeing images that I don't want to see. The premonitions, they come and I fear them. I don't want to have the ability that God has given me. I don't want to see the future. I feel cursed and think that if I share what I see folks will think that I am going crazy. But God has warned me for a reason. He sent an angel to guide me through the most difficult time of all times in my life. He openly handed me struggles and the ability to survive those struggles because He knew that I would someday come to meet Antwone and he would have to go back home with Him. Often I pray and ask in a soft voice, "God… could you spare Antwone and take me instead?" Tears roll down my face. "Listen, I know that I haven't truly lived like most of Your children, but I've seen all that I need to see, felt all that I need to feel, and experienced all that I need to experience. If You would take me and allow Antwone to live his life to the fullest, I would trade places as *we* speak." I mean every word. Internally I am bleeding profusely. I will do anything God asks of me just to have that one blessing. I pray under my breath, lying down, standing up, sitting, walking, talking, laughing, smiling, and listening. Yes. Any time I have a second's peace I pray because my gut is telling me soon things will change.

23

There are good days, so-so days, and bad days and I try to remain optimistic. By this time Antwone has a male nurse named Mike. Mike, tall, chiseled features, blonde neck length hair with a motherly disposition comes over to do his routine checkups on Antwone. They sit and have a chitchat and laugh. Mike is a breath of freshness at this time in our lives. I need all the help I can get because I feel myself dwindling day by day. There are two other women nurses that come on different days and that makes me feel comfortable because I have a lot of medical support. But I have to administer all of Antwone's meds. Things seem to be going rather well up until he starts falling as he tries to get up off the sofa. This is the second time and I hope it is because of the medication. Maybe the dosage is too high. Maybe his body doesn't react to it anymore. Maybe. I have so many maybes.

I immediately call his specialist and Dr. Stone advises me to bring Antwone back to Jaysen University and Medical Center. I take him to the emergency room. The medical staff run some tests to try and figure out why he keeps falling like a puppet. The end result is that one of his medications is too strong so they lower the dosage. Boy, am I relieved.

Within a couple of days Antwone falls ill again and is admitted back to Children of Tomorrow.

During this time I have to learn so much: how to administer meds through an intravenous drip line. How to change the bed sheets with Antwone in the bed. Change his gown while he lies in bed. I have to learn how to put pillows between his legs so that his knees and feet won't touch to prevent bedsores. I have to move his legs so that they won't stiffen. Brush his teeth with a soft swab. Bottom line, I have to play nurse, mommy, daddy, and single-aunty. And it is the hardest job to maintain. I am overwhelmed, but my youngster has so much faith in me. He believes that I can do it all and more. He convinces me that I can and will be his nurse, and there is no way that I can or will decline the role.

Deep inside, I am not certain of my faith in nurturing him in his state. I feel he needs professionals who have years of experience. I only have experience in being his single-aunty and it is not even a year's experience. So actually I am not even qualified to be handling all of this. Caring for him is a full-time job and the qualifications are strict and concise. I have to be on top of my game at all times. I have to be alert and focused. There are certain things that I feel comfortable doing, but there are things that I am foreign to. I am scared that I will make a mistake—a mistake that could cost me the worst penalty of my life—losing *him* by the hands of me. That is my worst nightmare.

Eventually my confidence level increases. Antwone seems stronger than ever after a few weeks, but every time he gets better, he gets worse. I am angry at his cancer—wishing that I could somehow leap into his body and punch it, beating it to a pulp, and then drag its ass out and push it over into the Passaic River to face its demise. If I had the ability I would do it in a heartbeat. And suffer the consequences of my actions.

24

One Saturday evening, Antwone and I are in the bedroom sitting on the bed while Tyree is in the kitchen eating dinner. Antwone turns to me with those big bright eyes and says, *"Ma, does God have toys in heaven?"*

My eyes widen. I'm at a loss for words because too many questions are coming about. Too many questions about death—a word I dread to hear. I pause and massage my face. I am caught off guard again with no type of answer to comfort him. I hesitate kinda in a flustered state of mind. Realizing that I can't answer his question because I have never lied to him, and I don't feel the need to embellish heaven because I have never been to heaven. I want him to respect me as his aunty, not his mother. I am not his mother. Only a mother can answer his questions. Only his mother, a woman who has carried him in her womb could answer such a profound question. Only a mother who has cared for him would know how to soothe him with words of wisdom. Something I cannot do. It hits me like a ton of bricks. I am not his mother, no matter how much I pretend to be. I'm not. And it hurts me dearly because his mother is dead.

"Um, Ant, um, I don't know how to quite answer your question." I feel like I am failing him bit by bit.

He breathes out deeply. Then out of the blue, he asks,

"Can you and Tyree come with me…to heaven? Then we can still be a family."

I shut my eyes feeling the saliva slowly flow down my throat. He catches me off guard again and all I can do is answer him with compassion.

"Ant, we will always be a family, but Tyree and I won't be able to come with you to heaven."

"Why?" he asks, as his eyes spread and flood with tears.

"'Cause we have to wait for God to call us home."

"But…how will we still be a family if we are not together?" One tears rolls slowly down his cheek and his little lips tremble.

"We will keep each other in our hearts. That will keep us together forever until God calls me and your brother home."

"I don't wanna be by myself, *Mommee*. I don't wanna die by myself."

It takes everything in me not to crack. I have to look him in his little face and try with all of my might to soothe him, and truthfully I don't know if I can sound convincing enough for him to believe me. *This is some heavy shit.* I speak with sincerity.

"You won't be. God won't let you be alone. You're special, Ant, and special people never die in spirit."

"They don't?"

"No…they don't. Special people become angels."

"So, I'll be an angel in heaven?"

"Yes." I clear my throat. "You're an angel already on earth."

"I am!" His eyes light up.

"Yep. My angel."

My voice cracks the whole time I am talking and I know that he knows it is not a comfortable conversation for me but as always I do the best that I can to comfort him. This conversation stirs within a feeling of losing a soulful part of me that I have just discovered. I lower my head feeling powerless.

I prepared Antwone's plate so that he can eat before going to pick Tyree up from the summer program at the YMCA. Antwone sits at the kitchen table and takes small bites of his food. Then not even twenty minutes pass before he says, "*Mommee*, I don't feel well." He stands up out of his chair, but I notice he can't figure out which way to turn to head back to the bedroom. Mike came by earlier and Antwone seemed fine. Maybe he's just tired, I think to myself. I stand still for a moment and in my spirit I feel that Antwone has just gone blind at the kitchen table. Unfortunately, the spirit never lies.

It is more than I can bear. I brace my fingers against the sink counter and count in my head not to blow up in front of Antwone. But I turn and realize that this child doesn't utter one complaint. Not one. He doesn't utter a sound. There is no anger shown on his face, cries of sorrow, no resentment, no frown or sigh of disappointment is exchanged. He doesn't raise hell, stomp his feet, have a tantrum, spit, squint his eyes in fury, punch the wall, kick the door, or swear underneath his breath, or cry. He simply waits until I grab a hold of his arm and guide him back to the bedroom, lay him down, and I return back into the kitchen to finish the dishes. Anger resides in me, but then it transforms into anguish so quickly. My eyes tear. I want to break a plate, smashing it to smithereens, but I don't because I don't want to disturb Antwone's peace. The child is at peace with whatever God hands him, and I am simply mortified, but I capture the essence of what Antwone stands for. The messages are sinking in.

Antwone is a gifted blessin' from God. It has occurred to me that he is a *mentor* for me to learn from. Just like Johnnie. Just like Storyteller. I have struggles beyond my expectations, but Antwone has taught me to look into the eyes of a child who has struggles beyond his expectations and mine. I find his message to be shrewd, profound, distressing, but it paves a way that I have never traveled. My life has only been a fragment of his and I gravitate to his calling. I am lifted far more than I'd ever imagined, and I don't have to imagine it because I am living it. It is a hell of a lesson to learn.

Antwone doesn't tell anyone that he is blind, not even Tyree. He pretends to see when Tyree slips in their favorite movie *Batman* in the DVD. And I don't say a thing. I just sit back and learn. After a while Tyree catches on that his brother is blind. And it is a relief off of my shoulders. They watch *Batman* a million and one times and each time Tyree tells his little brother what scene is about to come up and they laugh and joke as if he still had his eyesight. Their bond is something special. They have true brotherly love that is inconceivable in the eyes of someone like me. I am so impressed by them. It makes me feel like all the struggling is paying off because through hell or high waters nothing deters their ties. They don't allow bitterness or anger to consume them. They enjoy the quality times together and it lightens the load on me. I have so much love for them, more than they know, more than I ever anticipated.

After I settle down I contact the nurse, Mike to inform him that Antwone has gone blind. His reaction leaves me to believe that he knew eventually this was going to happen. Possibly he saw while he was here and didn't say anything. I am not upset because he didn't want to speak too soon on something that he didn't know if or when it would occur. It makes sense to me. If Antwone doesn't have any resentment from his blindness, why should I? I am learning more and more. It seems funny that I am being taught from a seven year-old boy about surrendering with a sense of peace.

All of Antwone's doctors are informed of his blindness and later that day one of the women nurses comes to the house to examine him. A day later, I am contacted by Hospice and they send a social worker named Mrs. Kramer to come to visit. Mrs. Kramer, a lily-white, tall woman with blue eyes comes and talks to Antwone and me and Tyree when he is home. Eventually a small crew of three comes to visit, wearing out their welcome. Sometimes Antwone gets agitated by them coming disturbing his rest. And when that happens, he gets bold and says, "Ms. Lady, every time you come, you say the say thing over and over. You ask the same questions over and over. I'm tired. Please, I'm tired." Mrs. Kramer closes her mouth and stares into space.

On one visit, Mrs. Kramer discusses assistance from Visiting Home Health Aide Services, for a home health aide that will be able to deal with our situation. She says they usually stay for two hours a day, depending on how often their needed. I opt to inquire about they're services because I can run errands and not worry about Antwone. It is not easy finding anyone, though. As soon as they find out it is for a child, most get discouraged. I understand that it will be most difficult. Children are so precious. I don't hold my breath waiting I just continue on as I've done.

Antwone adds amusement to the upcoming days. Anyone who comes to visit he charges them a quarter to see *him*. He sounds so cute, "A quarter, please." He opens his palm, waiting with confidence that he will achieve his goal. And once it is placed in his palm, he unzips his black pouch that he keeps near his side and drops his quarter in and zips it back, until another gullible soul comes waltzing in. No one would deny him his request because once he dazzles you with that boyish charm, deep smile, and eyes that glow like stars you are whipped under his spell. In your pants pocket, wallet, or purse your fingers rummage to find a silver quarter and make his day.

The days ahead are hard to bear. Antwone's health is slowly fading little by little. But he is strong-willed. The social worker from Hospice and the nurses come more frequently. Things seem hectic and I grow tired very quickly. The disappearing Sin returns looking as dreadful as when I first laid eyes on him. His toothpick, almost skeletal frame, sunken cheeks, gumball eyes are like looking at walking death. Getting high is his domestic partner. *Nodding ass.*

I often wonder what will make him stop. I heave a heavy sigh. And then I just let the thought fade from my mind. I continue to open my door to visitors, something I wouldn't normally do if I were here alone. I can't stand to have a flock of folks up in my house. Snooping, stealing, lounging around like this is the next hangout spot. I try to be cordial, for Antwone and Tyree's sake.

My cousin, Cedric, who is Skye and Never's brother, comes to visit with his girlfriend Carole. They catch a bus all the way from Jersey City, New Jersey, almost every weekend. Oh, Carole, she is a sweetheart, with high-rise weaves, chunky frame, with the style and grace of a voluptuous black woman, so helpful and patient. On most of the visits she sits and talks with Antwone and Tyree, and me. Cedric, the dark-skinned lover-man, loves to crack jokes at anyone's expense. The man is full of laughter, but I see in his eyes that he has had many, many hardships. They are both such a comfort. I smile at them wishing, drifting, dreaming of a relationship that they display. They seem in bliss. Some of my uncles, aunts, and cousins stop by unannounced. Old acquaintances of Sisal's come on the weekends with gifts in hand. One couple, Chip, with his snow-white hair and amicable ways and his lovely wife Dixie, stop by with gifts and alternatives treatments for Antwone that they hear about or find surfing on the Internet. Dixie, a tall, Caucasian woman with short dark hair, and light cream skin, sits beside Antwone humming and rubbing his tummy. I stand in the doorway and just listen to her serene tune of comfort. Oh, he is smitten with her. A few of my childhood friends—Jelly, Wisdom, Derwood, Larry, Rock, Bitty, Tracy B.—stop by on different occasions. Just to say hello, how are you doing, do you need anything. It is like a melting pot up in here. I appreciate their visits, and I know Antwone does too because his pouch is getting rather full. It makes the days most enjoyable; it's the nights that become tiresome.

My mind drifts, thinking that if I go to sleep Antwone will—well, it is heavy on my mind. So heavy that I creep into the bathroom in the middle of the night and stare into the mirror and sob full of anger, regret, disgust, resentment toward his cancer. I watch him day in and day out fight like a lion for his cubs, which is his life, and I weep with such disdain in my heart for this disease. This monster, that preys on the innocence of children. My flesh quivers so heartfelt, so mindful of life and death. Of how quickly it can dissipate. Tears flush out of my pores and I fall to my feet and lie across the cool tile and rest my burdensome soul.

25

I try to hold my head up high, but inside I feel like I am drowning. I sense that Antwone knows just by the look in my eyes. The eyes never lie. This is tough. And I don't know how much longer I can pretend to be this strong woman. I don't know how much longer before I breakdown. I'm trying to keep it together. Lord, why? I huff. I just want to stop feeling. I just wish I could for a minute or two. Just…just numb my pain. I scratch my scalp. I am way over due for a haircut. This is unlike me. I always keep myself up, but lately I haven't been feeling like myself. I've been this woman…this *unknown* woman who is playing the role of mommy. I must be losing my mind to think that I can pull this off. And these poor children depend on me to care for them when it should be the other way around. I have no idea of what I am doing. I am clueless. Lord, why were they placed in my hands? Why, because I'm man-less? That doesn't make a bit of sense because they need a man in their lives. Where's Sin? Out somewhere getting high. He has no concern for his children. He can't even stop for a second to come and visit them. I haven't heard him once tell them that he loves them. What kinda father is he? But regardless of what he doesn't do, the boys still love him. Even though he's the invisible man. I can't figure this shit out. And maybe that's it—I'm not supposed to figure anything out. I'm just supposed to do what was asked of me. Mind my own backyard and let the dice roll where they may. I nod my head up and down because it is finally sinking in. I have to use that "Do You" mentality. I used to be so good at that. Yeah, a hard cookie to crumble, but then I caught feelings for people and the insensitive me drifted off somewhere and now I'm left with this humane creature that I stare in the mirror at. Still, I wonder where she came from.

Antwone lies in his bed like his mind is a thousand miles away. It is a lot for him to deal with. I see it in him. He's not the same as when he first walked through my doors. He's growing up rather quickly, too quickly. His health is still depleting. Things are not good at all and decisions have to be made about what he wants to keep him comfortable.

"Mommee, I wanna go home."

Deep down I don't want him to come home for various reasons. But my main reason is that I have no idea of what to do should he get very ill. I'm afraid. But I can't express that to him. What would he think of me? I'm supposed to be the "mommy" in this. At least, that's how he looks at it.

"Ah, don't you think it will be better to stay here? You have all the things you need here," I say, thinking that I sealed the deal. I hear Avona's voice, *Ms. Thang, this is not a business! He is a child! A sick little boy. Get it together!*

Her words sink my heart. Here I am trying to weasel out of caring for him. What kinda person am I?

"Antwone, this hospital has everything you need."

In his defense he replies, "They don't have my family living here."

Ah, man…why did he set me up in this trap? There is nothing left to say. Home, that's where he belongs, I'm just gonna have to get a grip. I step out of the room and call Sisal from my cell phone.

"Hello."

"Hi, Sisal."

"Is everything all right with Antwone?"

"Yes…well, no…I mean, yes and no. His health is not getting any better. Sisal, he wants to be home."

"Oh, boy, that's a tough one. What have you decided?"

"I have options?" I say somewhat astounded.

"Sure, Avery. Your world has been tumbled upside down and it is okay to say, no."

"I can't say no to a sick child!
The boy wants to come home to…to…to."

"To die, Avery. The boy wants to come home to die. But did you ask him which home? He coulda meant North Carolina. Maybe you need to ask him, which."

I push the "end" button on my phone and stand in the hall pondering over Sisal's question. I never did ask which, I just assumed he meant mine.

I walk back into the room and Antwone is still staring into space. I keep forgetting the boy is blind. I smack myself over the head.

"Ah Ant, you sure you want to come home?"

"Yes, single-aunty."

"But, which home are you referring to: my home or back home in North Carolina?"

"Single-aunty, I just wanna go home."

Antwone leaves me hanging. I make arrangements with Children of Tomorrow to transport him home…my home. Then I stroke Antwone's face and tell him I have to leave to pick his brother up.

"I wanna see my brother. Can he come to see me?"

"They won't let him come because he has a little cold. But you'll see him when you come home."

Antwone smile spreads so wide I can see the inside of his mouth.

As I am entering the elevator there is this Caucasian woman waiting as well. She smiles at me and I smile back. Then the elevator door opens. She gets on and so do I. The next thing I know she is making small talk with me. I have never seen this woman before out of all of my visits here. It was like she just appeared out of the blue.

"Hi." Her smile is so pretty.

"Hello," I say a little standoffish.

"I want you to have this."

She extends this book, *Embraced by the Light* by Betty J. Eadie.

I reach in for the book and turn to the back cover and read that it's about a woman who had experienced a near-death experience. I look at her strangely.

"You're gonna need this to help you through," she says, still smiling with that beautiful smile.

I don't feel the impulse to question, decline, or simply dismiss her generosity so I simply say, "thank you," and leave it at that. I tuck the book in my handbag and keep it moving.

26

Antwone is transported home and I must admit I am struggling with him being here. I have so many thoughts traveling through my mind. And none are positive. This is a sticky situation that I walked into. I'm not blaming Sisal or Jo-Ruthie, but damn, when it rains it pours.

My vein is about to pop out of my neck trying to do the drip line to Antwone's IV and for some reason it isn't dripping. Immediately, I panic and pick up the phone to call the answering service to have a nurse assist me over the phone. It is about 3:00 in the morning and this nurse name Rosy is telling me what to do, but nothing is making sense to me. I get frustrated. I start crying on the phone because I fear if I don't get this IV something may happen to Antwone. In my hysteric state the woman asks me for my address and tells me that she is coming.

"Please, ma'am, don't cry. I'm on my way," Rosy says.

I need a break but I can't take a break because I have no one to help me. I am beyond overwhelmed with learning how to undress him while he is still lying in bed. To remind myself to change sheets while he is lying in bed. To make sure I maneuver his legs so that they won't develop bedsores. I just wanna scream with all of this responsibility. I won't fail him, no matter what.

Finally, the buzzer goes off and I gladly let her in. I hurry to open the door as I nervously wait for her to exit off the elevator.

Stepping off of the elevator is a slender, white woman with her blonde hair pulled back in a ponytail. She wears some wrinkled denim jeans and a plaid flannel shirt and loafers on her feet. She looks rather homely but what do I expect for 3:00 in the morning. Her eyes are big, beautiful sapphire blue with a look of sincerity beaming through. Her long strapped black bag dangles from her shoulder as she rushes to meet me at the door.

"Come in, please," I say.

She nods her head and I immediately show her to Antwone.

Rosy has a way with children and Antwone responds very well to her. She shows me where I had made my mistake and I smack my forehead because I was inserting the tip of the IV upside down that is why it wasn't dripping. I feel so stupid.

After time things ease off and the many conversations with my youngster make me realize that I have things under control. Change of life's circumstances can seem like a hindrance, but I realized the hindrance often comes from self. I had visualized things in my head being a hill to conquer. I had exaggerated it all promoting this catastrophe, and truthfully once I had things under a routine it became easy. My stress level decreased and I felt confident.

The SSI that I am receiving for Antwone and my savings combined I have to penny pinch for us to survive each month. The doors to Anonymous had to remain closed while I tended to the boys. Trying to run and promote my business, be a care provider, be a woman, is putting a lot on my once half-empty plate. A social worker, Mrs. Loretta, calls to say that she'll be coming to visit to talk with Antwone and me. I am a little embarrassed to have her come because my refrigerator is damn near bare. I can't keep up with housekeeping, the boys, grocery shopping, laundry, school; I tell you if I had hair I would be pulling it out. These demands that have been bestowed upon me are backbreaking. So backbreaking that when Mrs. Loretta came to sit and talk with me in the kitchen I became emotional in front of her, unexpectedly. I became a water bucket of tears. I started telling her about how stressful I've become. Mrs. Loretta extends her pallid hand up to her thin pinkish lips and scratches her throat that stretches like a giraffe like she has cat hair stuck in it or something. I don't catch on right away that she may be parched. I just keep on flapping my gums, until it finally registers.

I tap my forehead, "Oh, Mrs. Loretta, would you like something to drink?" I ask.

"Yes, please."

I raise my lethargic body from my chair and open the refrigerator halfway so that she can't see that it is bare. Lord, I don't want DYFS coming knocking on my door assuming that I am not feeding the boys. I pour her a medium-sized glass of cranberry juice and put the container back in the refrigerator and sit back down.

Out of the blue, Mrs. Loretta slides a five-dollar bill in front of me. She catches me off guard, as the look is evident on my face.

"Normally, we aren't supposed to give money, but in your case I feel compelled to."

Still I am stumped.

"Um, I don't understand," I say as I stare at the five-dollar bill. "Why are you giving me this?"

"Ms. Love, I know that this is a touchy situation you're in. I applaud you for taking your nephews in. Please, forgive me for prying but I notice your refrigerator is bare."

I know my face is red. I am so embarrassed. I lift my hands up. "Mrs. Loretta, allow me to explain. I don't need your money I just haven't had time to go grocery shopping. I can't seem to catch a break. Please take your money back. I appreciate your generosity but I am fine. We are fine."

Mrs. Loretta pulls the five dollars back and slips it in her purse.

"I hope I didn't offend you." She cracks a smile. "I'm just smitten with your nephews." She laughs softly.

I nod to acknowledge what she has said. But actually, I am a bit annoyed by her referring to the boys as my nephews as I consider them my sons.

"Antwone is a very precocious child. I can easily see that. He is the kind of child that knows why, when, and what he wants. It somewhat amazes me that he is only seven years old. But, what I would like to know is how much does he know about his sickness. The reason I ask is because he doesn't show any signs of resentment, sorrow, and any type of emotional distress that someone in his situation would display. Don't get me wrong I'm not trying to throw up any red flags for alerting. I'm just stressing what I've observed," she says, as she raises the glass and takes a sip of juice.

I absorb her words before responding.

"Well, I really don't know how Antwone or Tyree, for that matter, should be reacting to everything that has changed in their lives—my life. It's like; as long as they are together they gain strength from each other. It is difficult to explain in words, but I see it and truthfully I wonder how they manage to smile, laugh, and horseplay through all the ruckus of life. With their mother dying I thought taking them in would be the worst thing ever, but it has actually been a blessing. They are coping. And it may not be displayed in a way that you or I can see it; all I can think of is that they get some of their strength from the memory of their mom, as well as through their strong belief in God. Some things can't be explained and I guess this is one of 'em." I nod my head, content with my response.

Mrs. Loretta has a blank look on her face, and it is quite obvious that to her everything has a reason for its actions. With Antwone not displaying his makes her seek to analyze, instead of just letting things be as God wants them to be.

I miss going to Anonymous. I mean, I am not used to not

working. The days are longer with nothing to do but eat, sleep, watch TV, talk on the phone to the doctors, the pharmacist, Mr. Clyde, about my prescriptions, and run errands with Antwone and Tyree. My life is put on pause and anything that I want for me has to wait.

Out of the blue, Sin shows up wanting to see his boys. I pause before buzzing him in, reason being I have to look out for the best interest of the boys, and right now Sin has other things that are top priority to him, and his boys aren't it.

The phone rings and the doorbell buzz simultaneously. I answer the phone and then run to answer the door. Sin steps in. He looks like walking death. I point to the bedroom letting him know that is where Antwone is.

"Hello."

"Hi Avery."

The voice doesn't sink in until I listen to the words very carefully. "Xavier?"

"Yes, were you expecting someone else to be calling you?"

"No, no…I, I. How are you?"

"I'm fine; no need to complain even if I wasn't, now, is it."

"I guess not." I tilt my head to the side, pondering.

"I'm sure you're tied up right now, but I was wondering if you had about an hour to spare, today. I would love to take you out for a bite to eat. I can arrange for a nurse to come to your home and watch the boys, if you'd like. Something tells me you need some Avery time."

So quickly tears flood my eyes. I wonder if Xavier had been talking to Mrs. Loretta 'cause I was just telling her that sometimes I would love to have a moment to myself.

My voice cracks. "I don't know what to say Xavier." Tears roll down my face because I feel so overwhelmed. I wipe them away with the back of my hand. "Um, I would love to get out for a bit, but the boy's father just stopped by and I can't leave them alone with him. I, I, don't trust him. I may have to wait, but thanks for thinking of me. It means a lot."

"Avery, allow me to comfort you."

"What do you mean?" I ask quite puzzled.

"Well, let me bring comfort to you. I'll be more than happy to keep an eye on the boys while you go to the spa and get pampered. What do you say?"

"I, I, don't know what to say, again. Xavier, why are you doing this?"

"Avery, I see so much in you. You are such a loving and vibrant woman. And the way you are with those boys just fills my heart. I just want to do something to remind you that you are special and valued."

I completely lose it and start sobbing on the phone.

"Are you okay? Did I say something wrong, Avery?" Xavier's voice sounds alarmed.

"No, no, you are a very sweet man. No one has ever said such kind words to me before, except my friend Johnnie. Thank you."

"I will set everything up and I'll call you when I am on my way, okay."

"O-okay," I say in a hoarse voice.

After we hang up, I stand in place because I feel so blessed to have a friend.

27

"Are you awake, *Mommee*? Mommee, are you sleeping?" Antwone asks.

"No, no, I'm awake." I slide my hands down my face in the pitch darkness.

"You wanna talk, Mommee?"

"Okay."

"Mommee, I just want you to know that I love everything you've done for me. You do everything that I ask of you, even being my nurse."

"I know."

"Mommee, I know that you be tired of taking care of me, riding me around, feeding me, washing me up and stuff, but you do it anyway. Mommee, I want you to know that I really appreciate it all."

I lower my head and bat back the tears that I feel stirring inside.

"I know. You don't have to say that to me. I already know," I say, as my eyes drip tears.

"Yeah, I do. I want you to be happy, Mommee. Take care of yourself and my brother. Be happy."

"I will...we will." My voice cracks with tears easing down my face.

Please...please Lord, please, not tonight? Please don't take my baby...nephew from me?

I can't help but to think the worst.

"Stop talkin' about things you wanna do. Okay, Mommee. Stop that. Start doin' it. Just do it. I love you and Tyree."

How does he know that? I never spoke of things I miss and want to do, I think to myself.

"We love you, too."

We both are silent and go back to sleep.

The next morning I am paranoid hoping that Antwone didn't leave me. And he didn't. Tyree gets himself to school. I pretty much have my routine of getting up early to tend to Antwone. We listen to the television, mostly cartoons. I clean up while he sleeps. And when he wakes I feed him baby food, let him sip on some Ensure, and we talk until he gets tired. Lately he's been complaining that his stomach is bothering him and I rub his tummy to soothe him.

I continue to change his sheets, change his diaper and gown, and give him his little birdbaths. His weight is dwindling by the day. All I can do is pray. I get in touch with Sin and suggest that he come to see his kids. Around noon there is a buzz and I answer the intercom and it's Sin. I buzz him in. As soon as he rings my door and as I open the door I feel a sense of panic inside of me. Sin says his usual hello and heads straight for the living room. I know that it is difficult dealing with this but you have no choice. I try not to meddle and give Sin time to decide that he needs to be in the bedroom with his son, but Sin doesn't budge so I have no choice but to speak my mind. "Why are you in here when your son is in there." I point my forefinger. "Go in there and be with your son!" My tone is sharp, as well as the cutting of my eyes. I have very little tolerance for Sin as it is. His blue-black skin glosses with sweat. He has lost even more weight and he looks like he smells—funky. I am not trying to understand a damn thing. His body craves for drugs and he continues to feed his habit. Like life doesn't matter. His child, my nephew, is dependent on morphine to keep him comfortable, to keep him out of pain. I lose full control because reality sinks in.

"It is not fair!" I snap. "My nephew is in their fighting for his life and you…you." I have no more words so I just walk away.

Sin finally goes into the room, sits beside the hospital bed, slowly reaches in to wrap his fingers with Antwone's hands, and lowers his head sobbing uncontrollably. Antwone slowly turns in the direction of his dad and says, "Daddy, get yourself together. Get it together." Sin's sobs echo throughout my apartment. Snot is running from his nose. His eyes are bloodshot red. His body is shaking. My hands stroke my lips, eyes tearful, and I nod my head. *Yes. Talk to him, son. Tell him.* This is an emotional day for Sin because mostly every visit since Antwone has been bed-ridden he has not been able to face him. The pain is too great and the drug addiction has too strong of a hold on him. He is weak and I am not sure how he will be once everything—.

Sin stays for about an hour and then he tells Antwone that he will be back tomorrow to see him. As he heads for the door, he turns and just stares at me with a look of utter fear upon his face. There is silence between us as he exits.

That same day during the evening hours Antwone is laying still and then he says, "Single-aunty…Mommee, I gotta go to the bathroom."

I turn and look at him peculiarly, "Well, go in your diaper."

"No…I wanna go to the bathroom," he adamantly says.

I stand in place, trying to picture him achieving what he

requested. Antwone has been in bed for so long that I don't know what to expect. His body is down to a skeletal frame. His head is the size of a grapefruit and it is the heaviest on his body. I stare at him with such admiration and I help my little soldier up as he leans on me with his emaciated frame, crooked foot, slightly crooked mouth, blind self, and we take baby steps to the bathroom. It feels like eternity walking slowly to the bathroom. His head leans to the side because it is so heavy and his body so, so, so very thin. But we make it to the bathroom. My eyes flood so proud. I help him sit on the toilet. I lift him up and wash his hands as we head back to the bedroom for him to lie back down. This is a profound moment for me. A moment I will never, ever, ever, ever forget! I will always use this moment as my boost of confidence because it has taught me that even though my nephew is seven years old he has a strong will to defeat his ailment. I help him back in bed and throw my hands up to God to give Him praise.

Soon after Tyree walks in from school and I tell him the great news.

By the next day, Antwone can no longer talk. I truly have to make myself look at him because he is withering away. I am broken inside. But I rehearse his words and I stand strong and do what I have to do to keep him comfortable. It is most difficult.

I call Xavier but I get no answer so I leave a message stating that I have to cancel the spa because there is no way I can leave Antwone. I start to prepare dinner when my buzzer goes off.

"Hello."

"Avery, it's me, Xavier."

"Come in."

28

I decide to stop at Anonymous on my way to Mr. Clyde's to get a refill on my prescription. My appointment at the spa is at 4:00. As soon as I lay my handbag on the counter the phone rings. I flinch because my nerves are frazzled. I guess Xavier was right—I do need to relax.

"Good afternoon, Anonymous, Avery speaking."

There is silence.

"Hello."

"Avery...Avery Love, please?" the man says in a raspy voice.

"This is she." I cut my eyes down to the floor and stare at a fuzz bunny so I kneel down to pick it up. "Who's calling?"

"Avery...Is this the same Avery that used to be a paralegal at Bruman & Prescott law firm?"

"Yessssss. Who is this?"

"It's me, Therron."

My eyes light up, so surprised to hear from one of my old flames.

"Therron! How have you been! What has it been like forever since I've heard from you? How did you get my number?"

"Yes, I know. Avery...I heard that you started your own business. A friend of mine is a regular at Anonymous. I wasn't sure if it was you. I just took a chance to find out. Avery, listen I'm calling." He coughs a rattling sound.

"Therron, are you okay?" I ask.

"Oh, Avery."

"Is everything all right with you?"

He exhales hard through the receiver.

"Therron," I say, standing still as I hear a beeping sound in the background. "Therron," I repeat.

"Ye-s. I need to talk to you."

"How's California?!"

"Avery...listen!"

I remain quiet. I can hear him breathing erratically.

"Listen, I need to tell you something. Can you come see me at Englewood Medical Center?"

"Sure," I say, with a bewildered expression outlining my face. "Are you okay? Do you need anything?"

"Ye-s, just for you to come, today."

I glance at my wristwatch. It's 3:05; there is no way I am going to make it to the spa on time. My lips press together. "O-kkay. I'll leave now." I slowly put the phone back in its cradle. I lift the phone back up to call home, but then I place it back and leave out.

I hop into my Ford Five Hundred and head for Rt. 4 in deep thought as to what Therron could possibly want. I hope the man is not deathly ill.

I park my car in the hospital's parking lot and enter through the lobby and stop at the information desk.

"Good morning, ma'am, Therron Bolton," I say.

The middle-aged woman hands me a pass for the fifth floor, room 523 is written in bold. I take the elevator to the fifth floor and follow the arrows to room 523. I look in the small window and see one bed occupied, nearest the window. A fairly older man, but I don't see Therron so I stop one of the nurses making her rounds.

"Excuse me, Ms., but can you direct me to Therron Bolton's room. This pass has 523, but the man I see in that room doesn't resemble him."

The cashmere-white-skinned woman checks some papers on her counter and confirms that that is Therron's room. I try to restrain from showing any emotion. But I am shaking in my shoes.

As I am about to enter the room the same woman scratches her throat and points for me to look closely at the door. My eyes scroll down and my heart skips a beat as I read in bold letters: Acquired Immunodeficiency Syndrome. I drop my face in my palms and shake my head in disbelief. I hear the same lady scratch her throat, which makes me look her way. She points to the cart that has disposable gowns, masks, and latex gloves and advises me to use them. So I do. Before entering I take one deep breath, say a little prayer, and walk in. As the tip of my Charles David pumps step in I swear I want to snatch everything off and run as far away as I possibly can, but I don't.

My left foot steps in and then the right. I see these long yellow-looking fingers resting alongside this lean frame. The fingers raise and direct me to come in. So I ease in with caution trying to hold back the tears that are stirring up inside me. My feet move slowly as I can hear him breathing heavily. Still, he is not familiar to me. He looks like he has aged into a man in his seventies. His frame is skeletal so I turn and quickly look away. I swallow. Then I raise my head and greet him with a smile. God, it hurts to even smile. His skin is paper thin with red veins that resemble bait for a fishhook. Through his translucent skin that stretches over his face his eyes are embedded in their sockets. God, he looks permanently spooked. My eyes stroll back down to his fingers and his nails are brittle and broken and grayish with discoloration. They look like they can fall off at any minute and shatter to the floor into dust. His lips are fever blistered with sores and dry blood. Inside I am full of panic wondering who he is and why am I here. He motions those feeble fingers for me to come closer. I stand a few feet away from the foot of the bed and I wait for him to speak.

"A-Avery," he says.

"Ye-sss. How do you know my name?"

I see his cheekbone rise into a painful smile.

"It's me," he catches his breath. "Therron."

I am in complete awe. Honestly, I don't quite know what to say or how to react. So I turn away.

"Um, why am I here, Therron?"

He motions his thin fingers against his ghostly pale skin as we listen to the beeping sound of one of the machines he is hooked up to. I see he is being fed intravenously. I see his urine bag is nearly full with red liquid. He motions his fingers for me to come closer. And I remain still.

"I needed to see you. To tell you face-to-face that I didn't know." A tear leaks from his deepened socket and drools down the side of his face onto the thin collar of his gown and melts into its fibers.

"Know what?"

He speaks in a whisper, "Know that I was sick." His forehead wrinkles, making him look distressed.

I cut to the chase, "Therron, why did you want to see me?"

His eyes roll in the back of his head, "I wanted to…" His breathing becomes erratic. He heaves. He hyperventilates. I step back to get ready to call for help, but then his whole body shudders as if he is going into convulsions. I turn to rush to the door and he bellows with full force, "No!" I flinch as I hear him yell. Then he lowers his tone, "No, please, just…."

I step back and move closer and he slowly turns his head staring me dead in my face. His eyes sink deeper into his head and his body shudders again, and then shuts down. His mouth stiffens as if he had a stroke. The machine echoes that annoying beeping sound and a charge of feet bum rush in. I step backwards and exit out of the room. My hands grip the rail out in the hall and I start to hyperventilate. Tears flow quickly down my face. My whole body feels queasy.

My life feels like it is slipping from underneath my feet. I make my way to the water fountain to sip some water and I breakdown right then and there. Slowly, I make my way to the elevator, out to the lobby, and through the doors as my eyes strain to find my car. Once I spot it, I hurry to get inside and I look myself in the mirror and lose all control. I slap the steering wheel several times, punch the dashboard, stomp my feet, backhand the rearview mirror almost breaking it, and scream at the top of my lungs. My trembling hands cover my mouth. I start to gag and I quickly open the driver's door and empty myself out onto the ground. I cannot stomach all of this. Not now. I adored that man, I say to myself. I massage my distressed face. *All these years. All this time. How could this be happening? Why now? Why fuckin' now? I have the boys to take care of. I have me to take care of. I have Anonymous to take care of. But who is going to take care of me. Who? I can't....*

I put the key in the ignition and drive off with a cluttered mind and a punctured heart. I return home to be with my family.

29

The next morning my world of yesterdays is just that, "words of appreciation." The inevitable has not occurred, but it hits me hard that Antwone is a mute. There is no sound, no ability to make sounds come out of his mouth. No laughter. And what hurts me the most is that I cannot tell if he was afraid when it happened or not. He had no reaction, more of an acceptance. I can't tell anything. But the fact that in his time of yesterday he took the time to leave me with words that would encourage me to continue to strive for happiness—that was the best gift anyone has ever given me. It was an unselfish act of love. Antwone was generous and feeding my soul with his last words and the fact of how much he acknowledged all that I had done and still am doing even though he could no longer speak or see. I feel myself breaking.

The phone rings.

"Hello."

"Ms. Love, please?" a screechy woman's voice says.

"Speaking."

"Hello, Ms. Love, my name is Anita Freeman and I am calling from Visiting Home Health Aide Services."

"Yes."

"The social worker, Mrs. Kramer, informed me that you were interested in a home health aide for your little boy named Antwone. I heard wonderful things about him. Well, this young lady named Morning Glory is interested in helping you care for Antwone. I can schedule her for two hours per day, if you'd like."

I pause. "Sure, that would be helpful."

"When would you like her to start?"

"At your earliest."

"How's about tomorrow?"

"Tomorrow is just fine."

"Great! I'll give her your address and phone number and she'll call you with the time she will arrive."

"Okay. You have a great day."

"You, too."

We hang up and I am thrilled to have someone willing to help me care for Antwone. I will be able to run errands for at least two hours. The first thing I can do is go grocery shopping. Ma'am taught me how to make a meal out of a little. And that was what I had been doing. The boys weren't starving and I hope Mrs. Loretta didn't get the wrong impression.

The next day, I receive a call from this young woman who seems to have a pleasantness to her. Later, around 11:00 a.m. she rings my buzzer and I let her in. I answer the door in a pair of frayed jeans and a faded T-shirt. She has a mocha complexion, with beautiful doe eyes, a thick frame dressed in some white scrub pants, a colorful pediatric scrub top, and some white Nursemates shoes on her feet, and the friendliest disposition. I must admit I am a little leery at first. She is a stranger. I take her in the bedroom and introduce her to Antwone. I show her around the place so she will feel welcome. Morning gives Antwone a sponge bath, changes his gown and puts on a fresh diaper, feeds him, makes sure he drinks some Ensure, moves his legs, and sits and watches cartoons with him as he listens. I feel he is in good hands. Morning doesn't appear to be nervous or emotional in his presence. But deep down I am sure it is difficult for her to witness his state. *I wonder if she has children of her own?*

While Morning is here I run out to go check on Anonymous and since Whole Foods Market is down the street I pick up some groceries. I return home with several filled recyclable green bags.

The next day, Morning comes back and stays for her two hours, and I am able to breathe and regain a moment to myself. I indulge in Jenny Downham's book, *Before I Die*, and a cup of Celestial Seasonings peppermint herbal tea.

November 2nd brings me to a screeching halt. Morning arrives and stays for her two-hour shift. I don't have any errands to run so I hibernate in the living room until close to the time for Morning to leave. I check on Antwone as she is giving him a sponge bath.

"Ms. Love, I think Antwone has a fever," she says.

I rush over to him and touch his forehead and he is burning up. As soon as I am about to check his temperature the phone rings.

I rush to answer it.

"Hello."

"Hello, Ms. Love, this is Maribel. I am hearing impaired. I am on my way to check on Antwone."

I sigh deeply.

"Great. He has a fever. I was about to check his temperature."

"I'm close to your house. I'll be there soon."

"Okay."

I hang up the phone and go back to Antwone.

"Morning, you can go ahead on home. I'll take it from here.

Thank you."

"You sure? I, I, can stay if you'd like." she says a little concern.

"I'm sure." I smile to ease her nerves. Minutes later, the buzzer wails and I rush to answer it.

"Hello."

"It's me, Maribel."

I buzz her in and go to open the door.

This brunette-haired, white nurse comes fast-pacing it to the door.

"Hi, I'm Avery. Come in."

"Maribel."

I escort her to Antwone. She checks his blood pressure. His vitals. I even catch her sniffing his sheets to see if they reek of piss. I cut my eyes at her because that was somewhat rude. What she think—I going to leave the child in soiled sheets. Immediately, I grow not to like her. She doesn't say much at first, but when she does I have to listen very carefully to her speak.

"He has a 103 degree temperature." she says.

My eyes widen and I swallow hard.

"He will possibly *die* within twenty-four hours or so." She says rather nonchalantly. *Where has the sensitivity gone?*

I ignore her.

Roll my eyes.

Suck my teeth.

Press my lips tightly together.

Wave my hand behind her back.

Cross my arms about my chest.

I tune her voice out like a small child. I make noises in my head. My eyes wander around the room because I don't want to hear her foolishness. How insensitive to tell me news of the sort. Who does she think she is, God? Every other week I keep hearing from the staff at Children of Tomorrow that he isn't going to make it. How many times have they said that to me! Too many. I am sick of hearing the foolishness. Sick, sick, sick! Finally she leaves and says that she will call me later. I don't want to hear from her. I don't care to hear from her if she is going to be talking this craziness. Antwone is going to be fine. JUST FINE!

To preoccupy my mind I start tidying up the living room, then the kitchen, and then the bathroom. I turn the radio up hoping it will take me away for a moment or two. I need to distract my mind from that crazy talk. While I am mopping the kitchen floor I hear the phone ring.

"Hello."

"Hi, Avery, it's me Xavier."

"Hi," I say dryly.

"Is everything okay?" he asks.

"Um…." I breathe deeply. "Well, one of the nurses came by and she is telling me that…that…that… Antwone is, um." My voice starts to crack. "She says that Antwone is not going to make it." A tear scrolls down my face.

"Trust in God, Avery. Don't lose your faith. Just trust in God."

I sniff. "Okay," I say in a whisper as I place the phone back in its cradle.

In-between me cleaning I go in and check on Antwone to see if his fever has reduced. The radio is surround-sounding. I stand by his hospital bed and I gaze at his face—a child's face that's so full of life. So destined to be somebody great in this world. A leader. I see a leader. I reach out to touch his hand and it is warm. I lean in to give him a kiss on his cheek and I inhale a smell of death, hot, stinky, rotting death. It smells of waste inside out. I hold myself up. Literally wanting to crumble as I stand and undrape his history. I shut my eyes from the imagery. I turn my head from the sight. It repulses me. He is just a little boy. So fragile. So loving. So wise. A little boy. A little black boy. A seven year-old little black boy. I repeat in my head. My eyes greet the ceiling and I frown, why are you doing this to me? I don't want Antwone to hear me speak to God in this tone. I want him to remember me as kind. Why? I massage my face. Pinching my skin 'cause it hurts so damn bad watching him. Watching him slip away day after day after day. Why? What can I do to change Your mind? Look. I sniff in the snot that runs from my nose. LOOK, I am already sick. I am fighting every day to survive, but I will take on this little boy's pain and suffering and dying so that he can live a full life. Take me instead, please? Please? I whisper.

I gawk at his frame. I push the button on his cassette to give him a dosage of morphine. I gaze again. His bones I can touch as they poke out with a thin layer of skin to coat. I swallow. I see his ribcage as if it were being dissected for laboratory experimentation on bone marrow. His navel sunk in like a deflated basketball. His legs are like twigs. His knee bones touch. His feet blister with a few bedsores even though I constantly rubbed them down with Vaseline to keep his soles soft. His neck, long and thin as if a giraffe. His head bloated with liquid. His eyes glossy and dead. One is shut and the other remains open—his eyelashes curled and thick. His lips are chapped and white. His cheeks are round and full. His hand is still warm and welcoming and his beautiful skin so dark and flawlessly glowing.

I stand still and I hear him breathing. I lean in to hear him breathing. I place my face against his lips to feel him breathing. I want to wrap him up and drive far away so that God won't find him. My hands claw at my face as I feel my grip pulling away from me. I want to bawl into sobs. I curl in a ball and rock the pain away. Ma'am rocked and hummed a gospel hymn. I grab a chair and I rock, crisscross my arms about my bosom and I rock. And I hum and then lip-sync as I hear Amy Grant's voice in my head singing, "Imagine." and as much as I don't want to imagine it is evident that something is about to transpire. I gaze at Antwone and I strap my arms around my stomach and I massage it so endearingly as if he came out of my womb. I hold it tight, tighter, tighter, gripping it like an elastic band trying to hold on to the feeling of motherhood.

Don't stop breathing! Don't stop breathing! Don't stop breathing! Don't stop breathing! Mommee, needs you! Mommee, needs you! Mommee, needs you! Mom—. I shake my head from side to side. I stare at him. I lean in again and place my face to feel his hot breath evaporate in my skin. To feel combustive heat sweltering his insides. To feel him fight. I lean over his chest and I stare hard as his chest lifts and pause, lifts and pause as if he is hooked to a machine breathing for him.

"Ms. Love, do you want to resuscitate should there be complications?" Dr. Boyd had asked. *"I feel he has fought his fight and if that should come about I feel he should be able to rest in peace. It would be an unselfish act,"* Dr. Boyd said.

"No resuscitation," I said.

"Don't go, you might not make it back in time!" the social worker said.

"I'm looking for a particular outfit," I said.

"What's the occasion?" the salesperson asked.

WHAT'S THE OCCASION!

"Mommee, you can go and pick out my outfit but you can't buy it until after I'm—," Antwone said.

"He needs RITALIN," the Child Study Team said.

"Avery, Sisal wanted me to reach out to you to see if you could help out with Antwone and Tyree. I, I, know you don't have any children of your own. We just need someone we can trust. Someone already established. With your business and all we can't seem to find anyone else, reliable," Fever said.

"Avery, I regretfully have to advice you that you are HIV-positive," Dr. Fulmore said.

"No, no, no...stop, stop, stop, my unborn baby, my dying husband, pleasssssssseee!" I said.

"Avery, pack your thangs and be out by twelve. You have to venture out intuh the world of opportunity." Poppa said.

"He will possibly die within twenty-four hours," Nurse Maribel said.

"Mommee, I don't wanna die," Antwone said.

"Twenty-four hours!"

"Fifty-fifty," The surgeon said.

"NO, NO, NO, not Johnnie! Not my Johnnie!"

I come to.

Antwone's breathing is erratic. His chest heaves up and down, pause, up and down, pause. I stand to my feet and get close so very, very close just to see that sunken stomach rise. And I sigh so deep that I feel like my heart dropped to my feet. I cover Antwone from his neck down and I turn and walk out of the room for what seems like a few minutes to finish tidying up.

It has to be close to three o'clock and the radio is still flowing soulful tunes and then the strangest thing occurs. I hear these four young black men singing, "It's so Hard to Say Goodbye to Yesterday," and at the very moment something in me says go back in the room. So I do.

I pull the sheet from his neck down to his legs and his legs are the color purple. My eyes bulge and blink in disbelief. Oh, God! I panic to the four walls, to the floor, to the ceiling. Oh, God! I hear him breathing erratic, again. His chest lifts up and down, up and down, up, pause...pause...down, up and down, and then it stops. There is no more erratic breathing. No more up and down. Just pause. I stand in inaudible silence as I stare at his lifeless body. His deep dark skin. I hear his laughter in my head. I see his smile in my head. I feel his touch wrapped around my waist. I feel his kisses on my face. I feel his love in my heart, down my spine, and smothering me into smiles. I smile as I gaze at him as still-life art. A realistic portrait of cancer in its youngest...most vulnerable stage. I witness a child dying. I stand there giving my moment of silence as he lies still. I wipe the snot that drools out of my nostrils. Wipe my bloodshot-red eyes. I swallow that rock that is stuck in the middle of my throat. And I pick myself up, dust myself off, and I stagger to the phone like a drunken wino.

I pick up the phone and I call Nurse Maribel. I hang up. I pick up the phone and call Sisal. I call uncle Kye and his, fiancée, Lee, who is a Licensed Practical Nurse, answers the phone sounding a bit under the weather. And I say, "Um, he's gone." All I heard her say is, "I'm on my way!" and I hang up. I call Sin and hang up. I call and leave a voice mail for Wisdom and I hang up. I sit there and stare into space listening to the radio as Antwone listens with me.

Finally, Lee arrives and she gives me a hug. She goes in the room and she stares at Antwone.

"Look, his lips are blue. Poor baby."

Then it dawns on me, how am I going to tell Tyree? Who's going to break the news? Who's going to get him from YMCA? Oh, my goodness, who's going to tell that little boy that his brother has died? Lee volunteered to go pick Tyree up. I say, okay. It will give me time to think of a strategy.

For it to be the beginning of November the climate feels like spring. The day is pleasant enough that a jacket is not needed. Everyone comes to pay his or her respects. People stand in front of the building, some in the halls, some in the loft reminiscing about a brave little black boy.

"Avery, when do you wanna go get his outfit?" Sisal asks.

"Well, Ant, told me that I couldn't get it until after," I say with watery eyes.

Sisal hands me his credit card and I ask Wisdom if she wouldn't mind riding with me. We drive to Passaic to Barry's and as I walk in the looks on the people's faces are like they know without it being spoken. I give the receipt to the salesperson and she quietly goes to get the outfit. She extends her condolences and we leave out.

When we arrive back at the house people are still sitting up in the loft in disbelief. Everyone is very supportive. As I look among them all I see Xavier walking through. I meet him halfway and he grabs me and swallows me in his arms and smothers me with his warmth.

"Are you okay?" he asks.

"No...no," I say.

"You will be," he says, as he pierces my eyes with his. I cut my eyes and I see Lee with Tyree with his backpack on his shoulders and a baffled look on his face. Antwone is upstairs lying in bed and Tyree goes up to see him. Everyone is still as they hear his footsteps climbing the stairs. With his hard bottom shoes his steps sound like snaps of one's fingers.

The next day I call to have the hospital bed, and any medication, needles, and anything else that doesn't belong to me picked up. I contact Booker Prayer Funeral Home to make sure all the arrangements are intact: the casket, the flowers, his attire, his haircut, and the programs. After I take a long drive and let my thoughts have a moment to absorb all that has occurred in my life. It is mind-boggling, to say the least.

November 4th, Antwone's obituary is in the Herald News. Even with seeing his name in print it still doesn't seem real. But when I step in my bedroom it becomes as real as it can get.

Monday, November 6th, I have two scheduled viewings for Antwone. A black limo comes to pick up the family to take them to the funeral home in Montclair. I prefer to ride alone. There are many who come from out of state, from Children of Tomorrow, from the YMCA, PS 117, friends, strangers who heard that a little boy died in their neighborhood. It is a flock of people coming to pay their respects to Antwone, unlike Johnnie's wake and funeral. There were only two: Javis Cline and myself.

Tuesday, November 7th, around 12:00 p.m. the funeral is to start. It is raining like cats and dogs. The day is gloomy. I wear a fudge-colored pinstripe pants suit with a pair of chocolate brown shoes. Everyone is filtering in. I turn to my right and I see Sin standing by the white casket in a black blazer. He spots me looking at him and walks near me and asks, "How come you so calm?" I sarcastically reply, "Because I was there, so therefore I have no regrets. My heart and conscience is at peace." I look him up and down and walk away.

I greet folks coming in with nods and smiles—just what Antwone would want me to do.

The service begins and my cousin, Nigel, reads a scripture passage. My uncle Billy does the acknowledgement, a poem, and the obituary. Pastor D.J. Neville's does the eulogy. He's a friend of Sisal's. But I realize that when Pastor Neville's gets up to speak about Antwone he doesn't know a thing about him. There are many times that I want to interject and spread some love of Antwone around, but I don't. Selfishly I keep him all to myself.

There is no doubt in my mind that Antwone went to heaven—no doubt. He was a shrewd little boy. Uh-huh. So shrewd that during his stay at Children of Tomorrow he managed to collect toys for his brother because he knew that he would not be around for their next Christmas. Yep. He planned things out very meticulously. I always said he had been here before.

After the funeral service everyone drove with their lights on to Laurel Grover Washington Cemetery in Totowa, to lay my nephew to rest. It is still raining, but harder as everyone stands with their full-size black umbrellas to cover them from God's tears. After, we all go back to my place for refreshments.

Days after burying Antwone I find myself in this hollow hole of darkness. I think I am losing my mind. I hear little voices, children playing above my head, shoes clicking. I hear children laughing and giggling. Every morning I drive to the cemetery to apologize to Antwone for not dying before him. I feel much guilt. I am not his biological mom but I felt a motherly bond with him, more so than Tyree. Maybe because we spent so much time together. We got to know each other. We communicated and were very open about how we felt about life, death, and the world itself. All of this happened with a seven year-old. It was an experience that touched me so deep. I began to lose my way.

Sisal brings Tyree over in my distressed state. I haven't eaten all day. I am losing weight. I look awful. I get up and get dressed and watch from the window as Tyree plays with a remote-controlled car his brother left him. I see Uncle Diggs standing outside with Sisal and Tyree so I go out to say hello. Tyree is so excited when he sees me exiting out of the building.

"Single-aunty, the jeep had moved," he says.

"What?" I ask.

He lifts up a white jeep. "This remote control jeep that Ant gave me. It moves without batteries."

I look at him and wrinkle my forehead because I think it is cruel to pretend like that. I am not amused.

"Didn't I tell you not to say anything, boy?!" Sisal says.

I look at both of them and frown until I see Uncle Diggs eyes full of tears streaming down his face. *I have lost my mind*, I think. I feel woozy so I return upstairs, but before I do I realize a new package of batteries on the ground alongside the box the jeep came in. I turn around and Tyree places the jeep on the ground.

"Look, Single-aunty, look!"

God is my witness, the jeep drives around the parking lot as my eyes widen so big that I have to catch myself from falling to the ground. Tyree is smiling from ear to ear.

"It's Antwone! Single-aunty, its him!" He jumps up and down like he is flying on air. I am so spooked that I run inside, catching my breath before I climb the stairs. Tyree beats me upstairs by taking the elevator with the jeep in his hands. We enter the loft and he places the jeep on the hardwood floor. And the jeep rolls onto the black tweed throw rug in the living room. Then it reverses and rides around the living room. At this point I totally lose it. And I plop on the floor. Tyree rushes to run outside to grab Sisal and Uncle Diggs.

Thereafter, each day around 7:00 o'clock in the morning the buzzer sounds off. And every day I crawl out of bed to answer the intercom, but no one responds. And I crawl back into bed sleeping my life away. I have no energy to eat, bathe, or live. I am at the end of my rope.

The phone rings. I don't answer it. I put the covers over my head until I hear the answering machine pick up.

"Avery, I know that you are there. You haven't been at Anonymous. How do you expect to run your business if you are not open? You are being selfish. Think about the artists who come to Anonymous to get away. They come to share their passions with you. Where are they going to go, Avery? You have to pull yourself up, baby. You have to or you will lose more than you ever bargained. Yes, it's me, Xavier."

30

Within a few days, I receive a call from Sisal but I let the answering machine pick up.

"Avery, how are you doing? Listen, I am calling to say thank you. You have done a wonderful job for a family you had no knowledge of. I can't say thank you enough. I am leaving…we are leaving today."

I lift my head from underneath the comforter. "Yes, Jo-Ruthie, Tyree, and me."

I ball into a fetal position.

"I'm gonna put Tyree on the phone."

"Hi, single-aunty, I just want to say thank you for taking care of me and my brother. It was great living with you. You're the best single-aunty I ever had." In the background I hear Jo-Ruthie. "Bye, Avery."

I curl up small under the comforter and cry so full of emptiness. Everyone I have loved or come to know suddenly disappears out of my life: Poppa and Ma'am, Johnnie, Storyteller, Epidemic, Jewell, Therron, and Antwone. God, why are you doing this to me?! And now Tyree! *How could they just take him away from me so easily? I have grown to love that boy like he was my very own child. How could they be so cruel?*

Why am I so unloved? Why do people just use and abuse me? And discard me as if I am nothing, a nobody? *I hate living! I hate me! I hate life! I wanna die!*

Okay…Lord, Poppa and Ma'am, I'm coming to join you. I laugh out loud. I smack my ear. Stop laughing. Hush up all that noise. Hi Bitty, your mother home? I giggle. I hate Sin, Sin, Sin!

I run half-naked out into the street. I run fast, feeling the cold ground under my bare feet. I start dancing with only a pair of black Victoria Secret's boy shorts on and no bra in the middle of downtown Paterson until two female officers arrest me for indecent exposure.

In the backseat of their patrol car something snaps inside of my mind and me and I go on a rampage. I transform into someone I knew so long ago. Someone I dreaded to become.

The two female officers escort me into the precinct in handcuffs with a denim jacket covering my nudeness. I am fingerprinted. A mug shot is taken and the most humiliating part is that I am put in a holding cell until my arraignment before a judge, which won't be until tomorrow.

I hear the bars clank and I feel like a wounded dog locked in an unwanted cage. I lean my back against the cold concrete and stare at the marked-up walls feeling as though God has saved me from myself. Where would I be if I never ran out of the house? Who would know if I was missing? And would anyone really care? I feel so alone so uncomfortable within my skin. Then I think about Antwone at his last moments of life. And I wonder how he must've felt being diagnosed with cancer, later being paralyzed, then having a stroke, going blind, and then becoming a mute, and probably wishing to have that one last say before it was all said and done.

I feel so blessed because I had a best friend who thought of me on his dying bed. I feel so blessed because there was a little boy who taught me how to be strongest in my weakest moments. Because of a man I once adored swept me off my feet with his charm. All of whom died by the hands of disease, regardless if its cancer, AIDS, or God's will, no one should be discriminated against.

I lift my legs on the dingy mattress and wrap my arms around my knees and hum "Imagine" because I can't even begin to imagine what they are all doing in heaven. It makes me wonder as Antwone had asked: does God have toys in heaven? Wondering if He has toys for all the deprived, little children who had to grow up faster than their years. For the children who never had toys to play with. Even for adults who lived life on the straight and narrow, never even embracing the thought of playtime before business. The ones who are sticklers for work, work, work, thinking they have time to play later. Only to realize life has swept them by as they grow old, wealthy, and lifeless. It makes me wonder if Johnnie, Jewell, Therron, and Antwone, even Poppa and Ma'am, if they are looking down on me right this minute wondering what will come of me. Sometimes I wonder the same. My hands quiver as I smear the tears off my face and ease them down to the soles of my feet as I massage the tension away because they hurt just as I do.

How much can one take?

I've been *spittin' 'em out like babies from age four or five. I've grown, but if truth need be told I am at my wit's end. I can't take any more of these "babies." When Ma'am was troubled she used to say, "I be spittin' 'em out like babies," that would be her woes of life...the voices...the memories of all that cluttered her mind...the anguish...and love loss.* Yes, I truly am my parents' daughter there is no denying that.

Poppa would say, "You gotta talk to Jesus! He'll help through all of your troubles. You can't sit there and wallow in despair. The babies know how to shake you up. They count on you to fall and crumble and crack. Then you'd be no good to yourself or me. Honey, you gots to pull yourself up by the strings and stand tall and strong." And I never knew what he was talking about up till now.

When you're hurting like the pain is going to bleed out your soul. You have to talk, cry, scream, shout, and most importantly you have to bow down on your knees and pray like it is your dying day. Pray my babies, pray. And you spit out your troubles jus' like a woman giving birth for the thirteenth time. You follow what I'm saying. So I have to redeem myself. I have to…to let my spirit rise above all that was trying to stop me in my tracks. All the deaths. All the disease. All the destruction of drugs. The mental illness. All the negativity. I have to stop in the midst of my pain. I have to stop! 'Cause those babies would keep on following me. I have to stop right here in this holding cell. A holding cell. Ain't this a blip? God stopped me in a holding cell. Locking me in so that I can't run anymore. Woo, Jesus! I cackle.

I think about what Xavier had said about those who come to Anonymous to vent, express their woes, expose their passion for the arts. People like me. If they can't be free in the churches. And if they can't be free in the workplace. And if they can't be free within their own families. And if they can't be free with their children. And if they can't be free within the grassroots of their stomping grounds. And if they can't be free within themselves. Where will they go to be "truthful and free" if I become a hermit in my own nest? Where will they go? This is bigger than me. This is bigger than You, and You, and You. It is widespread all over the world. Where will they go with no place to let out those babies? Where?! I'll tell you, six-feet under. It will be babies toppling over babies in small, medium, and large sized caskets. That's where!

No, no, no! My arms swing recklessly cutting up the air.

My fists tremble. My body trembles. My lips quiver. My soul unravels out of its cocoon. Yesssss, I am shaking 'em out of me! I kneel on my knees 'cause I feel my spirit wanting to have a moment with Him. I speak humbly, "Lend me Your ears?" And I get out what ails me before it eats me up.

Can U hear me?
'Cause I really need U to hear me,

You see, I'm ready to climb out of this hole
Try and control my destiny.

I wanna reach within myself
Pulling out everything that thinks the lesser of me
I want U to take me in Your arms and rescue me
Shake me 'til my skin sheds
Eyes bulge out of their sockets
Lips quiver
As the Holy Ghost takes a hold
Of my weary soul,
And tap dances into my life.

"Thanks for listening."

***

Who is she? This woman I've become who slept around to fill the void of loneliness. It seems my mind drifts in many fantasies. This time I'm glad it was not my reality. Just the thought brings tears to my eyes because it goes against everything I stand for. Sweet revenge against my ex Grand will not do me justice. I'm sleeping with the virus every day of my life. Why would I want someone else to live my history? No, that is not me I've come to know and admire. I'm trying to live by example. To teach and tell the truth about my status so that others won't have to suffer by something they never saw coming.

Grand and I shared a moment that was well protected. And as much as I regret to say I didn't tell Grand about me being HIV-positive.

Why? Fear of him rejecting me.

I kid you not; I would *die* before *I* subject another to this life I live. Maybe it sounds like I've just contradicted myself, but this life is a hard life. It's a stigmatized life.

The guilt I feel.

What is left of me is a woman still in search of me. I am not bitter. I am learning how to forgive and move forward. I can't change what has happened to me. But I can continue to live the life that I have. Yes, so much has happened and just as before I stand alone, trying to weather the storms of this life I live. Living with HIV. Living as a black woman who yearns to be loved, liked, and instead of bruised by life.

I question as any other human being who lives a life of loneliness, "When will 'true' love enter my domain?" I dunno.

The guilt keeps pressuring me to call Grand. To tell him the truth, so I do.

I press the ten digits to stretch out the time. Deep down I am praying that he doesn't answer, but he does.

"Hello," he says.

I can hear children in the background.

"Hello," he says again.

"Uh, Hi. It's me Avery. Well, um, there is something I need to share with you. Is this a bad time?" I am hoping he says yes.

"No, go ahead and say what's on your mind."

"Um," I sigh. "Ah, I don't know how to quite tell you this, Grand."

"Tell me what?"

"Ah, well, um, well, ah, I'm…I'm…."

I can hear the little girl saying, "Daddy come play with me."

That hits me deep in the pit of my stomach.

"I'm…Grand, I'm HIV-positive. I…. "

All I hear is, *CLICK!*

***

I dust myself off and resume back to me. The woman I have grown to love. And it doesn't happen overnight. Each day is a new day for me. I pray a lot. I reflect back on the old me and I write in my journal, Sis, about what I expect from the new me. I have to make some changes within myself. I'm still a work in progress.

I return to Anonymous.

The first thing I do is reopen the doors and by Saturday evening a flock of people come gathering in. And it feels so good.

I walk on-stage in my ripped-up Lucky Brand jeans and an H&M black T-shirt with a huge smile painted on my face because living feels good.

"How's everyone doing this Saturday evening? Good I hope! This evening we have the baddest poets here to plant some seeds in our heads. First off, we have a newcomer by the name of—" I pause for a brief moment. I am speechless as I see Xavier walking on-stage. I gather myself and introduce him, as if I never knew him. "Ladies and Gents, let's give it up for the gentleman who refers to himself as, 'The End'."

"Hello," Xavier says. "I want to dedicate this to a woman I

195

admire. I find her very interesting, but I feel the need to allow her to see the deeper side of me. The 'me' who has been hurt and maybe, just maybe she won't feel so alone. Maybe she'll feel the connection that we share, even though she tries to deny that it exists. Maybe?" Xavier takes a deep breath and looks me piercingly in the eyes. God, I feel the connection. I feel it strong, deep in my soul, but I am so afraid to get close to him. To be hurt by another man. I don't think I can deal with another failed moment in my life.

God, please, take him away from me. Please? I'm not ready for this. I'm not equipped for this "relationship" stuff. I'm not. Please? He is a good man and I don't deserve him. Not now. Not yet.

Xavier distracts my thoughts with his deep voice. "My brothers and sisters this piece is called,

Wo-Man   Part 1

Woe is he for she use to make his heart sing,
Dreams of her in the mid-night hour,
Full of hope and power,
To love her unconditionally,
Oh, how he use to love she,

Sweeping he off his manly feet,
Into the arms of her space to keep,
Befriending never wanting it to end,
And she creeps away into the mist of air with another him,
"Farewell my dear"…as she struts into another him's arms,
He bluntly being smacked in his face,
As him entertains the space between her legs,
Engaging in poetry with him,
Huh, makes he want to spit venom in her face,
As he tries to relinquish the thoughts of her,
But can't.…
She used to be his love, his gem,
Shining with a glow of sun,
He thought that he was the only.…
The only one who could make her heart dance?
It is by chance that she was caught off her guard,
Entertaining in her backyard with him,
Sleeping in the willow of him's stream,
Oh, how he dreamt for it to not be true,
Bloodshot red eyes made he realize,

How much she thought of he,

Between their sheets she lies with him,
Intertwine, as she rode him, springing her back to please,
Forward and back, back and forth,
Staying on course as him closed his eyes, wetting his lips,
being captivated by her lovemaking,
Never conceiving, but believing the thought of fornication,
he does,
Realizing what lies in the canal of (their) pussy willow,
Upon his pillow lies a stranger's head,
Within (their) bed disrespect, neglect, and abandonment is fed,
Resenting the thought of the love that was embedded in his heart,
Catching a spark that has been drenched with specks of rain,
Draining his brain to contemplate,

What's next…where did the mistakes begin?
Trust dwindled…love escapes…loss befriend.
Upon his distraught face sketches of what was, is,
and will not be,
Setting he free as he rubs his hands to end,
Walking in a state of distress,
Upon his heart reads, 'damage' temporarily,
Preoccupying his mind with books of self indulgence,
Loving he,
As he love another,
Time is essence,
And he is the essence of love—
Filling his soul with life's experience."

Everyone claps and whistles. I am a bucket of tears as I look at this man, this wonderful man. *God, what is wrong with me?*

Xavier continues to stand in place trying to regain everyone's attention. "Listen, I am not quite through. You see, I have been hurt deeply, but then I had to figure out a way to let go of the pain. To let go of her without being another statistic of a black man being incarcerated. So I sat and really thought about all that burdened me and I, I asked myself, The End, how can you free yourself and love again? YES, I asked myself that question and here is what my spirit said to me,

"REIMBURSEMENT Part 2

Karla Denise Baker

Here he sits peeling back the skin that has hardened,
Within his soul he feels anguish, but soothes his pain diligently,
Closing his eyes as the memories are rehearsed,
Her body being touched upon by him, her other lover,
He was once weak, but now he has regained his strength,
Believing in his heavenly Father to put his hands upon his head,
Oh, how the heat penetrated down to his heart,
Warming he within,
Thoughts came upon as he tore a check from the book,
With his pen he writes "reimbursement" to her,

Here is the repayment for the loan:

The rent/mortgage that we shared,
For the food that was consumed,
For the laundry that she washed,
For the gas that filled the car,
For the luxury of being able to make love to her,
For the times that she consoled,
For the tears that she wiped,
For the smile that she gave,
For the shoulders to lean on,
For the laughs that we shared,
For expressing concern,
For the cares,
For feeling temporary love for her,
For sharing our space with another man,
For giving herself putting it in him's hands,
For kissing, hugging, and believing him's fairy tales,
For achieving the goal of burning he's soul,
For breaking he as his heart crumbled into pieces of misery,
For leaving he behind to conquer his dismay alone,

Here is the reimbursement for setting he free,
Life couldn't be sweeter as he signs the check
towards new beginnings,
Sealing it within the envelope and mailing his past away,
Stamping it with a picture of her for remembrance,
Sighing… then mailing it to her new address,
Reimbursement in full…
As he moves forward in life,

Forwarding his past to its proper receiver,
Waiting for confirmation of his endorsed check,
He is single,
Freeing his mind and body to love again."

I lose complete control of myself, my feelings. I ask God to guide me into the arms of this wonderful man, Xavier Combs III. This man who accepts me for me—HIV and all. This man who helps those like me. I sway my head from side to side, no, no; I cannot afford to let him go because of fear. I won't. I promise you, I won't.

I arrive home a little after eleven; kick off my shoes and plop on the bed when the phone rings. I reach over on the nightstand to answer it.

"Hello."

"Avery. This is Grand. Man, you hit me hard with that. Woman, you really hit me hard. But I must confess something to you."

"Okay." I feel lighter after telling Grand. I feel like nothing can get me down.

"I'm also HIV-positive."

My mouth hangs open.

"You remember that chick I ditched you for?"

"Chocolaty girl. Yeah."

"Yeah, seems chick gotta around. But that is not how I became infected." He pauses. "I got locked up. Yeah, did a bid and during my incarceration I was *gang raped*. Most men won't even share this kind of horrific experience. Funny how I'll share that with you but I couldn't share my status with you. I can talk about it now, but back then I wanted to forget, you know. I didn't know, Avery. I didn't know that I was infected. I did my time and got my life back into proper perspective. I was blessed with a great job as a counselor at the HIDDEN-VICTIM COUNSELING CENTER-HVCC helping those like me. Men who have been raped; whether by molestation, gang rape, or incest.

"Well, at the time I didn't know I was like *them*. I met a beautiful woman and I fell in love. Avery, the messed-up part of this is my wife, well, we are separated now, but I gave it to her and she passed it on to our unborn child. Precious is four. Yeah, life's a bitch. Avery, I couldn't even admit to the men I counsel about my status. I was too embarrassed. And the messed-up part of all of this is that 'we' you and I, both know better and neither would share because of fear. We wanted to be selfish and have a moment of peace inside. Wanting to feel the warmth, the want, the need, to be loved. I miss my wife. I miss her scent, her laugh, and her smile. I feel trapped most of the time, you know. Shit is hard. Man, I'm not the man I used to be, Avery. I've changed a great deal since that *boy* back in the day. I just wanna say I am sorry for hurting you and treating you so badly. I guess *Karma* is a bitch."

"Yep, Grand, I guess *she* is."

31

I'm dying.

32

"I am no longer attracted to you, Avery."

Those very words cut slowly through the white meat of my being.

I sit on the saffron-colored sofa in the living room in a daze reliving *his* words. He used to recite Walt Whitman. He captured my heart, not instantly, but he captured my heart. My eyes wander the walls of my one-bedroom apartment in Montclair, New Jersey, while he lives in *our* suburban home in Upper Saddle River, New Jersey. His words haunt me as I hear his voice so vividly, so abruptly. My fragile heart sinks down to the pit of my stomach replaying it all in my head.

33

I sit here thinking. Thinking about all the women who walk in my shoes at this present moment. How brave they are by releasing their demons. Gosh, I wish I had it in me to be that brave. I bow my head and wipe the tears from my blackened eye, as I grip the banister to lift myself up off the floor. My bare feet are nearly cut by the broken pieces of the ceramic lamp. My balance is wobbly, as my head feels woozy. I can barely see out of my left eye as I head into the guest bathroom. I hear the door squeak open as I flick the light on and squint my eyes from the brightness. I stand before the mirror no longer recognizing myself. Who stares back at me is a woman who I can't even *stomach*. How could you stay? I have no words. I just stare at her...and I ask myself, *would I love him more if he didn't beat me?*

Dry blood stains the sides of my face, from my eyes down to my broken nose and curves and greets my busted lips. Finger imprints color my skin purple almost like a neck choker. It hurts to cry. So I whimper as my body shivers so tired, so very, very tired.

I can't do this...I can't live this...I...can't. I won't.

My eyes stare at the ceiling and I say under my breath, Johnnie, you are my inspiration. You are my guardian angel. You're probably wondering how all of this came about. I don't even know where to start. Where do you start, Johnnie? From childhood to adulthood? I swear I hear a voice say, "Start from when the pain first started. Use me. Use me Avery to guide you." I break down in tears feeling so low. Feeling so empty.

I slowly exit the bathroom and enter my home office hunched over. I turn on my computer and ease myself down to sit and I stare at the computer screen until it hits me. Just like his *iron fists*. POP! SMACK! POW! Something hits me in my spirit and I placed my fingers on the keys and I begin to imagine it all as if it were just yesterday. I shut my eyes tight feeling the pain shoot through my head. My eyes burn. I taste the dry blood against my tongue. I open my eyes and stare at my first sentence.

The pain started when I let go of me.

I nod, as my head throbs. It is a start in the right direction. And I am not looking back. It is time. Once again, it is time to expose myself.

34

Love is blind...

Hellman drags me up the stairwell banging my knees in the hard marble and throws me down to the floor. Thank God it is carpet to support my fall. He yanks the Ashley dresser drawers open and shoves my belongings in the Versace luggage bag. His size twelve feet walk into the walk-in closet and snatches my clothes off the wooden hangers and balls them up and shoves them in until all of my clothes are stuffed and then zips the bag up. Then he grabs another bag and tosses all of my shoes in and grabs me by the wrist as he squeezes it hard and pulls me down the stairs as I trip over my feet and stumble down, tumbling, as my face smacks into the hard flooring nearly chipping my front tooth. He drags me by my wrists and pushes me out the door with nothing but one hundred and twenty dollars to my name and a change of address form in my hands. What happened to the man that was so eager to vow to become my lawfully wedded husband, I wonder. What brought this on? How come the sight of me repulses Hellman? His soon to be wife, Mrs. Hellman Middleton. The renowned fashion photographer. What happened?

I sob as I sit in front of our home. It is dark around 2:00 a.m. as I stagger to my feet, and drag the luggage bags across the gravel, open the door to my Mercedes Benz and set the luggage bags in the passenger seat. My trembling fingers wrap around the steering wheel and my head lowers, so full of dismay. My heart thumps hard as if to burst through my skin. *What happened? What had I done?*

Then is when I hear the sound of a car approaching. Then is when I see this stretch limo driving up to my home. Our home. My eyes don't deceive me as I see pale, toned legs step out and a slim figure stands tall. My eyes literally pop out of their sockets as I see.

The door swings open to 7111 Fullerton Drive as Hellman's arms reach out and whisked *him* up in his arms and swings him around and around as his brunette hair flows in the night air. They look so full of bliss. His lips press against his as they walk in and shut the door. I try to compose myself, but the sharp pain in my chest is unbearable. *How could I be so stupid! Why, why, why...did I let him get away?*

Tears rush from my eyes as I put the key in the ignition, back out of our driveway, and drive to an unknown destination. I am beyond heartbroken. I have *died* because I let my circumstances blind my fate. *I* chose the wrong man. And I am dying a slow and painful death.

Each tear that drips off my chin is a reminder of the chapters of my unfulfilled life. So many opportunities I let fall to the wayside because of Hellman. I wanted to be a devoted wife. I vowed to take care of him. To love him unconditionally. Yes, I felt obligated to live out those sacred vows once we said I do. So why couldn't Hellman? My mind is flustered as the thoughts clutter and my head pounds. My whole world is tumbling down right before my eyes and there isn't a soul that can catch me before I fall flat on my face.

After all I have given up to become a homemaker. I lower my head and then lift up my chin and stare blankly into space as the migraine throbs. I just wail. Where did things go wrong? And how can I make it right, I wonder. How can I regain that youthfulness Hellman once desired? Tears continue to stream down my cinnamon-complected face.

I run my quivering fingers across my scalp and huff as the hot air escapes from my mouth and brushes against my full pouty lips. I wipe the tears that flow from the creases of my brown eyes. Hellman hurt me in the worst way possible—by vindictively seducing him, the notorious whore who loved to indulge in men who did not belong to him. He sought out for the fine and daring bachelors, but for some unknown reason his taste buds were fetching for Hellman. The lean, muscular, and tan-complected man with abs that made him melt in his Marc Jacobs. I wonder what he has that I don't. Even a blind man can see that he has it all: an Empire, looks, body, ambition, and bank. Who am I kidding? He is a self-made millionaire of twenty-five lingerie stores called Teddies. He can buy his way to the top. He is infamous for getting what he wants and he feels no remorse for his actions. I drift in thought. I am hopelessly lost without the man who holds the key to my heart—Xavier.

How did all of this happen? Where had I gone wrong? It is still so very real to me. I brush my quivering hand across my world-weary face wondering how I can right the wrong.

***

I was deliriously baffled when my fiancé spoke with a pokerfaced, "*I am no longer attracted to you, Avery.*" He chose to end our relationship. It took me by surprise because we had never talked about *his* unhappiness. I transformed into a plain Jane; I'll be the first to admit. Apparently, he expected me to be jazzed up with designer wear. I had long stopped wearing makeup because he had long stopped looking at me. I wasn't trying to enhance myself because I had got lost in taking care of him. I came last to me.

My fiancé said that he had met someone else. It hurt just hearing those words but it hurt even more when I found out that the "someone else" was none other than *him*. That tore me in two.

At first it was devastating to accept. Morning and nightfall, I cried like my insides were rotting out. I ached a majority of the time because he was my first, everything. I put a lot of emphasis in trying to please him and not enough in pleasing myself. I was oblivious to what a relationship entailed. Based on my upbringing, it seemed acceptable hearing about Ma'am dealing with having a third party. I thought that was what it was all about when you're in a relationship—giving. Giving when you don't want to give. Giving when it makes you feel sick inside. Giving when you see how much it makes him happy, yet you are miserable. I thought if I learned how to cook his favorite foods, kept the apartment immaculate, and washed his dirty clothes that it meant something. That I would be appreciated, valued, and compensated with unconditional love. But that was not the case.

After a few months of soaking my pillowcase with salty tears, and after a few months of praying and devoting quality time to me and pampering me with some much needed tender loving care I began to feel something. I can't quite put my finger on what. Being single was *unbearable*. It took some getting used to because I had never been totally alone, other than when I was in mother's womb, and after my parents had died. It was emotional, scary, a desolate time in my life. I had to face being unchained and unshackled to a lifestyle that I thought was inadequate. I couldn't cope with the freedom that was handed to me. I fought with my conscience day in and day out, half-starved for the mistreatment that he had delivered. I was trying to somehow reconnect with it hopeful that he would come back and continue his task of punishing me because punishment meant he cared enough to acknowledge me. I yearned for him to devote some of his precious time to making my life a livin' hell. I was immune to dysfunction. It made me stay in my comfort zone because it seemed to fit my life. I was terrified of freedom. I did not know it because I had been held in captivity. Yes, different forms of captivity. Freedom meant I could do as I damned well pleased. I was a vulnerable woman, scarred inside and out from all the dysfunction that had damaged me. Freedom was my worst enemy.

I drifted in thought of the soundtrack on *Waiting to Exhale* with Mary J. Blige singing "Not Gon' Cry" I didn't want to cry, but that was my only outlet. I felt insignificant. I felt like a rock had been dropped on my heart. And when I looked in the mirror I saw it: misery, a hideous, lost soul staring back at me with a grin on her freakin' face. It was a breaking point for me, but not influential enough to get me to the next phase of rebuilding me into a stronger woman. I had relied on him and it left me dependent on something that was harmful. How could I get strong? I didn't know but I knew that I was single. I was a vibrant woman, a woman in her prime, a woman who had been murdered within herself. I didn't know how to handle it. He was all I knew. All I had put much effort in and he just left me for someone new—someone with a slimmer frame, an attractive face and long hair and cashmere-white skin. Someone who opened his legs and invited him in to have some pumpkin pie. I found myself crumbling right before my eyes. I was falling hard. Man, I could most definitely relate to Whitney Houston singing "Why Does It Hurt So Bad" because it hurt like aw hell.

Gradually I gave myself a makeover. I started dressing better. Looking better. I even let my hair grow back. I started wearing makeup again. Men began to glance at me, but I would look away because I was not ready for anyone new. I was just getting used to the new me. And plus, I didn't trust men. They had a habit of loving you and leaving you for the next set of bigger titties or plumper ass. That meant nothing to me because I had finally embraced single and I was lovin' it! But I had to start all over after letting Anonymous go. How naïve could I have been to think that we were going to build together. I couldn't forgive myself. I just couldn't.

***

I adore Xavier Combs III. The man who uttered how much he loved me, but *I* chose to remove myself from his grip and walk into another him's arms. Why? Stupidity! I met someone who shared the same blood as me. A man who lives my history. I felt at home with him—more at peace. How stupid was I. I let a good one get away. Why? Fear. And I settled for him—Hellman Middleton. He is a man who did not sincerely share his heart with me. No. He'd spread himself around. I think he plotted to steal me away from Xavier. Had I known I would have fallen into Xavier's arms and told him how much I loved him. How much he was the chosen one. I wanted *him*. God I wanted him. But I wondered if his love for me would fade with time. If one day he would awake having reservations about our relationship since I was infected and he was not. He deserved better and I could not give him better. I huff. I could only give him tainted *love*. Not better.

Many negative thoughts ran through my head so I allowed myself to be wooed by Hellman. Believing that *we* would share not only the same blood, but also believing that our love would bloom. How wrong was I. Hellman words made incisions deep in my soul. Made me bleed within my skin. Still, I drowned in my own blood. I'd lost me and became submissively wounded as I buckled my knees and clasped my arms around his shins and pleaded for him not to leave me. *What happened to me?* His green eyes stared cold at me, as he stood erect with a nonchalant expression on his distinguishing face. I stared up at him with bloodshot eyes. Begging to be given another chance to right the wrongs. Me. I'd promised to join a gym. I'd promised to buy some new clothes to spruce myself up. I'd promised to visit the salon. I'd promised to take a striptease class. To watch porn. To pleasure him more in the bedroom. I'd promised it all and more, but Hellman showed no interest. It was over just that quickly. And I became undone.

I needed help. Guidance. Protection. And I had neither. Every night I cried because I hated my life. I hated me. That's when I decided it was time to end it all. Cut my losses because life was some hard livin' and I couldn't withstand the pain. I'd rather take my chances and rot in hell.

I had taken some pills. I don't remember what kind. I remember looking at my our picture and vomiting on the floor. I saw an image of Xavier in my head. I'm gonna miss you honey, I thought. For some reason I picked up the phone while lying on the floor. I dialed a number and then I sprawled out on the floor as a woman answered. I dropped the phone and cried so full of agony.

"Hello, hello, hello," the woman said.

"Please, Ms., please say something." I had no words.

"Ma'am what's your home address."

"It's...," I said, and then hung up the phone.

Soon after the police arrived at the house. I remember one officer, a white man opening the refrigerator and finding nothing but a bottle of Beringer 2002 White Zinfandel from my girlfriend Lois's bachelorette party, an aluminum container of red potatoes, broccoli, and corn on the cob with catfish. I was rushed to St. Barnard

University and Medical Center. The police notified my fiancé and he came to the hospital pissed off. He was yelling at me and saying that I needed to get myself together. I needed help and I knew I needed it desperately. He wouldn't listen to me. I needed someone to soothe some of the pain that was eating me up inside. I had had enough of the torment from him. I couldn't deal with the emotional roller coaster I was riding, swerving out of control. I was having nightmares of the sexual abuse, of the physical and mental abuse. I was sinking and I could no longer pull myself up. I needed help.

My fiancé continued on ranting and then he called me *stupid*. Then he said something that really put my panties in an uproar with, "Think about what your are doing to me." WHAT! What was I doing to him! I tried to love him. I gave him all of me. I was left with nothing, but all of this pain. All of my life I was fighting with my own demons. I took care of him, first and foremost. Couldn't anyone take that from me. NO ONE! I had no one to care for me and I sunk deeper and deeper. I sought out help from the hospital since I was there. Yes, I admitted myself. And he was furious. I was a mess. I looked a mess. I was giving up without fully knowing that I was giving up until I picked up the phone and called that number. I was losing my mind.

Once upstairs and in my room this white nurse had come in and given me a vanilla Ensure. She looked at me and placed her hands on her wide hips and said, "Honey, we have work to do." She wasn't lying either. I had a lot of work to do to regain some sense of me.

There were group sessions but I never participated. I stayed in my room just staring out the window, wondering how my life became so ugly. How I became so ugly and bruised? I was alone and so afraid of my own shadow.

Come morning I met with an older white man who was a psychiatrist. His name was Dr. Boner. He asked me a few questions about my childhood, teen years, dating, and marriage that I candidly answered I figured he could pinpoint my anguish. Help me bounce back and balance out my life. I assumed a lot about that man. Unfortunately, it didn't help me much by expressing myself because I had somehow convinced him that I wasn't crazy. Somehow I did just that. Dr. Boner felt that I didn't belong in St. Barnard so I was discharged. I was released to wander back into a world of obscurity, afraid for my life.

The man that I loved dearly was embedded in my heart. *Where could I go from here?*

35

April

It is about 11:46 p.m. when my cell phone rings. I am surprised the damn thing is still on because this is like the 5th or 6th time it has been turned off by Sprint. If I go over by a minute they shut my shit off. How the fuck am I supposed to find a job if they won't cut a sista a break? Anyway, it rings while I am engrossed in a book of erotic pleasures. My eyes are buried in someone else's imagery of getting their freak on. And their depiction of it all has me hot between my legs. My eyes cut to the side to see exactly who is interrupting my "stimulation" time. I see six letters in bold, TRAVAR. I smirk just a little. It is certainly an unexpected surprise to be hearing from him. I mean we just bumped into each other a couple of days ago. He's still fine as ever.

Travar Atkin, a tall glass of water I had met in His and Her Incense Boutique. The same Travar who now owns a gazillion gentlemen's clubs. Uh-huh. I want to guzzle down all of his caramel more than a couple of times. But I have to be careful 'cause he is sinfully delicious. He knows how to do everything I love. Not like. Love. He teases my nipples, sucks them, and caresses my thigh. I always dreamt of him sticking his dick so far up inside of me until it got stuck in my throat. Breathe. Even now I have to take a breather from him because he'll make a prissy freak likely to fall in love with his fine ass. And I am not trying to go there. I have enough on my plate, at the moment.

First, I am currently unemployed. Let's just say the "ghetto-girl" came out after the publishing company I'd worked at for almost nine months canned my ass. This uppity chick who swore up and down that she was white, but was every bit of black as the color, kept making smart remarks to me as if I was a dumb bitch. What she didn't know was that I was from the 'hood. Obviously she had gotten things twisted until I set her straight. She wanted me to kiss her ass and I basically told her, "Missy, you can't afford for me to kiss your ass." Next thing I knew she was escorting me to the door. So I went straight to Unemployment Services to file a claim. And weeks later I received a letter in the mail stating my benefits were denied *"indefinitely."* Come to find out that bitch's lover was my claims examiner. Fuck! I shoulda whipped it on her ass and called it a fuckin' day, but that part of me was behind me. Danell was history.

I am into church again and my faith is strong. Employment is not easy to find, but I am going to keep at it. Gosh, I miss Anonymous.

Each and every interview I go on everyone has a preference. Either you aren't slim enough, fat enough, cheesing enough, serious enough, fake enough, real enough, smart enough, dumb enough, blah, blah, blah. Secondly, I am what one would call a dreamer. I have aspirations that go far beyond working a 9 to 5. I can't see myself slaving for $9.00-$10.00 an hour or even $30,000-$90,000 a year for the rest of my life. Listen, if I am going to be sweating bullets I had better be working for my damn self. That's exactly why I am unemployed for the 1st, 2nd, 3rd, 4th, shit, I might as well stop counting. Let's just say it has been more than I care to recount after Hellman kicked me out.

See, I have legitimate reasons for each uneventful moment, but those employers weren't interested in what I had to say. Why, 'cause I was black? I didn't know but I guess they thought I was stuck on stupid or desperate. Automatically, *I* was judged based on some bullshit! Uh-huh. Some he say, she say shit. I am getting too young for this. Yes, that's what I said, young 'cause I am not getting old. If I don't share my age one would never know. That's how good I look, still do, but even with looks I still can't find a job.

If you really want the truth, those people hated on a sista. I didn't know why, but it was getting on my damn nerves. What did they want me to do, get on my knees and beg for a job? Puuuuuuleasssssseeeee them to death with my palms curled up so that they could smugly say no because they were on the other side of the fence: Employed. That is exactly why I have to continue to dream because if I don't I will have lost all faith. And that is something I am not trying to lose.

So the majority of my day will be spent surfing the Web trying to find something that will pique my interests. Something I haven't tried before but am willing to give it a go at. Well, most of the time I am willing but I have no say in who hires me. Honestly, I feel like I am walking in circles. And I can't afford to keep doing that. I have rent to get up for the next month and I have no idea how that is going to get done. I had put my Friend-with-Benefits on pause after I saw him holding hands with another woman. I guess after constantly hearing "I love you," after every conversation I must've been feeding into his manipulation. But surely that changed with the quickness. I regained myself. I was broke but I still had my dignity.

I must admit I did well for a chick that didn't have a job for three months. My rent was paid up. I got a brand new computer. I was going to fancy restaurants. I got a few new pieces of clothing. I had some money in my pocket. All of that I got and I was jobless. And the only reason that occurred was because one Sunday my girlfriend Lois and I were going to this spot called Village Underground and Fletcher wanted to tag along. I figured what the hell. No harm done, right? It wasn't like I was going to take him home and make passionate love to him. Our dating never consisted of "lovemaking" because he was so eager to slip it in that he came before I could even blink. It was pitiful. So as you could probably imagine I never had an orgasm with him. Some things you just dealt with and that happened to be one of them for me. He was a roughneck—what more did I really expect.

Honestly, I thought just maybe my sensual side would work him over to be gentler with me. But he knew nothing about gentle, mellow; calm…everything was fast, hard, hostile. I tried to mold that man but it was taking too damn long. Shit, I wasn't getting paid and I damn sure wasn't working under the table so I had to cut that shit loose. Lemme tell you something I got more pleasure taming my own kitty.

Well, Village Underground was pumping. There were many cultures in the mix and I guess you can say I stood out among them all. Anyway, Fletcher was chilling until this man approached our table. Actually I caught his eyes as we were walking in. The brotha gave me a compliment, something on the lines of, "Oooh, sexy, how you doin'? Love that sexy do!" Next thing I knew, Brotha-man was standing by our table gaping at me. Well, Fletcher was a tad bit annoyed but what could he say we weren't together. Brotha-man took it a bit far by tapping my side and that was when shit was about to pop off. Fletcher sat up and him and Brotha-man had words. I had to stop the feud before it got out of hand. And let me tell you it was close. Things simmered down and I got pissy drunk. That night was a blast. That's all I remember.

When I woke up the next day all of my clothes were off. I was butt naked in the bed and Fletcher was lying beside me. I looked up and my thong was at the foot of the bed, bra was at the head of the bed, clothes were thrown on the fall by the door. My breath smelled like vomit. Those apple martini's were no fucking joke.

Sometime after all of that Fletcher started buying me shit. That's how my rent got caught up. I think I was leaning toward trying to rekindle things but deep down something most definitely was missing. That fire. Yes, in the bedroom. Fletcher was up there in age and I needed me a young buck. Someone who could hang with my youthful self. Someone who didn't mind eating pussy. Fucking me doggy-style. Someone who could reload for hours and fuck me so good until the rubber dried up and cracked from all the friction. And that is what Travar has burning inside of him. Oh, that man is a animal and I know that he will be a beast in the bedroom. I have never found another like him, other than....

Travar has that sensitive part of a man and I find that to be so attractive. So yes, with him I have to be very, very careful because I can easily fall head over heels for him and get my heart broken again.

Ring, ring, ring...
I better answer this phone.
"Hello."
"You're speaking to Avery, who's calling?"
"Oh, how are you doing, Travar?"
"Fine."
"No, just sitting here reading."
"You don't say."
"No, I don't have any company. Who gonna come here?"
"Yeah, that's nice. So how many bars do you own now? Twenty!"
"No, no I live in Montclair. No new man in my life. I'm just sitting here reading a book, fantasying about a man." I chuckle.
"Who? Washington. Perry. Underwood. Shit, I'd even settle for Obama."
"Tomorrow. I have no plans for tomorrow."
"Out for lunch. Well, I don't know. Um, well, okay."
"You can pick me up at 1:00. My address is...."
"Okay, see you then."

After we hang up, I pause for a brief minute. Avery, what are you doing, I ask myself. You know damn well that man has some potent shit that you can't handle. You will never learn, will you, I think to myself.

I walk into the kitchen and open the refrigerator and I am not a bit surprised to see that it is bare. I am broke. And if Travar wants to take me out for lunch who am I to turn down a free meal. I grab the saltine crackers off the top of the refrigerator and nibble until I am full.

Lords knows I can't wait to have a real meal come tomorrow.

36

Travar and I had spent the weekend together and he is dropping me off. As we drive up Elizabeth Road I see my ex-fiancé sitting on the front porch. I kinda panic a bit because I thought something happened. It is early in the day. Well, Travar never really comes inside unless we are planning on having protective sex. I hop out of the car and head towards the gate to go to the side of the house to my apartment and my ex-fiancé follows me. I ask is he okay and he says yes. I ask is everything all right with work and he says yes. I ask how *he* is doing and he says fine. So I take a load off my mind and drift back to my romantic evening and morning with Travar. My ex-fiancé walks into the quaint apartment with me. I see his eyes roaming the small space like he is looking for something. I lock the door. Once he hears the *click* from the lock he asks,

"Where you been?!"

"Out." I say.

"Who was that guy?!"

"A friend."

"A FRIEND!"

"Yep, a friend."

"Did he *touch* you?!"

I am silent feeling a tad bit embarrassed by him asking such questions.

"Did you have *sex* with him?!"

Again, I am silent, cutting my eyes from side to side.

I am caught by surprise when *he* goes ballistic. He starts throwing things around in the room like a mad man. The whole place is in disarray. I stare in his eyes and there is this rage burning his pupils. He has transformed right before my eyes. My body quivers by his look. I have never seen that look. That belligerence. I can hear my heart beating so rapidly that I think I am going to have a heart attack. I keep a distance from him, but then his dark hand yanks my arm and he manhandles me as he flings me onto the sofa. I fall on my back as he stands over me. The beats in my chest grow louder, my sweat glands burst, eyes pop fully as I know something bad is about to happen. The scent of fear mingles with my perspiration. It outlines my eyes as spittle glides across my lips with my tongue. I sense horror, danger, and plead to God in my head. I plead by who stands before me. No, no, no! I don' wan' it! Back and forth my head sways against the soft throw pillows. He stands and glares at me as his zipper slides down, as his pants inch down to his knees, then his feet. His hands pry my legs open, his hands grip my panties and rips them off with one yank and throws them to the floor. I inch back on my heels trying to move away. Trying to get away but I have no outlet. The wall is blocking my escape. The look in his eyes is dark and cold. My body twists, arms tug, legs motion up, up, up, and open wider as if I feel a muscle spasm coming unglued. There is a cramp that zooms through my whole body, as my eyes squint from its pinch. His breathing is heavy almost like a dogs breathing. A thirsty dog. A hungry dog. A mean dog. Emotions are brewing inside and out of me. My arms swing like two boxing gloves are on the ends, but it doesn't stop him.

He leans in and sniffs me as if he is getting ready to eat a home-cooked meal. Then he makes me do it. I shake my head no, no, no. There is no hope left for me. His hand claws at my upper arms, his knees pry to keep my legs open as his boxers run down his legs and his hardened dick stares at my open hole. Flood of tears blur my vision. I have no options. No, no, no! Pullllllleeeeeeeeaaaaaaasssssseee please, it's me…your future wife! Nothing matters. He is a different person. He grips it and jerks it and then leans over me and sticks it in my mouth. I almost bite the head as I nearly gag by his dick swelling from being aroused. My eyes widen even more not believing that he is forcing me to suck his dick. There is a film of glossy sweat on his forehead; there is no conscience in his eyes. Flood of tears blur my vision. I have no options. No, no, no! Pullllllleeeeeeeeaaaaaaasssssseee please, it's me…your fiancée! Again, nothing matters. He is ruthless. *I'm gonna die! I'm gonna die! I won't get to say good-bye to…!* I scream as his hands muffle my mouth with force. The memories. The trauma. The stench. The taste. I am relieving it all over again. I feel my jaws lock from suctioning his dick. I try to loosen my legs, but he weighs them down as he pries them open again and forcefully and savagely sticks his dick inside of moist pussy. I am still moist from Travar. And out of resentment he snaps, "You gonna give *my* shit to somebody else, huh!" I see the wrinkles form on his forehead, the darkness in his green eyes, and the mean streak of revenge twists his face as if deformed and I know. *I'm gonna die. I love you…!*

Aggressively he pumps his dick, rotating it, forth and back, back and forth, harder, and harder, till my eyes burst into tears. He opens my legs wider to get a better feel as tears roll down my cheek. The veins in his temples bulge like they are going to pop. I urge them to pop so that he will bleed to death. I want them to pop so that I can run, but they don't pop. The forceful thrusts tear my delicate skin. The secretion stings the delicate tissues as I squint from the pain. Quickly I am drying up as his thrusts, humps, and pumps get vigorous. I bite down on my lips breaking the skin. Feeling the saliva burn. The sofa pounds against the wall. No one is home in the next room. I pray, and scream again with everything in me and he cups my mouth with one hand and dares me to scream again.

"I'll kill you Avery. I'll kill you bitch!"

My body trembles. I have no way out. It is evident, so so evident.

I scream again, "Sttttttttttttoooooooooooopppppppp!" as my teeth chatter. I try my best, twisting, kicking, swinging, and screaming but no one is home. No one can hear me outside. His body shudders. His eyes squint. His wrinkles stand out across his forehead. His thrusts grow stronger, faster, harder, as come gushes out and into me like graffiti against a canvas of emptiness. I am undone in my skin. And then I hear *it*. Three knocks at the door. I pant with a streaky face. I sniff back in the snot. Hellman quickly stops. Pulls up his boxers, then his pants, zips them and acts as if nothing happened as he let's me up. I sit up and lean over to grab my ripped panties and tremble putting them back on. I stagger to the door and say, "Who is it?" and I burst into tears covering my mouth as I hear a male voice. Xavier's voice. How did he find me, I wonder. Hellman walks past Xavier as if nothing ever happened.

Xavier steps into the apartment, looks around at its disarray, looks at me, and stands in awe with eyes that pierce to kill. Then they soften as he looks at me again. I sit feeble in the corner so broken.

"Oh, baby, baby." His arms wrap around my trembling body as he drives me to the hospital to report that I have been raped by my ex-fiancé.

How often does it happen that a woman is raped twice in her lifetime?

A police report is filed and the police are on the prowl for Hellman. I won't be stupid this time. No. He is going to get what he deserves.

Xavier drives me home and I lay in a fetal position on my sofa and cry, as he is in the kitchen simmering me a hot cup of herbal tea. There is a knock at the door and my body flinches. I am afraid to answer the door. I walk toward the door and listen, but I don't hear any voices. Xavier stands close. I say, "Who is it?" There is no answer. I quiver in my skin. I am afraid even more. I give it one last try, "Who is it?" and then I hear a manly voice say, "Me." I swallow a gulp of spit down my throat and search the kitchen with my eyes for a weapon. I know who *me* is. It is the rapist. He is back to finish the job.

Xavier dials 911.

Tears ease down my face as Xavier leans against the wall with a knife in his right hand. I take a chance and unlock the locks, and ease the door open only to find *him* standing outside the door. His sturdy hand reaches out to give me a bouquet of flowers, as a form of apology. And then he runs off. The flowers tremble, as do I. I lock the door as my body slides down to the floor and I sob as I feel my will has failed me and my soul has died. All I need is a casket to confirm my death. May *I* rest in peace?

37

I have found sweet peace through all the misery. I died, yet I am reborn because I love *him* wholeheartedly. He sweeps me off my feet and swoops me away, so very far away that I am lost in love. I am wrapped in him exclusively. I am fading in his lust, salivating his taste for me, drowning in a kindness that loves me so tenderly—so genuinely. I lost my identity. So oblivious, I become someone else. Someone he yearns for me to be. Someone he love bites with those thin lips and tongues with seductiveness that makes my clit purr and ooze juices of my love out. I thought I had dried up, but I was so wrong. I am fl-oo-ding. His juices that stroke me so unselfishly inebriate me. His touch teases my nipples and finger licks my pussy and devours the dripping juices as if sherbet ice cream. It is magnificent how he captures my heart and nurtures me. He molds me. Chisels me with sensitivity and love knowing, that I am *damaged goods*.

H.Y.M.

He takes me under his spell and makes me forget about *H.Y.M.* The man who killed my spirit. He mends me back into this…this person that I mirror with teary-eyes. This woman I never knew existed beneath all of the scars. He takes me under his wing and pampers me with love and affection. I've changed. I've become his love cat.

38

"Baby, it's time for you to get up." Xavier says, carrying a breakfast tray of sliced oranges, an English muffin, and herbal tea. I toss and turn my body and then open my eyes and smile. I sit up and lean against the headboard feeling so loved. *God I love him.*

"Lemme freshen up before I eat, hon." I leap out of bed and zoom in the bathroom. Seconds later I come rushing out.

Xavier is sitting on the bed with a huge smile on his face.

"Avery."

"Yeah, babe," I say, as I take a sip of herbal tea and sink my teeth in a piece of English muffin.

"Avery, you know I love you."

I nod.

"Do you know how much I love you?" he asks, as he kneels down on one knee.

Tears flood my eyes as the muffin falls in the plate. My mouth is open wide. My eyes spread so big and heart feels so full.

"Avery, will you marry me?"

I blink. Catch my breath. Blink. Catch my breath, and then I blurt out, "Yes. Yes, I'll marry you!"

He grabs me and lifts me up and twirls me around and around in the air.

As I am floating in the blissful breeze I hear the glass crack and my flesh burns as if on fire. Xavier cradles me in his arms as I feel blood gushing out of my chest.

Xavier shields me, as he grabs his cellular, "PLEASE, please, send an ambulance, QUICK, QUICK!!!!! 4444 Montreal Drive, QUICKLY!" His face is drawn and broken. Tears engulf in his eyes as he snuggles my head in his chest holding me tightly. He sniffs my hair and kisses my lukewarm forehead.

My eyes flutter as his face fades in and out. The liquid oozes like a faucet of running water. A chill of coolness sweeps through my body as his hand clenches mine. I hear a faint whisper in my ear, "Avery I love you."

I vaguely see a beam of light coming through. There are spirits: Johnnie, Ma'am, Poppa, Storyteller, Jewell, Antwone and Therron. I feel light as a feather as if I am floating outside of myself. I stare at his endearing eyes as he cradles me in his arms, humming an old hymn, with tears dripping from his eyes. There is stillness. There is somberness as my eyes close, as I feel his heart shattering like glass.

Xavier whispers in a crackling voice, "Baby, I guess you can say, if he couldn't have you, no one could. I love you, Avery. Baby, I love you, please. Please Avery, don't leave. Don't leave...." Not able to compose his emotions he hunches his broken soul over my lifeless body, rocking me back and forth witnessing the *love* of his life slip away.